MY KIND OF PERFECT

(FRIENDS LIKE THESE BOOK 3)

HANNAH ELLIS

Dedicated to the memory of Neil Walker
My kind of person

Chapter 1

I wasn't particularly surprised when I walked into work to find my middle-aged colleague, Anne, dancing around the room with my accidental personal trainer, Jason.

"You realise this is a Thursday morning in a travel agency and not a Saturday night in a club?" I had to speak loudly to make myself heard over the sound of Beyoncé blaring out of a pair of portable speakers lying on Anne's desk.

I dropped into my office chair and shoved my bag into the cabinet by my feet. Jason and Anne were really throwing themselves into the dance moves. Thankfully, the window was almost completely covered by posters and holiday adverts so passers-by couldn't see in.

Anne beckoned me over with a wave of the hand. "Come and join in."

"What are you doing?" I asked.

"I read an article about productivity in the workplace," Jason said, still bopping around the place. "It claimed that starting the day with music and dancing improves staff motivation which leads to increased productivity. It creates a happier workforce, which is good for everyone. Greg agreed I could test the theory on you two."

Greg was the boss in our little shop. There were

just the three of us - Greg, Anne and me. We'd been working together for years and balanced each other well. It was always a relaxed atmosphere in our little travel agency.

"Anne's always happy," I pointed out. It was an annoying trait as far as I was concerned. She was constantly chirpy, even first thing in the morning. It baffled me, but I'd grown used to it.

"That's why *you* need to get up and dance!" Anne said.

"Oh! So this is all for my benefit, is it?"

"Mostly, yeah." Jason threw his arms up in the air and spun around, showing off his ridiculous clothing ensemble. This morning he'd opted for yellow shorts (very yellow and very short) with a tight orange T-shirt and leg warmers. The rest of him could freeze but apparently he needed his calves to be well wrapped up. He'd just managed to tie his silky blonde locks back into a ponytail, albeit with strands falling forward over his bright blue eyes.

"Well, I won't be dancing at work." I managed to keep a straight face as I watched Jason shimmy up to Anne with some dirty dancing moves. "It's very unprofessional if you ask me."

"Told you," Anne said.

"Told him what?" I asked, with the distinct feeling that I was walking into a trap.

"I said there's no way you'd dance. I know you so well. It's okay! Some people aren't as good at letting go as others."

Jason winked at me. "I said I bet you had some moves."

"I do, as it happens."

"Prove it," he challenged. The song ended, and as the next song kicked in, I reluctantly rose from my chair and began an awkward dance toward the middle of the room. Anne gave a little cheer and moved towards me, shaking her shoulders so her sizeable bosom bounced in front of her. I did a twirl in order to move away from her, and laughed at how ridiculous my morning was. I relaxed and found myself getting lost in the music, suddenly not caring that I looked like an absolute lunatic. I let myself go and it could easily have been a Saturday night on a sticky dance floor somewhere.

Getting carried away, I stepped onto the chair and then my desk. Technically, Anne and I shared a desk. It was one long table, which curved down the length of the room like a wave. Anne and Jason cheered me on and I danced my heart out, strutting my stuff along the entire length of the desk.

I was flinging my arms around wildly when I noticed Greg standing in his office doorway, watching me. His arms were folded against his chest and one eyebrow was slightly raised. Greg was a serious sort of guy but he was also a big softie. I knew I wouldn't be in any trouble, but he could definitely put an end to the fun with just a look.

Jason moved to stop the music as Greg's presence killed the atmosphere. I was left feeling slightly awkward as I stood on the desk looking down.

Greg's stern expression didn't change as he held out his hand with a five-pound note in it. Jason took it from him, then turned to high five Anne.

"He didn't think I could get you to dance," Jason told me with a grin.

Greg remained unsmiling as he looked up at me. "I argued you were far too professional to dance at work."

"It's because I'm so dedicated that I did it!" I protested. "I was totally against the idea but Jason told me about the article about increased productivity …" I glared at Jason as I stepped down from the desk. "You made all that up, didn't you?"

I went back to my chair as he and Anne collapsed into fits of giggles.

"I only did it to improve productivity," I said again.

"So you think you could be more productive?" Greg asked.

"No! Of course not … but …" I realised I was digging myself a hole so I stopped talking and turned on my computer. "See, I've got work to do. I'm not standing around giggling like some people." I glared at Anne. The corners of Greg's mouth twitched to a smile before he disappeared into his office at the back of the shop.

"You were right," Jason said to me. "You do have some moves!" He snorted as he re-enacted some of my dance moves, making Anne even more hysterical.

"Don't you have a job to get to?" I asked him. Jason was a regular visitor to our shop. He'd jogged in one day to book a holiday. He and Anne had hit it off and he kept coming back as though it was some sort of social club.

Somehow, he'd also talked me into some personal training sessions. Initially I'd hated every second of our workouts but they'd grown on me, mainly because Jason was such a sweet guy and a lot of fun to be around. His impromptu visits to the shop were always well received. He'd sit and drink coffee with us as he gossiped about his clients and told us stories.

He groaned as he moved to the door. "I've got a session with Little Miss Chihuahua. I'll be back later with stories no doubt." Jason had a strict code of confidentiality when it came to his clients. He wouldn't use their real names but had nicknames for them all. He'd hinted that we'd know Little Miss Chihuahua, who insisted on bringing her tiny dog to her workout sessions. He claimed to have a few celebrity clients, although there was a good chance Anne and I would never have heard of them even if he did name them.

"See you after work," he called to me as he headed for the door.

"We can skip today if you're too busy, I don't mind!" I was trying my luck and we both knew it.

He laughed as he waved back at us and took off running up the road.

"He's a funny one, isn't he?" Anne chuckled as she made for the coffee machine in the corner of the room. "He really brightens the place up."

"Greg and I not good enough for you?" I asked.

"Oh you're all right, I suppose." She grinned as she handed me a coffee. "Have you got anything nice planned for the weekend?"

"Not really. Just the usual: my Saturday shopping trip, and then a visit to Mum on Sunday. Come to think of it, I have quite a boring life, don't I?"

"Oh, not at all! What about Brian? Won't you do

something fun with him?"

Unfortunately, my lovely fiancé had been fairly absent for the last few weekends. "Probably not." I'd intended to sound casual but didn't quite manage it. "He's still busy with some big project at work." He'd been working all hours recently and when he wasn't working, he was too exhausted to do anything.

"Oh, Marie, that's terrible." Anne came and perched on the opposite edge of my desk. It was her customary position when conversations got serious. I hadn't meant to make out that things were so bad they warranted an edge of the desk chat.

"No, it's fine!" I cheerfully waved a hand in front of my face and hoped she'd retreat. "Once this project is over, things will calm down." I forced a smile. Deep down I knew that once this project ended, another would begin. Brian worked in investment banking and his job was high-pressured and demanding. He was currently knee-deep in some big acquisition and it was eating its way into his social life and our relationship.

"You should talk to him, or things will only get worse. You don't want to marry a workaholic. Get him to cut back. He should at least have weekends free to spend time with you."

"He does usually, it's just the last few weeks that have been hectic. It'll be fine."

"They'll write that on your gravestone. *It'll be fine.* Sometimes you need to address your problems head on instead of waiting to see what happens." Anne was always spouting little gems of wisdom like this. It was like having my own personal agony aunt.

"Thanks for the advice. I will definitely think about it. Now come on, isn't it time to flip the sign to *open*? We'll have a queue out there if we're not careful." Anne chuckled as she moved towards the door. We both knew that we wouldn't have any customers for a while. The first hour was always slow. It would be phone calls and admin work for the next hour or two.

I thought about Anne's words as I looked through my emails. She was always full of unwanted advice but she'd got me thinking this time. Maybe I should talk to Brian. His workload had been steadily increasing and it was frustrating never to have his full attention. The trouble was he seemed stressed enough without me nagging him.

"Are you excited about Grace's visit?" Anne said, interrupting my thoughts.

"Yeah, I think so." My best friend Grace was flying in from New York to start planning her wedding, which would take place the following spring. I'd taken some time off work and told her I'd help out. I wasn't really sure what that would entail. Theoretically, I should be busy planning my own wedding. Brian and I had decided to get married abroad but we were struggling to choose the destination so there wasn't much planning going on.

"You don't sound too sure! Are you worried you'll miss me?"

"Ha! That has been playing on my mind! Actually, I get the feeling I'll be busier than I ever am at work. Just don't tell Greg." I paused as I thought about Grace. I should have been excited to see her, but her upcoming visit was making me nervous more than anything else. "It's never very relaxed with Grace these days." I chewed the end of my pen. "I feel like I'm constantly making excuses for myself and my life."

"Oh, but she's your best friend. I'm sure you'll have a lovely time. It'll be nice to have a proper catch up."

"You're probably right." I hoped I was overthinking things. Grace had been my best friend since primary school and she'd just always been in my life. I sometimes wondered, though, if we met now, whether we'd be friends at all.

I decided I ought to be productive and dragged my thoughts back to work. I spent an hour replying to emails before our first customers of the day arrived. As usually happened, the day got steadily busier and the time flew by. Before I knew it, I glanced at the door to see Jason arriving. I grabbed at the phone on my desk and pretended to be deep in conversation.

"Sorry, Jason." I screwed up my face as I moved the phone to my shoulder. "I'm in the middle of something here. I think it's going to take a while. Shall we postpone?"

"Really?" He stared at me with a hand on his hip. "We're still going through this little charade every time?"

I tried to look indignant before I gave up and replaced the phone on the desk. My acting skills clearly needed some work.

With a sigh, I went to change into my jogging gear.

Chapter 2

"How was your day?" I asked Jason as we ran down the main shopping street, dodging pedestrians as we went. My running skills had definitely improved. When I'd first started with Jason, I couldn't talk while jogging. My lungs didn't allow it.

"Oh, I've got this new client, Miss Whippy. She's a total nightmare."

"Miss Whippy?" I asked. "Like the ice cream?"

"Yeah. If you saw her hair, you'd understand. She's trying to get in shape for her wedding, like you."

"Good one, Jason!" We both knew that I was not trying to get in shape for my wedding. In fact I had no real desire to get in shape at all. I'd made peace with my size twelve figure a long time ago. I was no supermodel, but I'd never seen the point in obsessing over a bit of extra weight. After being bullied into working out with Jason, I'd gradually come around to the idea of a bit of exercise in my life. I felt healthier for it and I enjoyed the chats with Jason. Although, recently he spent a lot of time teasing me about my inability to choose a wedding destination.

"Come on, Marie, I'm dying to get myself a new hat!"

"Who said you're invited?" I laughed at him. I

wasn't entirely sure the hat comment was a joke either, what with Jason's odd dress sense. I'd never seen him 'off duty', so I couldn't really imagine him without sports clothes on, but he definitely prided himself on his unique and fairly effeminate style.

"How are the driving lessons going?" he asked, changing the subject. I registered the cheeky grin on his face.

"Anne told you, didn't she?"

"Told me what?" he asked with a look of mock-innocence.

"I don't need to drive anyway. I've already told Brian. I've managed this far without that particular ability. Why start now? It was all his bright idea in the first place."

"Come on," he said. "Tell me the story."

"How do I know that you don't have a nickname for me and tell your other clients entertaining stories about my life?"

"Oh, I definitely have a nickname for you! And yours are the best stories. Don't let me down now."

"Fine," I said. "So the driving instructor claims he has some sort of 'three strikes and you're out' rule, but I actually think that him giving me the boot is more a reflection on his teaching skills than my driving abilities."

"So you really did get dumped by your driving instructor? I didn't know if Anne was having fun with me."

"Clearly Brian found me the worst driving instructor in town."

"Clearly! So what were your three mistakes? Something about a lamppost, was it?"

"Reversed into it," I confessed. "Then there was an incident with the wing mirror … apparently they're more effective when they're attached to the car. I also scratched the door a bit on a tree."

"You drove into a lamppost *and* a tree?" He spluttered out a laugh.

"No, I didn't drive into a tree. I just parked badly and opened the door a bit too fiercely. He overreacted on that occasion."

"And the dog?" He didn't look at me as he asked.

"I knew I shouldn't have told Anne about that. I only told her because I was slightly traumatised. But the dog was fine. Hardly a scratch on him and I think he learned a valuable lesson about road safety."

"Stay off the road when Marie's behind the wheel?"

"Shut up! The dog really was fine. I only nudged him. In fact, I think technically he ran into the car. People overreacted again."

"I believe you! Anyway, that's four things, not three."

"Yeah but when the wing mirror happened he told me to pull over and was muttering about how he definitely couldn't teach me anymore, so I got a bit angry and opened the door pretty wildly into the tree …"

"Wow! Two scrapes in one lesson? I guess you're not his favourite person." He snorted with laughter. "Come on, let's put in a bit more effort for the home stretch, shall we?"

"No, I'm okay thanks." He'd already sprinted away from me. My fitness level really had improved a lot since I'd started training with Jason. The first few weeks were torturous. There was even a day I jogged right on to a bus just to get away from him. I don't really know what had come over me but I was gasping for breath and being shouted at by Jason, so when the bus pulled up at the stop, I dropped back and got on it.

Given how much I hate buses it felt like an 'out of the frying pan, into the fire' situation, but at the time I would've done anything to get away from Jason. I'd felt his eyes on me as the bus drove past him. It wasn't even going in the right direction. I got off a couple of stops later, when I felt like I'd put enough distance between me and my sadistic personal trainer. I'd wandered slowly home, feeling slightly guilty, but confident I would never have to see Jason again.

Unfortunately, he wasn't so easily deterred. Eventually, I resigned myself to having exercise – and Jason – in my life.

Jason was jogging up and down the front steps when I caught up to him.

"I'd invite you in," I said, "but …"

"It's fat club night. I know. And sadly I don't qualify to join." He gave me a cheeky grin as he lifted his T-shirt to flash his six-pack. "See you soon," he called over his shoulder as he jogged away, leaving me smiling after him.

Chapter 3

"I've got an idea!" Sophie said, as she jumped up and down on my couch. I eyed her suspiciously; who knew what might happen when Sophie had an idea? "I'll just throw this cushion – beautiful by the way – and whichever brochure it lands on is where you get married."

"Don't throw the cushion." I took it from her and plumped it up. It was one of my mum's delightful creations. She'd made it for Brian when I first met him. It had a knitted square with a 'B' on the front and I'd somehow become quite sentimental about it. I had a lot of homemade cushions from my mum but very few of them were on display.

"That's a ridiculous way to decide where I get married," I told Sophie. The living room floor was scattered with holiday brochures. I'd decided that I at least needed to have a location for the wedding by the time Grace arrived for her visit. I had to show her that things were moving forward, even though they clearly weren't.

I'd managed to narrow my search down to about twenty different resorts in various locations but I wasn't sure how to decide. I thought maybe my fat club friends could help me. We always met here, in what I still thought of as Brian's house but was actually my place as well. I'd moved in almost six months ago and the Thursday evening meetings had moved with me.

I'd first met my fat club friends totally by accident. I'd intended to go to a speed dating event in a hotel but the guy on the reception desk thought it would be funny to send me into a slimming club instead.

Somehow, and it's all a bit vague now, I'd managed to get into an argument with the woman in charge and when I stormed out of the place, Sophie, Linda and Jake followed me. I'd later found that they all had slightly strange reasons for being there and only Jake had actually been there because he needed to lose weight. I tended to scoff at Sophie's theory that it was fate that brought us all together.

"Let's just do what Sophie says," Jake said. "Maybe you'll actually reach a decision that way. At the rate you've been pondering things, you may never get married at all."

"It's an important decision." I scowled at him. He'd lost a bit of weight since I first met him. Jake worked in an old people's home and had fallen head over heels for their in-house chef, Michael. I think that had finally given him the incentive he needed to shed the extra pounds. I guess it also helped that Michael was a great cook and made sure that Jake no longer lived off fried food. They were a solid couple now and it was nice to see Jake so happy with his life. We'd all taken to Michael immediately and I was sure the two of them would live happily ever after.

"Oh, come on," Sophie said, bouncing up and down on the couch. "The quicker you decide, the sooner we'll be sunning ourselves on a beach somewhere with cocktails in hand."

At Christmas, Brian and I had decided that we'd get married on a beach somewhere and just take our closest friends and family. It had seemed like a major breakthrough in the wedding planning at the time. I hadn't expected it to be so hard to pick a destination. As a travel agent, picking somewhere should have been easy, but I just couldn't decide.

"I think Sophie might have a good idea for once." Linda pulled herself up from the armchair, fishing in her sleeve. "Here, use this, though, not a cushion." She offered a dainty white handkerchief to Sophie.

Sophie held it up suspiciously. "I hope it's clean." At one point I would've laughed at that fact that one of my best friends was a gentle lady in her fifties who carried handkerchiefs in her sleeves. I was pretty used to my unconventional friends by now though.

Linda tutted. "It's clean."

"Go on then, Sophie," Jake said. "Let's find out where we're off to."

"Okay, here goes …" The hanky fluttered through the air and landed on a brochure.

"Okay." I picked up the brochure and flipped to the folded down page. I felt three sets of eyes on me. "That one's out then. Next!" I handed the hanky back to Sophie who stared blankly at me.

"Where are we going?" she asked.

"I don't know, but we're not going to Mexico." They all stared at me so I kept talking. "It will have to be a process of elimination because we're not going here." I waved the brochure around. "It's too far away. Try again, Sophie …"

Sophie looked to Jake and Linda who shrugged. She glared at me as the hanky fluttered onto another brochure.

"Oh good, I didn't really fancy Portugal either. This wasn't such a bad idea after all."

Sophie groaned. "It's going to take forever."

"It will if you don't hurry up," Jake said.

Sophie threw the hanky repeatedly, eliminating Majorca and then the Dominican Republic, Lake Garda, Hawaii, Thailand and Fiji.

We were getting low on brochures when Brian wandered in, wearing a dark suit and looking decidedly weary. I'd met Brian around the same time as my fat club friends and he'd always been a part of our Thursday evening get-togethers.

He pulled off his tie and gave me a quick kiss. "What's going on this evening then?"

"We're deciding where you're getting married," Sophie told him from her place on the couch. "And it's not …"

"Sicily!" I said, picking up the brochure nearest to the fallen hanky and adding it to the pile of discarded ones.

Brian smiled as he draped an arm around my shoulders. "Well, it looks like you finally found a sensible way to decide!"

Five minutes later, I was standing with the winner in my hand. "Mauritius," I said unenthusiastically.

"That's good, isn't it?" Sophie asked through a yawn. I took a seat between her and Brian on the couch.

"What's wrong with Mauritius?" Brian asked.

"Nothing really …" I hesitated wondering how much of a fool I would sound, "but–"

"What's this?" Sophie snatched the brochure from me and retrieved the Post-it note which I'd stuck to the page. "Woman lost her hat." She squinted as she read my handwriting. "What does that mean?"

"I just read a review about the place and there was a woman–" I was interrupted by an array snorts and giggles from around the room. "What?" I demanded.

Jake chuckled. "You can't get married in Mauritius because you read a review by a crazy lady who lost her hat there?"

"I don't know why you sound so shocked," Sophie told Jake. "This is exactly the sort of thing Marie would base a decision on. I'm not sure how you ever manage to sell any holidays!" She grinned at me.

"She didn't *lose* her hat," I told them adamantly. "There were gale force winds the whole time she was there and her hat kept blowing away. She spent her entire holiday chasing it."

Brian moved to plant a kiss on my forehead as the rest of them gave me pitying smiles.

"I just don't want to have my wedding dress flying around my head, that's all."

"So me throwing a hanky around all evening was a complete waste of time?" Sophie asked. "We're no closer to a wedding?"

"No, it's fine. If it makes everyone happy we can get married in Mauritius. Who cares what *I* think?"

Brian clapped his hands together. "That's settled then. Mauritius it is." I gave him a friendly shove.

"You'll figure it out," Linda said kindly.

"Always the optimist, Linda!" Jake laughed and I threw a cushion at him.

"We could throw you a surprise wedding if you want?" Sophie offered.

"No, thanks!"

"Phew! I don't fancy planning a wedding; you're not making it look like fun. I'm making tea … who wants a cup? I hope you've got biscuits." She bounded out of the room as we shouted drink requests at her.

"I'll help," Jake said, following her.

"She's cheered up," Brian remarked once Sophie was out of earshot. She'd been pretty moody for the past few months. It seemed like she was fed up of working at the health spa. She'd started there as a trainee as soon as she finished school and seemed to enjoy it but I got the feeling they were taking advantage of her now. She worked hard and was struggling to get any recognition for it.

"How's work now, Sophie?" I asked when she came back in carrying drinks.

"Terrible," she said cheerfully. "But I've decided that I'm definitely going to open my own beauty salon."

"That's more of a long term plan though, isn't it?" Sophie had been mentioning this idea for a while now but I'd dismissed it as a pipe dream.

"Well it was, but now I'm wondering what I'm waiting for. I know what I want. I just need to stop talking and do something about it. I don't want to stay at a job I hate just because I'm too scared to take a risk."

"Well, I guess that's a good attitude … isn't it?" I

looked around the room for more opinions. I actually wasn't convinced at all.

"It's very ambitious," Jake said, tilting his head to one side. That was fairly diplomatic.

"I know. But I know I can do it and I don't want to work for someone else forever. It will happen. I can do anything I put my mind to! Why shouldn't I just get on and do it now?"

"It's a lovely idea," Linda said. "Once you're all set up, maybe I could work for you too. I could be your assistant ... pass you things and what-not."

Sophie stared at Linda for a moment and I was glad she was engaging a 'think before you speak' approach rather than shooting Linda down and reducing her to tears. "Maybe." She nodded vigorously. "I will definitely keep you in mind when I get to the point where I can afford to employ someone to pass me things and what-not!"

Luckily Linda wasn't brilliant at detecting sarcasm so she happily sipped at her tea and gave Sophie one of her slightly condescending smiles accompanied by a shrug of the shoulders.

"What do you think, Brian?" Sophie asked. "You know about business and stuff. Do you think I could do it? I just want a little place at first ... in town somewhere. I'll start small and build it up."

"If anyone can do it, you can." Brian smiled at her and she beamed back at him. I thought he'd been a bit vague in his answer. Surely someone other than me thought that it might not be as easy as she was making out.

"I've been looking at premises in town. A lot of my clients would follow me so I'd have customers immediately. I just need to raise some initial capital. I'll either have to get a loan or find an investor." Her words hung in the air for a moment and I glanced at Brian who didn't react. "Anyway, I know I can do it." She smiled and picked up her cup of tea.

"How's Jeff?" I asked to change the subject. "I haven't seen him for a while." Jeff was Sophie's boyfriend. He'd been the joker working at the reception desk of the hotel, who'd sent me into the wrong room. He'd played the same trick on Sophie. When she finally decided to give speed dating another go, she'd bumped into Jeff and ended up dating him instead. The relationship had been pretty rocky at the beginning but it seemed pretty stable now. I guess it took Jeff a while to learn how to deal with Sophie and her mood swings.

"He's fine," she said with a smile. "It's a good job he works on Thursday nights or he'd want to come to fat club too. I've told him it's an exclusive club but he seemed to think I was joking." She didn't even pause before changing the subject and launching into a longwinded tale about one of her colleagues. Sometimes it seemed like she didn't stop for breath.

I always enjoyed Thursday evenings with my little gang of friends. They were quite unpredictable. Occasionally the evening would end in some bizarre argument, usually started by Sophie who seemed to enjoy winding us up. It was always a nice atmosphere between us though, even with all the teasing. I'd come to think of them more like family than friends.

"I think we'd better go," Linda said in response to

Brian's yawning.

"Don't mind me," he said. "I just had a long day."

"Are you sure we're not just boring you?" Sophie asked.

"A little bit," he said, smirking.

Sophie gave him a shove as she stood up, "Come on then. Let's leave Brian to his beauty sleep."

Brian and I stood on the front steps and waved as we watched our friends climb into Linda's car and drive away.

I followed Brian into the kitchen. "You know Sophie's going to ask you to lend her money don't you?"

He peered in the fridge for a minute before pulling out a beer. "I think she's been building up to it for a while. She's not exactly subtle."

"That's going to be awkward."

"How do you mean?" He popped the cap off the beer and took a swig.

"Saying no to Sophie. You know what she's like. She'll take it personally and it will be a huge drama."

"I actually think she might do well with her own salon."

"You wouldn't lend her money though, would you?"

"I'm thinking about it."

I struggled to hide my surprise. "Seriously?"

"Maybe. She's miserable at work."

"That's not really a good reason though. Lending Sophie money is a terrible idea."

"Who else is going to help her? Her family can't afford to and I can't see her getting a bank loan. I don't see why we can't lend her the money."

"It's not just about money though. It's Sophie. I don't think you've thought it through properly." I was shocked that Brian would even contemplate lending money to Sophie.

"She just needs someone to believe in her." He leaned on the counter. "With a bit of help I think she could do well."

"But you don't have time to help her," I said. "All you'd be doing is throwing money at her. That's not going to help her. You'd just be setting her up for a fall." I moved around the kitchen tidying random things as I tried to avoid eye contact. The kitchen was annoyingly clean and tidy so I ended up repositioning the herbs on the window and wiping an already clean surface. Still, it was better than having to look at Brian. I felt like I needed to put my foot down on this occasion. "Sophie's got no idea about running a business."

"I can help her out with the business side of things - it's not rocket science. She's good at what she does and I think she can pull it off. She just needs some capital to get her going."

"But what happens in six months when she's blown all the money?"

"I'll take the chance." He shrugged and I wanted to throttle him. I could see that he was tired and that this was probably not a great time to discuss it but I was really annoyed by his attitude.

"But it's not just the money you'd be taking a chance with. How's Sophie going to feel when she fails at her business venture *and* she can't pay you back?"

"We could give her the money as a gift. Then you won't have to worry about what she does with it."

"I'm going to presume you're joking." I finally turned to look at him but only caught a glimpse of his back as he walked away.

I grabbed myself a beer, taking a long swig before following Brian into the living room and joining him on the couch. "Can we talk about this rationally? Because it feels like you're not thinking very clearly."

"I just think Sophie's got no one looking out for her." He looked up from his phone. "She's so ambitious and she's got potential and I don't want her to lose that because there's no one showing any interest and helping her."

"Well, that's nice," I said. "But do you honestly think that if you give her a load of money and tell her she can do it, that she's going to have a successful business?"

"I don't know …"

"She's only twenty. I know she thinks she has loads of experience but she still has a lot to learn."

"You might be right." He looked at me and frowned. "I just don't really know how to say no to her."

I laughed. "I know. She's got you wrapped around her little finger!" I moved over and gave him a kiss. "Why don't you sit down with her and go through all her plans and if you think it's a sound business plan, and she really knows what she's doing, then lend her the money?"

"You're very sensible, these days, aren't you?"

"Yes." I snuggled into him as he pulled me

towards him. "Nice that you finally noticed!"

Chapter 4

It didn't take long for Sophie to come asking for the money and I wasn't at all happy about being right about it. She knocked on the door on Saturday morning and launched straight into her pitch.

"I was thinking about my idea of setting up my own business …"

Brian handed me a coffee before taking a seat on the couch next to Sophie.

"I'm seriously looking into everything. I've been researching how much it is to rent a shop in town and trying to figure out how much money I would need. Obviously, I don't have the money so my next step is to get a loan or find an investor …" She trailed off.

"It seems like you're thinking it all through properly," Brian said. I kept quiet and sipped my coffee, awaiting the inevitable.

She looked at Brian and made a decent attempt at sounding casual. "I was wondering if you might consider lending me some money? I'd be making a profit in no time, so you'd get all your money back."

Brian made a vague attempt to sound surprised at the suggestion. "I don't know …" He glanced at me and I avoided eye contact, concentrating firmly on my coffee. I was staying out of it. Brian could be the bad guy.

"I'll have to have a think about it," he said. I glared at him briefly.

"Of course." Sophie beamed. "You definitely need to think about it. The thing is, I've found great premises. It's right in town but on a side street so the rent is manageable. I don't want to rush you into a decision but I don't want to miss out either." She turned to look at me and I smiled sweetly at her, confident that lending Sophie money would be a road to disaster.

"Have you got the details of the place?" Brian asked.

"Yeah, it's all in my phone." Quickly, she stood and pulled her mobile out of her pocket.

"What about the rest of your business plan? I'd need you to go through everything with me before I could decide."

"Of course. I can go through it all with you now. I have it all planned out."

I could almost see her hopes rising. Thankfully, there was a knock at the door.

"That'll be Linda," I said.

"Oh, yeah." Sophie grinned at me. "I forgot about the Saturday shopping trip."

"We're just going for lunch," I said. "Linda's working this afternoon."

"Have fun!" Sophie called.

Brian followed me into the hallway, where I grabbed my coat and shoes.

"Don't be long," he whispered.

"I won't." I kissed his lips. "Try not to break her heart."

"I'll do my best."

The weekly shopping trips with Linda had started shortly after I met her. She'd been having marital problems at the time and used the shopping trips as an escape from her husband, George. I'd somehow been dragged along with her. Strangely, I'd become slightly sentimental about my Saturdays with Linda. I found them comforting. I wasn't wild about shopping but I enjoyed the chats with Linda and our little refreshment breaks. I especially liked the days when she was working so she only had time to have lunch with me.

"How's George?" I asked once we were settled in the cosy little teashop, sharing a pot of tea and tucking into a plate of assorted sandwiches.

"Oh, he's fine. Boring, but fine."

"I thought things were good between you these days?"

"They are. Everything's fine. We're just getting old."

"You're not that old." She chuckled at my weak attempt at sincerity. "How's work?" I asked in a bid to change the subject. Linda had gotten herself a job at one of the little boutique clothes shops that she used to drag me into on the weekend.

"Boring." She sighed. "Sorry, Marie, I'm in a cheery mood today, aren't I? I just feel a bit ..."

"Bored?" I took another bite of my sandwich.

"Yes! I feel like my life is a bit dull."

"You always seem pretty happy with life." It was something I admired about Linda. She was always on a level; never moody or complaining. She just got on with things.

"Oh, I am. I just heard some bad news this week. An old school friend of mine passed away. I hadn't seen her in years. She'd been ill for a while apparently. I only heard about it from a mutual friend."

"Sorry."

"I didn't even know her anymore," she said, waving off my condolences. "It got me thinking though; life is short and I am quite happy plodding along, but sometimes I wouldn't mind a bit of excitement or ... just a change I guess. Maybe I should try something new. Make the most of life."

"Sounds like a midlife crisis. You're not going to take up sky-diving or anything, are you?"

"No, I don't think I'll go that far. It's just unsettled me a bit. Anyway, what's going on with you? How's Brian?"

"He's fine." I hesitated and I saw Linda register it. She was a good listener and I usually ended up telling her every detail of my life without prompt. "He's working a lot at the moment and I'm starting to feel like I never see him. I'm rattling around that big house on my own most evenings. I'm sure it'll all calm down, but it's hard for me to relate to. I go to work, do my job and go home. Brian never seems to switch off. He's working on some big project at the moment and I feel like it's turning into an obsession."

"Did you talk to him about it?"

"No. I don't want to sound like a nagging wife before we're even married."

"You don't need to nag," she said. "Just talk to him about it. Tell him how you feel and find out how he feels."

"That sounds very grown up and sensible. You might have over-estimated me."

"Well I guess you could always bury your head in the sand and occasionally have a sly little dig at him. Eventually you'll have a big argument and everything will be out in the open …"

I grinned. "That seems more realistic."

We laughed and quietly turned our attention to lunch. I always enjoyed the quaint little tearoom that was Linda's favourite. It was old-fashioned and suited Linda's personality. We spent a nice hour chatting and enjoying the bustle of the tearoom.

Even though I'd promised Brian I wouldn't be long, I would've liked to put off going home for longer. I was slightly concerned that Sophie might still be there, trying to convince Brian of her plans.

Knowing Brian, he might already have agreed to buy her a beauty salon.

Chapter 5

The raised voices were a bad sign. I heard them as soon as I opened the door and it crossed my mind to turn and run away. Finally, my sessions with Jason could be put to good use.

In the dining room, Sophie and Brian sat at the table with the laptop and some papers spread out before them. "What's going on?" I asked.

"You told him not to lend me the money, didn't you?" Sophie said, glaring at me.

"What?" I was determined to keep my cool and not get into an argument. Casually, I continued into the kitchen and switched the kettle on. The kitchen and dining room were open plan so I could still talk to them but it felt like a safer distance.

"I know what you're like," Sophie snapped. Her eyes were on me the whole time. "You told him to say no."

"Calm down," Brian said. "That's not true. If it seemed like a good business plan I'd go for it, but from what you've told me, it's not going to work. The numbers don't add up."

"But I can make it work." She snapped her gaze to Brian. "I know I can. Why can't you trust me?"

"It's not about trust," Brian said. "I don't think you really know what you're getting yourself into."

I took my cup of tea and joined them in the dining

room. "Taking a loan from a friend probably isn't a great idea either."

"Well it's a bit irrelevant, isn't it?" She stood abruptly and gathered up her things. "Since you've poisoned Brian against me." She stomped to the door. It was all a bit predictable. Shouting something melodramatic and storming out was trademark Sophie.

I sat down next to Brian and sighed. "That was really lovely to come home to."

"Sorry." He grimaced. "You were right. She'd lose all the money *and* be a nightmare."

"Nobody really likes it when I'm right, do they?"

"I went through her business plan with her, but she hasn't got the first clue about running a business. I'm not sure why I ever thought it was a good idea. I might be losing my mind."

"Good job you've got me."

"You don't have to rub it in." He leaned over to kiss me.

"I'll drink my tea and then go and find Sophie," I said.

"She may never forgive us for this one."

"She will. She's pretty sensible when she's not being dramatic. She'll see reason."

Sophie lived at home with her mum, stepdad and younger siblings. I'd never actually been inside the house before and I was slightly hesitant about it. I picked my way through the selection of kids' bikes which littered the front path and tried not to look too much at the small front garden which was overgrown and scattered with sweet wrappers and other assorted bits of rubbish.

I half hoped there'd be no answer when I rang the bell. A big, bearded man opened the door while shouting something over his shoulder. When I asked if Sophie was home he nodded vaguely. Then he turned and walked back into the house, shouting for Sophie as he went, and leaving the door open for me.

"Come in and shut the door," he called. I dutifully did as I was told.

"Do you want a cuppa?" he offered as I lingered in the hallway. I followed his voice to the kitchen to find him filling the kettle.

"No thanks." I hovered in the doorway.

"Have a seat." His voice seemed to command rather than offer. I moved to the little table under the kitchen window but wasn't keen to sit down. It was strewn with so many food remnants that I was sure I'd see living creatures crawling around if I looked hard enough.

"I'm Roy, by the way."

"Marie." I pulled a chair slightly away from the table to sit down.

"I've heard all about you," he said. "Sophie didn't mention you were coming over." He put his head out of the kitchen and shouted for her again.

"She didn't know. I think I upset her and I wanted to apologise."

"I wouldn't worry. She's got a thick skin."

"Well it was about her business idea and I think she's a bit sensitive about it." I was going to stick to my theory that she was overly sensitive and not that I was less than tactful.

He turned to face me and leaned against the counter. "Just don't lend her money, whatever you do."

His smirk annoyed me.

"Well Sophie's determined and I think she'll do whatever she sets out to do," I said quietly.

He laughed. "Trust me on this one. You'd never see your money again."

I stood up awkwardly and looked out of the window, wishing Sophie would appear.

"She has all these grand ideas," he said. "Pipe dreams. They'll never amount to anything."

My body tensed. "Sophie is very good at what she does and with a bit of help she could have a very successful business."

"If you bet on that, you're a fool." The kettle clicked and he poured steaming water into a mug. "She might be good at what she does but she's not destined to be more than a make-up artist - or whatever it is she does – at someone else's bloody health farm. She doesn't understand business. There's no way she could run her own."

I was opening and closing my mouth like a goldfish when I noticed Sophie standing quietly in the doorway. Roy followed my gaze and at least had the decency to look awkward before he turned and moved to sit at the table with his coffee.

Her eyes filled with tears. I moved towards her but she took a step back when I reached out to her.

"It's okay," she whispered. "He's right. I don't know how to run a business."

Roy tapped the side of his coffee mug. "I just meant it's not going to be as easy as you make out,

Soph." She glared at him until he turned to look out of the window.

"Why don't you come and stay with us for a while?" I said quietly. I was desperate to get out of the place but hated the thought of leaving Sophie there. She looked up at me with big sorrowful eyes, shaking her head as she fought back more tears.

"Go on," I said. "Pack some things and let's go." My voice cracked slightly as I turned her towards the stairs. She finally hurried upstairs and I waited, hoping she would do as she was told, and quickly.

I went back to Roy who was staring out of the kitchen window. "If you can't see how much potential Sophie has, then you really don't know her at all."

"I think you should leave," he said without looking at me.

I waited outside for Sophie. She finally emerged with a bag draped over her shoulder. Roy was behind her, calling her name with increasing determination.

She took my arm and propelled me down the street beside her. Roy stood at the front gate, watching us go. "Sorry about that," Sophie said when she finally slowed down.

I waved down a taxi on the main road. Neither of us spoke on the drive back to my place. Sophie stared out of the window, determinedly avoiding eye contact with me.

"I should never have asked you to lend me money." Sophie broke the silence as we stepped out of the taxi.

"We're not lending you the money," I snapped.

"We're giving it to you. It's a gift and you can do what you like with it. Brian and I think that you can run your own business and that you'll be brilliant at it."

Tears streamed down her face. "I don't know if I can though. I don't know anything about running a business. What if Roy's right? I might mess everything up and lose all your money."

"Brian will help you learn the business side of things. You'll be great. I know it." I raised an eyebrow. "And I doubt Roy has ever been right about anything!"

She coughed out a giggle amidst her crying. I took her bag from her shoulder and ushered her into the house like a child.

Brian appeared in the hallway as we hung up our jackets. "You okay, Sophie?"

"She's fine." I picked up her bag as I nudged her towards the stairs. "Sophie's staying here for a while."

She trudged up the stairs without a word.

"We're giving her the money," I said to Brian. "And whatever else she needs."

"Okay." He looked puzzled as he wrapped his arms around me.

"You were right." I rested my head against his chest. "If we don't help her, I'm not sure who will."

Sophie lay in bed for the afternoon. I ventured up a few times to check on her but she insisted she was fine and was adamant that she wanted to be on her own. At dinnertime I told her she had to get up and eat. She went into the bathroom and splashed her face before following me downstairs.

Brian had decided on a civilised meal at the dining table and Sophie took an audible breath as she sat down.

"Sorry about today," she said. "I'll just stay here tonight if that's okay? And I don't want your money. I'll figure something out." She picked up her knife and fork and I smiled as I saw the determination back in her eyes.

"You can stay as long as you want," Brian said. "And you'll gracefully accept the money and help we're offering." She opened her mouth to protest. "No arguments." He pointed his fork at her. "Now eat up and then I'll tell you the plan."

A smile spread across Sophie's face as she picked up a chicken leg and took a bite. "Does this mean I have to start being nice to you?"

"No!" Brian and I said at once.

Chapter 6

Brian got his laptop out and moved to sit next to Sophie as I cleared away the dinner things.

"Let's be realistic," he said. "You don't know enough about business to set up on your own at the moment." Sophie nodded her agreement. "And I don't have time to give you all the help you'll need. So I looked into it and found you a business course. It's specifically for people who want to set up a small business."

"What about work?" Sophie said quickly. "I can't afford to go back to school. I need the money."

"There's an evening course which you should be able to fit in around work."

"How much does it cost?" she asked.

"We'll pay for it," Brian said.

I smiled. "You can pay us back when you a rich business woman."

"I will, I promise. I'm going to work really hard."

"You'll need to," Brian said. "It won't be easy to set up on your own."

"I know but I can't wait to be my own boss. Where's the course?"

Brian turned the laptop to her and she read through the information on the website.

It seemed like the perfect solution and I was so happy Brian had found a way for us to help. I could definitely imagine Sophie running her own beauty salon, but sometimes she needed someone to rein her in and be realistic. She always seemed to trust Brian's opinion.

Once Sophie had pored over all the information about the course, we moved into the living room and settled ourselves with a glass of wine. Sophie went into overdrive talking about her plans. It was nice to see her so full of energy and excitement again.

I waited until Brian had gone up to bed to quiz Sophie about her family. Apart from the occasional comment, she didn't go into details about her home life and I was suddenly interested.

"I wasn't very taken by your stepdad," I said.

"Roy's alright." She twirled the wine glass in her hand. "He was having a bad day today. He'll apologise later."

I wasn't convinced but decided not to comment. "What happened to your real dad?" I asked.

"My mum got pregnant with me when she was eighteen. She was with my real dad for a while but it didn't work out. He stayed in touch and I see him on and off. He's okay. He's just really unreliable. It's hard trying to have a relationship with him so I kind of gave up caring. I know where he is if I need him but I've stopped expecting anything from him."

"You don't have much luck with dads do you?" I thought about my family and decided that the absence of my father may have been a blessing. I'd never known him and I'd never had much interest in finding out about him.

"Roy's been a good dad," Sophie said. "I didn't have a horrible childhood or anything. He's been around since I was six and he treated me like his own. I always felt like he looked at me the same as he did his biological kids."

"So he's horrible to them as well?" I blurted out.

She shook her head. "I had a huge argument with him this morning. I was in a terrible mood when I left here and I took it out on him. You came at a bad time. I owe him an apology just as much as he owes me one. I'll go and talk to him tomorrow."

"But he was so mean." I'd been really shocked by the way he talked about Sophie. I hated that she was making excuses for him.

"You know me though …" A smile played on her lips. "Can you imagine what a nightmare I would be to live with?"

"I guess you could be a bit difficult." My lips twitched to a small smile. "But that's no excuse for the things he said."

"I used to get on really well with him." She lifted her glass to her lips and finished off her wine. "Sometimes Mum even complained that we would gang up on her about stuff. Then, not long after I met you, Roy lost his job. I'd been saving up and almost had enough money to move out, but Roy couldn't find work and Mum's wage didn't cover the bills so I started giving them most of my wages."

She tucked her legs under her on the couch. "That was fine at first, but the longer it went on, the more I resented Roy for it and the more he resented me for it. His pride has taken a beating, having his stepdaughter providing for his family instead of him. He's home all the time and he gets depressed and we argue a lot. It's not really his fault. Apparently no one is very keen to employ a fifty-year-old builder."

"Why didn't you ever say anything?" I always felt like I knew every detail of Sophie's life - from what she ate for breakfast to what colour underwear she had on - but apparently she kept the big things to herself.

"It's not easy to talk about. And I kept thinking he'd find a job and things would get better."

"Well, you're welcome to stay with us." I was slightly annoyed that she hadn't filled us in on how bad things were.

"Thanks. I'll go back tomorrow though. I need to sort things out and be a bit nicer to Roy. It'll just cause more friction if I move out at the moment. Plus, I think you'd get sick of me pretty quick!"

"That's true."

I grinned and ducked to avoid the cushion she threw at my head.

Chapter 7

I was standing in the kitchen on Sunday morning when someone knocked on the front door. I'd been sipping coffee and complaining to Sophie about Brian's snoring

"You need to get a doorbell," Sophie said. "Who has a brass knocker?"

"We do," I replied. "It's in keeping with the area." There was mocking in my tone and I glanced at Brian as I repeated his words.

"Let's not have this conversation again," he grumbled as he moved to answer the door. "I don't want a doorbell."

"It's pretentious, if you ask me," Sophie shouted after him.

There was warmth in Brian's voice as he greeted whoever was at the door. I strained to hear who it was.

Sophie put her coffee down and moved into the hallway.

"Mum!" she said. "What are you doing here?"

A short, dumpy woman came in and kissed Sophie's cheek. "Just wanted to check up on you."

"I'm Marie," I said.

"It's great to meet you at last." She beamed at me. "I'm Maggie."

I did my 'I don't know how to greet you' dance in

my head and she gave me a kiss on the cheek and a tight embrace without hesitation. I think I would've gone for an awkward wave but her hug endeared her to me immediately.

"Do you want a coffee?" Brian asked.

"I'd love one," she said with a sigh.

I led her and Sophie into the living room and she looked around before parking herself on the couch beside Sophie.

"It's a gorgeous house," she said. "I'm so envious!"

"Thank you." I thought of the contrast between our homes.

"Enjoy it while you can. Once you have kids you can say goodbye to clean and tidy! What I wouldn't give for a tidy house … just for a day. Whenever I turn my back to clean one room, the rest of the house gets trashed." She smiled warmly.

"It's a pigsty!" Sophie looked at me as she laughed. "You know. You saw it yesterday."

"Sorry you got in the middle of that." Maggie looked at me sadly before turning to Sophie. "You will come home, won't you?"

"Yeah, of course. I'm coming back today."

"Roy told me what he said. He feels terrible."

"Did he tell you what I said to him?" Sophie bit her lip.

"He said you'd had an argument … Why? What did you say?"

"It doesn't matter. I wasn't very nice though. I'll talk to him."

"It's hard to believe Roy's not her real dad." Maggie looked to me. "They're so alike. Feisty and argumentative, the pair of them!" She put her arm around Sophie and gave her a squeeze. "Anyway Roy's got a job so hopefully things will get back to normal."

"Where?" Sophie asked. "Not the one down south?"

"Yes," Maggie said, rubbing Sophie's arm. "He's going to take it on a three month contract and see how it goes. He'll come home at weekends."

Sophie cast her eyes downwards. "That's just because I had a go at him."

"No. He needs to get out of the house and feel useful or he'll go mad. It's just for three months and he'll keep looking for something close to home."

"I don't want him to go because of me," Sophie said.

"He's not. He's not angry with you. He's angry with himself. Everything will get better." She took the coffee that Brian handed her, cradling two hands around it and taking a sip "Well this is like heaven." She sank back into the couch and grinned at me. "Coffee, clean house and no screaming kids!"

Sophie looked at Brian. "Biscuits?"

"I can see why she likes coming round here so much," Maggie said as Brian went back to the kitchen.

"I don't know how she does it," I said. "I don't get that sort of treatment."

"Yes you do," Brian said as he reappeared. He placed the tin of biscuits on the coffee table before grabbing a chocolate one and perching himself on the arm of my chair. I leaned forward to get a biscuit and he sneakily nudged me out of the way to steal my seat.

"You see what I mean?" I moved onto his lap and put my arm around his shoulders.

"Have you set a date for the wedding?" Maggie asked.

"No!" we said in unison, then laughed.

"I'd love to get married again," Maggie mused.

"Mum!" Sophie said.

"No, silly, not to someone else! I mean I'd love to go back and do it all again. It was so much fun."

Maggie stayed for an hour regaling us with stories of her wedding and her kids. She was so warm and down-to-earth, and I was sad when it was time for them to go.

Brian opened his laptop as soon as they'd left.

"I'm going over to my mum's for a bit," I said. I always went to visit my mum on Sundays and Brian usually joined me, although in the past couple of months he'd not managed it much. "Do you want to come?" I asked.

He looked up at me and grimaced. "I've got a lot to do here. I'm meeting with Graham Clifford tomorrow and I need to make sure I'm prepared." He nodded at the computer. "Sophie and her drama set me back a bit."

In the past couple of months, I'd heard the name Graham Clifford far too often. It was starting to sound like nails on a blackboard. He was the Managing Director at the firm and when he said jump, Brian asked how high.

"It's fine," I said quickly. "Don't worry about it."

"I'll come next week. Promise." His head turned

in my direction but his gaze was locked on the laptop screen. "I'll drive you over there though."

"I can get the bus." There was no way that would happen, not on a Sunday. The Sunday bus service was probably my lowest ranking form of public transport. Absolute nightmare. I'd get a taxi but I didn't have time for the lecture about being a public transport snob.

"Just wait one minute." He held up a hand to me with his attention still firmly on the computer. I went and got my shoes and jacket on and returned to hover in the doorway.

"I'll just get the bus. It's fine."

He hesitated before snapping the laptop shut and jumping up. "I said I'd drive you." He pushed his feet into a pair of trainers by the door. "I really wish you'd learn to drive."

"I did learn." I gave him a cheeky grin as we walked out of the door. "I just didn't learn to do it without hitting things!"

Chapter 8

At Mum's house there was a note attached to the front door telling me she was at her allotment. I sighed and walked to the end of the road. From there I took a path through a few trees and came out on open hills at the other side. After a few more minutes, I reached a row of walled allotments tucked away at the bottom of the hill. Mum was renting a small allotment at the end of the row. There was a homemade sign on the gate announcing her 'Doggy Day-Care'.

She was going up in the world. Her little dog walking business had expanded into a surprisingly popular day-care for dogs. She didn't stop there either. On Saturday mornings she could now be found wandering the hills, carrying a whistle, with a gang of seriously dedicated dog owners following her.

She'd somehow become the go-to dog trainer in the area and offered a dog obedience school once a week. I'm not sure what qualifications a person needs to be a legitimate dog trainer but Mum had decided that reading two books on the subject was education enough. To be fair, the business had really taken off. She'd been affectionately nicknamed 'Ellie the dog whisperer' by the locals.

"Hiya, Marie!" Joan in the next allotment called

out as I pushed open the gate.

"Hi, Joan! The courgettes were lovely thanks." Courgettes were the offering I'd left with on my last visit. There were always some vegetables going spare in her little garden and I never left empty-handed.

"I'll have a look and see what I've got for you today. Your mum's in the van. It's naptime."

"Thanks!" I headed to the old caravan sitting at the end of the mud patch that was her garden and knocked quietly on the door. She treated the dogs just like children and let them sleep in the bed which took up half of the caravan.

"Hi!" Mum whispered, stepping out from the caravan and giving me a hug. "I said I'd look after Rex. It was a last minute thing."

There was a little wooden picnic bench in front of the caravan. We took a seat side-by-side and Mum produced a bag containing mugs, a flask and a Tupperware box filled with sandwiches.

"Where's Aunt Kath?" I asked, eyeing the sandwiches nervously. Mum's cooking was indescribably bad. Actually bad was probably the wrong word; it was totally weird. She added random ingredients, coming up with her own ridiculous concoctions. Aunt Kath usually visited Mum on Sundays and I relied on her to cook us something normal.

"She's got a cold and didn't want to be sitting outside in the elements. She said to say hello, and she'll see you next week."

"Okay." Mum pulled the lid off the sandwich box and slid it nearer to me. "I'm not very hungry." That was a lie but I couldn't bring myself to eat one of her sandwiches. "I just ate before I came."

"Maybe later then." She covered the sandwiches and poured us both a tea as I wondered what crazy sandwich experience I'd just dodged. She'd once heard about American peanut butter and jelly sandwiches and decided to make me one.

Unfortunately she hadn't realised that what Americans refer to as jelly is not the wobbly pudding that we're used to. Although that was pretty tasty compared to the time I'd specifically requested a tuna, mayo and sweetcorn sandwich. When she realised that she didn't have sweetcorn or mayo she thought sugar and ketchup would be acceptable substitutes.

It was quite a pretty little allotment that Mum had found for herself. We were overshadowed by a birch tree standing tall in the corner of the plot, and a smattering of bluebells were dotted around our feet. Mum was doing well in her little doggy venture and being outdoors suited her. She had a healthy glow.

Growing up, I'd watched her jump from job to job, doing whatever she could to pay the bills. She'd worked in shops and cafes, and even had a cleaning job at the hospital for a while. She seemed much happier these days. She was free to be herself and clearly loved the dogs. I was glad she'd moved the dogs out of her house, and this little place she'd found so close to home was perfect.

"How's Brian?" she asked.

I shuffled round to face the wind, pushing the hair from my face. "He's fine. He had some work he needed to finish today."

"He works too hard. He's not been answering my calls you know?"

"He didn't mention you'd called. He's really busy at the moment though. He'll get back to you soon, I'm sure." Brian was usually really patient with Mum's random phone calls. "Try calling again later," I suggested. There was a time when I would've begged her to leave him alone and stop calling him.

She pulled a tin of biscuits out of her bag and offered me one. My eyes roamed the box, searching for the smallest one before I hesitantly took it and eyed it like I was handling an explosive device. It looked oatie and inoffensive but I'd learned to be wary of anything my mum made, regardless of appearance.

"So why are you working on a Sunday?" I asked.

"Rex's parents needed to get some things done and they feel bad leaving him alone all day so I said I'd take him."

"Hmm." I wished I'd not asked.

"But as a little thank you treat, they're taking me to Crufts next week!"

"That's nice of them." I was pleasantly surprised. Rex was Mum's favourite pooch - a scruffy little mutt who seemed to be forever at her side. He was having a nap in the caravan as we chatted. I'd always felt that the owners – or parents, as Mum liked to refer to them – were taking advantage of her so it was nice to hear that they were showing their appreciation. A day at the world's largest dog show would surely be like heaven to my mum.

"Yes, they are lovely. I can't wait!"

I gingerly nibbled at the biscuit in my hand and was surprised to find it tasted fine. I took another bite and chewed slowly, reluctant to let my guard down after one tiny bite.

"Did someone give you these?" I gestured the biscuits. I was now convinced that Mum hadn't made them at all.

"No, I made them myself. Why?"

"No reason. They're really nice." I smiled at her. Maybe all the fresh air was having a positive effect on her. Maybe she'd followed a recipe and stuck to ingredients which would be considered normal for biscuits. The smile stayed on my face as I popped the remainder of the biscuit in my mouth and shook out my hair as the breeze caught it.

"Mum!" I screeched and leapt up from the bench. "What's that?" I jumped around and spat biscuit from my mouth into my hand like a child. My mouth burned and I blinked through tears to try and bring Mum back into focus.

"Oh, you got a chilli pepper, did you?" She looked completely innocent as she peered at me over her cup of tea.

"Oh my God! Mum! Why did you put chilli peppers in perfectly good biscuits?"

"I was following a recipe in the cookbook that I got for Christmas … but I thought they sounded a bit boring. I actually can't eat these though. I thought the chillies would just spice them up a bit, but it's too much, isn't it?"

"A little bit, yeah! Why didn't you throw them in the bin?"

"I didn't want to waste them. I thought you might

like them."

"Don't offer them to anyone else. Throw them away!"

We had another cup of tea and I spent an hour playing catch with Rex, who'd woken full of energy. It was a lovely blustery day and I felt quite content with the world. I wandered the hills with Rex and laughed at him as he barked at a squirrel up a tree.

"What would you do with it?" I asked him. "It's almost as big as you!" He barked his contempt at me and we headed back to Mum's plot to find her cleaning the outside of the caravan with a mop.

"I'm going to go," I said. "Brian's probably missing me by now."

"Okay. Do you want to take those with you?" She motioned to the box of biscuits on the table. "Brian might like them …"

"No." I smiled cheekily. "Actually, yes. You're right; Brian might like them!"

"There are carrots for you there …" Joan called as I left. I reached for the paper bag sitting on her wall.

"Thanks, Joan. See you soon." I smiled at her and waved to Mum before setting off up the hill and across the field, pulling out my phone as I went.

"Hi, Helen!" I smiled into the phone. "I need a lift home from my mum's."

"No problem, babe. I'll send Dave. How are the driving lessons going?" I enjoyed the fact that I was on first name terms with the taxi dispatcher and the drivers. Not only that, we also knew far too much about each other's lives. My friends thought it was hilarious but I liked it.

"I've given up. Driving's not for me. Plus I like to

support local businesses. I can't just ditch you guys, can I?"

"I heard you hit a dog!" She cackled her over-the-top laugh.

"How on earth do you know that?" My mind whirred as I tried to figure out how it could've gotten back to Helen.

"Dave drove your colleague home the other evening and she was telling tales! She's a laugh that one."

"Since when does Anne call you?" I was annoyed at my reaction to this revelation. It irked me though. It felt like she was trying to steal my friends.

"She's called a couple of times recently. She said that we came highly recommended!" She laughed again. "She talks a lot, doesn't she? Even gives me a run for my money."

"Yeah, she can definitely talk." Anne was the only person I knew who could tell a story without a beginning, a middle or an end.

"I've got another call, Marie. Dave will be with you in five minutes. Take care."

I shoved the phone into my pocket and continued my cheerful little walk back to Mum's house where I sat on the front wall to wait for Dave. He didn't take long.

"I almost didn't come," he said as I climbed into the passenger seat. "What with me being a dog lover and all!"

"The dog was fine," I said beaming. "I'm quite sure Anne embellished the story for you. She spun you a good yarn no doubt."

"She's going round town ruining your good name

with tales of animal cruelty."

"I wouldn't put it past her." I grinned and relaxed into a pleasant drive home. I told Dave the real story of driving into the dog and he bantered with me good-naturedly. I always enjoyed the drive with Dave. He was easy to chat to and was warm and friendly. It was infinitely better than getting the bus.

I planted a kiss on Brian's cheek when I walked into the kitchen. He was perched on a bar stool by the island, with the laptop and a steaming cup of coffee in front of him.

"How's your mum?" he asked.

"She's good," I said. "It was really nice out there today. It feels like miles from civilisation." I leaned against the counter and wondered whether Brian was listening to me. He smiled vaguely, signalling that he'd not heard a word. I raised my voice slightly. "Mum said you're not answering her calls."

"I'll call her when I get time. She always seems to catch me at a bad time."

It annoyed me that he suddenly thought it was okay to ignore her calls. I knew that her random calls could be a bit annoying but it was Brian who'd convinced me it was just her way of showing that she cared.

"Just give her a call, please."

"I just said I would."

"Yeah, when you get time. Which could be never!" I was being argumentative but he didn't seem to register my annoyance as he stared at his computer.

Reaching for my bag, I pulled out the biscuit tin and slid it across the countertop to him. "There are biscuits there if you want one."

"Did your mum make them?"

"No, Aunt Kath." I casually walked out of the kitchen. By the time his death threats reached my ears, I was smiling to myself on the couch

"Seriously! I'm going to kill you!" he repeated as he appeared in the living room. I was creased up with laughter and could barely catch my breath.

"Kath made them, did she?"

I jumped up to get away from him. "I meant Mum! I got mixed up."

He chased me around the couch a couple of times before leaping over it to grab me and pull me down with him.

"That was mean," he said sulkily.

"I'm sorry! But you weren't giving me enough attention. I'm feeling very neglected." My voice was light but there was truth in my words and we both knew it.

"Sorry." He pushed a stray strand of hair behind my ear. "No more work for the rest of the day. I'm all yours."

"Really?"

"Yes." He planted a kiss on my cheek. "Just don't try and poison me again!"

Chapter 9

I phoned Brian as I walked out of work two hours early on Wednesday. "You've not forgotten Grace arrives today, have you?"

"Nope!" I could hear the smile in his voice. "You reminded me a few times. Including this morning. Plus, Grace emailed me. I don't think I've had chance to forget." I had to remind myself that Grace had been friends with Brian before I met him and that her friendship with him was not just through me.

I'd taken Thursday and Friday off work to help Grace with wedding planning and she was coming over that afternoon to go through everything she needed to get done. I'd been quietly amused by the fact that Grace was making a plan of how she would plan her wedding. That was typical Grace though; thorough and organised were her middle names.

"Will you be able to come home early?" I asked.

"To make sure we look like a perfect couple with a perfect life?"

"Yes!" I laughed. "She always finds fault with my life."

"You worry too much. Who cares what Grace thinks?"

"I do, unfortunately." And that was my problem. I really did care what Grace thought. "Can you just come home at a reasonable time for once?"

"I'll try," he said.

I don't know why I always felt like I had something to prove to Grace. She'd been my best friend since primary school and knew me better than most people. But I almost felt that she knew another version of me; like she still saw the schoolgirl version of me and refused to see beyond that. They say you'll always be a child in your parents' eyes and I guess that's how I felt around Grace. Maybe it was because Grace always seemed so grown up and serious. I felt slightly silly around her and had the feeling I needed to impress her.

Grace had always done well at whatever she set her mind to, whether it was school, work or relationships. She seemed to excel at everything. Now she was leading a high-flying lifestyle in New York and I couldn't even try and match up to her. At least I had Brian. That was one thing that seemed to impress her.

I hadn't been home long when the familiar sound of the brass knocker hit my ears. Grace was early and it annoyed me. I should've been excited about seeing my old friend but I was upset that she'd ruined all my plans by arriving too soon.

She banged loudly on the knocker again as I patted myself down in the corridor. I was such a mess. I took a deep breath and plastered a smile on my face as I opened the door. Maybe she wouldn't even notice that I was wearing an apron and a head to toe dusting of flour.

"You're just in time!" I grinned, trying not to sound flustered. I reached to give her a hug and transferred a generous amount of flour onto her. "You look great!" I said, ignoring her puzzled look. "It's so good to see you! Come on in … how was your flight?"

"What on earth have you done?" She followed me into the kitchen, completely ignoring my question. To be fair, the fact that every single surface was coated in flour was a little distracting.

"Oh, this?" I waved a hand. "I just spilled some flour." I laughed as though it was completely normal.

"*Some* flour?"

"Well, all of it."

"How did you manage to spill - sorry not spill, explode - a whole packet of flour?"

"Linda is trying to domesticate me! She keeps giving me recipes to try. I'm getting quite good at baking actually." That was a complete lie. "I thought you'd be impressed when I had some homemade delights in the oven and the place smelled like a bakery. Bet you're glad to know I've not changed too much!" Linda had given me a few recipes but I'd never attempted to try any of them before.

Grace started giggling and then struggled to stop. I tried to laugh too if only to make myself feel that she was laughing with me and not at me.

"You're such a sight," she said. "I never understand how you can live with such chaos in your life but I always enjoy watching you."

"Come on. You need to help me clean this up before Brian gets home." I stood in the middle of it all, pleading with her.

"Marie, I'm not even sure where we should start!

The poor kitchen."

"Well I thought that if we wiped everything from the countertops onto the floor and then sweep it all off the floor? And then maybe repeat a few times."

I threw her a cloth and she shook her head in amusement. "It's nice to be back."

We'd only just started our attempt at cleaning when I heard the front door open and close again. Typical! The one time I wouldn't mind him being late and he arrives early. I wiped furiously at the kitchen counter, but only managed to smear the flour even further.

"I didn't think he'd be home so soon." I pulled the apron over my head and shoved it into a cupboard before smoothing down my hair. A smile played on Grace's lips as she watched me. Now I'd have to deal with teasing from both of them.

"Let's just act normal. He might not notice. Sometimes he can be very unobservant." I threw my cloth in the sink and we moved towards Brian. Maybe we could shield the kitchen and he wouldn't see it.

Brian wandered casually through the dining room, towards us, glancing into the open-plan kitchen without reacting.

"Look who's here!" I announced with a flourish. Maybe Grace's presence would detract his attention from the disaster zone that was the kitchen.

Brian raised his eyebrows at me before turning to Grace with a grin. She moved to hug him, and I felt a pang of jealousy as she embraced him tightly and lingered slightly too long. I had to remind myself again that they were friends first.

Grace met Brian at work and I was jealous of their friendship long before I met Brian. With the kitchen chaos, I'd not even asked Grace how she was. As I watched her hug Brian, I felt that something was wrong with her. She'd not conveyed that to me, although maybe the flour and my stress levels had been a barrier.

"Nice to have you back, Gracie." Brian finally pulled away from her. "So what happened here then?" He planted a kiss on my lips. "I take it the flour won the fight?"

I bit my lip. "Sorry. I might have messed up your kitchen a bit."

He gave me a look and I quickly corrected myself. "Our kitchen! I meant *our* kitchen. I couldn't find the scissors so I tried to tear it but the whole packet ripped and it was like a flour bomb."

They laughed and exchanged glances, making me feel like a child amongst the adults. "You tell her," Brian said, grinning at Grace.

"You just roll the top down," Grace said. "It's not sealed, you just unroll it to open it."

I looked at them both and tried to gauge whether they were joking. Brian had his arm around my shoulders and gave me a squeeze before I wriggled away from him and continued wiping at the mess. I guess I hadn't fooled Grace with my lie about my baking abilities.

"I presume something delicious came out of all this?" Brian looked doubtful.

"No!" I snapped at him. "I exploded the flour and then Grace turned up early so I didn't get anything done. It was going to be a quiche. Now we're all going to starve!" I threw my hands up dramatically and Brian enveloped me in one of his bear hugs.

"I brought muffins if anyone wants one?" He held up a paper bag as he moved away from me.

"Go on then," I said. "I'll put the kettle on."

Brian went to get changed, leaving us to continue our not very effective cleaning strategy.

"So how's everything in New York?" I asked.

"Good." Grace sounded falsely cheerful and sighed before she continued. "Work's pretty crazy. I keep getting these migraines; tension headaches the doctor calls them. He says they're stress related and I need to cut down on work but it's easier said than done. Some time off should fix me up though. I'm so excited to get all the wedding preparations under way."

"I'm sure you'll feel better now you're home. And the wedding planning will be fun!" I tried to sound genuine but I wasn't really finding it fun to plan my own wedding so I struggled to find enthusiasm about Grace's, especially as she was such a control freak. I secretly thought it would be a nightmare.

"Actually, I'm really keen to look around the venue as soon as possible. Do you think you could do a trip to the coast with me?"

"Yes!" I didn't have to fake enthusiasm about a trip to her parents' beach house. I had fond memories of the place from the few times I'd been with them when we were growing up. "I've been getting excited about it. I love the beach house. It's been so long since I've been."

"I just hope everything is how I recall it. I remember seeing a bride in the hotel gardens when I

was a child and being sure that's what I wanted. I
haven't been back in years though. My mum says
it's as beautiful as it always was. The hotel offers a
wedding package and I've already provisionally
booked it, so everything should fall into place."

I was fairly confident that things *would* just fall
into place for Grace; they usually did. I decided not
to dwell on the fact that I would probably still be
trying to organise my wedding when Grace was
celebrating her tenth anniversary. A trip to the coast
would be good though.

Grace looked at me excitedly. "Could we go
tomorrow?"

"Tomorrow?" I tried to hide my reluctance. "I
presumed you'd want to wait until the weekend?" I
moved to start sweeping the floor, keeping my head
down so she couldn't read my face.

"I can't plan anything else until I've been and
checked the venue so I need to do that first. I don't
want to waste any time. I thought you'd taken time
off work?"

"Yes, I have. It's no problem. Tomorrow is fine! I
just thought you might be jet-lagged." I focused on
the sweeping and found it rewarding to watch the
pile of flour grow to a sizeable mound.

"I'm too excited to worry about jet lag. I've made
an appointment at the bridal shop for 10 a.m.
tomorrow so I thought we could have a look at a few
dresses, and then I've arranged to meet a couple of
the girls that I used to work with. We can have a
quick lunch with them and head straight off from
there."

"Great." I tried my best to sound enthusiastic. "I

can have a look at dresses too. I can't buy one yet because Linda wants to take me to get my wedding dress but I can have a look. If I find anything I'll go back later with Linda."

Grace looked at me like I'd said something utterly ridiculous.

"What?" I asked.

"I was talking about shopping for *my wedding dress*," she said slowly.

"Yes." I matched her speed. "I need one too. For *my* wedding."

"But we'll shop for yours nearer the time. You don't need to look tomorrow."

"Okay. I just thought that while we're there I may as well have a look."

"Marie!" she snapped. "It's not a 'while we're there' activity, it's not just any old shopping trip. You need to make an appointment and take it a bit seriously. Not just wander in like you're buying new jeans."

"Right. Okay. Sorry." I felt stupid as she stared at me, clearly expecting me to say something more. I wondered whether to tell her she was a crazy control freak and that the world didn't actually revolve around her. "I just thought it would be fun to try on dresses together. I'll go another time. It's fine."

"It's probably bad luck to start dress shopping before you've even set a date anyway." She turned to rinse her cloth in the sink.

I chuckled. "You think I'll try on a wedding dress and come home to find Brian's gone off me?"

"No. But there's a lot of superstition surrounding weddings. And what I really meant was, you should set a date. How long are you going to make poor Brian wait?"

"Poor Brian?" She was annoying me now. "Brian's fine. It's easy for you. You've always known where you want to get married. I have to search out the perfect spot."

"I would have thought you would just pick anywhere. I'm surprised you're being so fussy. Are you sure this isn't your organisational skills letting you down again? I can help if you want."

"No it's not that. I just ..." I searched for a way to explain to her. It seemed like she didn't understand me most of the time. I didn't know where I wanted to get married but I also knew that at some point I would find some inspiration and I would just know. Grace would never understand my approach. "We've actually been thinking about Mauritius," I said, improvising.

"Really?" She failed to hide her surprise.

Brian rejoined us at exactly the wrong moment. "I thought we couldn't get married in Mauritius because some woman lost her hat?"

I sighed and bent down to sweep the flour into the dustpan. "Not just her hat! Everything kept blowing away. What if we have the same weather and I end up with my wedding dress blowing over my head the whole time."

"I think it was fairly freak weather for Mauritius though."

"She also lost her luggage." I made a face at the flour that seemed to be multiplying on the floor.

As a travel agent my recent obsession with holiday review websites was not really a great thing.

At work I found myself wanting to refer customers to dodgy reviews, rather than the stunning pictures in brochures.

"Anyway, Mauritius is still an option," I said.

"I think it sounds wonderful." Grace seemed genuinely impressed by the idea. It was a shame it was never going to happen.

"I can't wait for dress shopping tomorrow!" I turned the conversation back to Grace, albeit continuing with the lies. I swept up what I thought was the last of the flour and deposited it into the bin.

If I'm honest all I really thought was that the bridal shop better be like the ones in films and serve champagne.

Chapter 10

I was supremely proud of myself. I'd been a great best friend. I was full of enthusiasm, and was surprised by how much fun the dress shopping was. I gushed at dress number four which was exquisite and looked like it was made for Grace. It had a touch of the old fashioned about it with its intricate lace detail. I'd also gotten fairly excited at that point because I thought that would be the end of the dress shopping and it had been entirely painless. Grace just wanted to try a few more though, which was fine, of course.

I helped with zips and a million tiny buttons. I held things and fetched things and 'oohed!' and 'aahed!' all over the place.

The trouble was, we were now almost three hours in and on dress number thirty-three, which was also a reprieve of number four; the one I knew was meant for her. My enthusiasm had wandered off about an hour ago and I felt like I would be physically incapable of smiling for much longer; my facial muscles had never had such a workout. I was only glad I hadn't been entrusted with the job of recording the dresses by number, description and star rating.

Grace's mum had that thrilling task and had been scribbling furiously in a notebook all morning. I'd tried to chat to her a couple of times but she made it clear she needed to concentrate and waved me away. She was a serious woman and I'd never found her to be particularly friendly.

I'd even been extra good and turned down the offer of champagne when we arrived. It was 10 a.m. and no one else was going for it, so I followed the crowd and went for coffee. I managed to keep that up until dress number eighteen and then I'd pulled on the owner's sleeve like a child and begged her for a glass.

She didn't seem impressed by my late and lone request but when I'd hinted that we might take our business elsewhere she'd relented and opened a bottle. I was surprised she'd succumbed to my threat so easily. I'd have thought it was clear by looking at me that I wasn't about to encourage Grace to start the process all over again elsewhere. I was good and refrained from asking her to forego the glass and just give me the bottle and a straw.

It was definitely going to be a long day. I was already a bit annoyed with Grace for the way she assumed that I would do whatever she told me for the time she was home. I felt like her lap dog. Of course, I'd taken some holiday time from work (as instructed) and I was all set to help with the wedding stuff, but I was finding Grace's attitude fairly hard to take.

Grace was standing in front of the mirror trying to decide if number four slash thirty-three was *the* dress. I took a moment to sit in the throne-like armchair and take a swig of champagne. When we'd arrived, I'd thought the over-sized, bejeweled armchair was ridiculous. It hadn't taken much alcohol for me to drape myself over it like I was queen of the universe. I was now thinking of getting one for the living room.

The champagne buzzed through my system as I gazed over at my best friend. She looked stunning in the wedding dress. My mind wandered and I smiled to myself as I thought of the previous evening when I'd sat slouched on the couch with Brian.

"Brian, they are going to kill me!" I'd been panicking all afternoon and announced my fears to Brian as soon as Grace had left. "I didn't know what to say to her. I knew how she'd react if I told her I couldn't help her plan her wedding because I had a fat club meeting."

I ignored the smirk on Brian's face and kept talking. "How am I going to explain to Sophie, Linda and Jake that I can't make it? I've not missed a Thursday yet. And it's tomorrow, I can't even break it to them gently."

"I'm sure they'll understand."

"I don't know what you're looking so smug for. It's you who'll have to tell them."

He looked suddenly concerned. "Why me?"

"Because I won't be here."

"You have to tell them. You can't just leave me with them."

"Just don't say anything," I suggested. "Maybe they won't even miss me."

"You need to call them and apologise. Cancel this week. I can't cope with them alone."

"I'm sure you'll have a great time!"

"Maybe I'll just go out for the evening."

"Don't you dare." I shoved him playfully and he pushed me so I landed on my back on the couch.

He pouted as he pinned me down and nuzzled my neck. "Don't leave me."

"I'm sorry but you're going to have to deal with them on your own for once."

"Unless I don't let you go!"

I wriggled but couldn't manoeuvre myself out from under his weight. "Get off me!"

He tickled me and I squealed as I squirmed under him.

"So you think you can keep me here until tomorrow evening?" I asked him breathlessly.

"You've left me no choice!"

"I'll give you about two minutes before you decide you're hungry."

He eyed me seriously. "How could you possibly know I'm hungry?"

"You're always hungry. Now get off me!"

"What are you going to do if I let you up? Bake me a quiche or something? Because I think we might be out of flour!"

"Hey!" He relaxed his hold and I sat up and pushed him away from me. "I may not be able to bake a quiche but I'm perfectly capable of ordering you a good takeaway."

"I can't argue with that," he said, and then paused. "Do you want me to call?"

I grinned. "Yeah, please!"

"Marie!" Grace's voice interrupted my thoughts.

"Yeah?" I sat up straight.

"Can you help me undo this?" she asked impatiently.

I drained my champagne and sighed as I stood up. "Please …" I added under my breath. Well it was supposed to be under my breath. I smiled sweetly and think I got away with it.

***

"Did you find a dress?" Grace's ex-colleague, Vanessa, asked.

We were in a quaint little Italian restaurant. Grace and I had arrived twenty-minutes late but no one mentioned it. Vanessa sounded really enthusiastic about the wedding; much like me three hours ago.

"Possibly." Grace smiled coyly. "I'm going to go back next week and have another look before I decide for definite. It's gorgeous though isn't it, Marie?"

"Perfect!" As if I'd say anything else.

"And when's the wedding? Next year?" asked Teresa, a tall, striking brunette in a power suit.

"Next spring," Grace said. "I'm saving up my vacation time so we can have a few days here for the wedding and then have a couple of weeks somewhere exotic for the honeymoon."

The champagne had made my head a bit foggy and I only half listened as the conversation moved to work. I looked around the restaurant as they chatted about people and things that I didn't know anything about. Occasionally, I tried to tune in to the conversation and nod along with what was being said, but I was getting more and more bored as the lunch went on.

Teresa suddenly looked in my direction. "I can't believe you're marrying Brian!"

It hadn't really occurred to me that as Grace's ex-colleagues, Teresa and Vanessa currently worked with Brian.

"Well, I am!"

"We never thought he was the marrying type, did we?" Teresa looked over at Vanessa who nodded her agreement. "I think all of the women in the office have had a crush on Brian at some point, but he never dated anyone from work."

"That's good," I said. "Or lunch could've been awkward." I laughed, but no one else seemed to see the humour.

"When's the wedding?" Vanessa asked.

"We haven't set a date yet. Probably next year sometime. Maybe this year. Who knows?"

"I don't think it could be this year." Grace smiled, making me feel like a complete idiot. "Especially not with your organisational skills!"

"The thing is …" I could feel the anger rising. "I don't have great organisational skills but I'm pretty good at throwing things together. I just go with the flow and see what happens. It doesn't bother me if things aren't perfectly organised." I was trying to sound like the most chilled out person in the world and hopefully make Grace sound uptight while I was at it. I'm not sure why I felt the need to validate my choices but it felt like I was being attacked.

"Well you've been engaged for over six months," Grace said, "and you still have zero plans for the wedding. It seems a bit of a stretch to think it might happen this year."

"I guess you have to plan it around Brian's work as well," Teresa said, tilting her head to one side.

"How do you mean?" I asked.

"Well he can't just take time off whenever. Things are crazy in the office at the moment and I don't think it's going to ease off for a while. It must be hard, marrying such a high-flyer. Everything must get a bit overshadowed by his work."

"He's always the first in the office and the last to leave," Vanessa added, seemingly just to make me hate her.

"He's very dedicated to his job," I agreed. "But I think he'll manage to take a bit of time off to get married. I'm fairly sure things won't fall apart without him around for a week or two. You'll just have to hold the fort for a while." I forced a smile and wished lunch was over.

Vanessa smiled condescendingly before turning to Grace to ask her about her job and life in New York. I went back to pretending I was listening to them as I watched the other people in the restaurant. It seemed to be a popular place for business lunches, with lots of people in suits looking stuffy and serious. At least I wasn't the only one not having any fun.

By the time we got into Grace's car for the two-hour drive to the coast, I was emotionally drained and hoping for a nap.

"You're very defensive about Brian and the wedding," Grace said as she accelerated down the slip road to join the motorway.

"Am I?" I'd just got comfy and my eyes were heavy.

"Yeah, I thought you were a bit rude at lunch."

"How was I rude?" I didn't want to get into an argument with Grace but I felt like she was trying to goad me.

"You were snappy and defensive. And I don't know why you seem to look down on anyone who has order in their life. Not everyone wants to just plod along and hope for the best."

"I don't look down at people." I laughed, finding the statement quite ironic. "But some people seem to have a problem with my relaxed attitude."

"Well it's not just that you're relaxed, you're also completely unrealistic. No matter how small your wedding is, you will have to plan it. And you do need to think about Brian's work schedule. He can't just drop everything like you can."

"I would have to book time off from work as well. I don't know why you think it's such an issue for Brian to take time off."

"You can't really compare your job to Brian's though," she said.

My heart rate shot up immediately. "Why not? I have a good job."

"You know what I mean … your job's not ..." She paused and I wondered whether she wanted to say important or well-paid. I'd never realised before what she thought of my silly little job. "Well it's just not as demanding as Brian's job, is it?" That was diplomatic of her.

"No, but I don't know what that's got to do with anything. Brian's not going to put his job before our wedding."

"I just don't think you understand how it is when

you're high up in a big firm. Sometimes your job comes before your personal life. That's just the way it is if you want to do well."

"That might be how it is for you," I told her sadly. "But Brian's not like that." I turned to look out of the window hoping that would bring an end to the conversation. I felt a bit sorry for Grace that she felt work could be more important than anything else.

Annoyingly, an image of Brian with his head in laptop kept springing to my mind. It was only in the last couple of months that his work had become really hectic, and he kept assuring me that it was just a temporary thing. I closed my eyes and hoped that the trip to the coast would be more fun than the morning had been.

Chapter 11

Even though I knew it was completely ridiculous, I couldn't help myself: I squeezed my eyes tight shut and wished myself away. I decided it could just be one of those things that no one has ever tried because it seems so unlikely. Ideally, I'd transport myself to a tropical island with palm trees and white sandy beaches. If I could open my eyes and find myself on a sun lounger with a cocktail in my hand, I'd be one happy lady.

I could still hear the screaming around me so it didn't seem to be working yet. Squeezing my eyes tighter, I tried a different approach. For the first attempt at teleporting myself, I was probably being a bit ambitious with my destination.

Anywhere. The word reverberated inside my head. *Anywhere but here!* I carried on and this time shouted the words in my head. *Absolutely anywhere! Just not here!* The sudden silence came as a shock and I'll be a honest; there was a millisecond when a teeny tiny part of me thought maybe I'd just discovered how to teleport myself.

"Marie! What the hell are you doing?"

That was my first clue that I was still standing in the same room as Bridezilla and had not, in fact, achieved teleportation. Slowly, I opened my eyes and looked at Grace and the poor woman she'd been tearing strips off. They were both staring at me. At least I'd managed to get Grace to stop screaming.

"I was …" I hesitated, trying to think of an appropriate response. Obviously, it's wrong to lie but there are some situations where you know that the truth isn't going to help anyone. "Just trying to think of a solution to all of this," I finally said. That wasn't even a lie, but Grace's idea of a solution was perhaps slightly different to mine. "It does seem like an honest mistake," I said, in an attempt to diffuse the situation.

I winced as Grace slipped back into screaming mode. "It is definitely a mistake and someone needs to be held accountable."

"I'm very sorry." The poor woman took a deep breath, clearly doing her best to stay calm. "As I've already explained, we have your wedding booked in, but it's for two years' time and not next year. I can only apologise. There really is nothing I can do about it. The circumstances are beyond my control."

Grace had insisted we go to the hotel to have a look as soon as we'd dropped our bags off at the house. We'd quickly learned of the mix up with the wedding date.

"I want to get married next spring!" Grace yelled. "Out there in the gardens, just like I've been dreaming of since I was a little girl. Somebody needs to fix this."

"Actually …" The hotel manager cowered slightly as she turned her computer in our direction. "In your original email you'll see that you wrote the date which we have in our system."

Oh no! It was Grace's mistake and not the hotel's.

I could see her peering at the computer screen, struggling to believe it could possibly be her error. Grace doesn't make mistakes.

I decided that as best friend and bridesmaid, it was probably my duty to step in now.

I gently took Grace's elbow. "How about we go and calm down and talk things through so we can decide what we do from here."

"I don't need to calm down. She is telling me that I have to change all my plans and it's not fair!" She pulled away from me and stormed out of the room.

"Did she just stamp her foot?" I asked the poor hotel manager.

"I think so."

"What a nutter! You'd think she was about five years old, the way she's carrying on."

"I've seen brides get like this before. Wedding planning doesn't bring out the best in people."

"It's probably hard to believe, but she's generally one of the most cool and calm people I know. I used to think she was part robot because she hardly shows emotions. She just ruined that theory."

The hotel manager gave me a sympathetic look. "Good luck with the bridesmaid gig!"

"Thanks. I'm really sorry about all that. Keep the booking as it is. Hopefully it'll all be fine once she's calmed down." I made my way across the hotel lobby in the direction Grace had gone.

She was sitting on a bench in the hotel's garden, with her phone pressed against her ear. I lingered at a safe distance until I saw her remove the phone from her ear. I was fairly confident that whatever I said would be wrong so I tentatively put a hand on her shoulder and waited.

"I can't believe this is happening." She wiped at her damp cheeks. "I spoke to James and he can't understand why I'm so upset. He says we can get married a year later or somewhere else. He just doesn't get it. I'm so glad you're here, Marie. You get it, don't you?"

Again, the truth didn't seem like it was going to help matters.

"Of course. You want your perfect wedding and you were all excited about it being next year. That's understandable." She nodded. "We will figure this out, I promise."

She managed a lopsided smile and I decided I was pretty good at this bridesmaid thing. "Come on," I said. "Let's go back to the house and crack open some wine. We can pretend we're on holiday."

"I'm sorry," she said. "I told you this would be fun, didn't I?"

"Yes, you did. But we only just arrived, it's not too late to keep your promise." We bumped shoulders as we set off away from the hotel and through the gardens. The hotel gardens eventually joined the public gardens which ran almost the whole length of the cliff top.

The view took my breath away. "Look at that. It's amazing." I stopped to take it in. There was something majestic about the rough North Sea. It mesmerised me.

"Come on," Grace prompted, unmoved by the view.

The sea air whipped at my face and I smiled to myself. I'd been here with Grace for holidays when we were kids. Her parents had bought a house there when Grace was a baby and they usually spent a large part of the summer in it. It was only a little fishing village but I always found it idyllic. I loved the beach and the gusty sea air. My mum was never big on holidaying so this was as good as it got for me.

"I think I'm going to have a walk along the beach to try and clear my head," Grace said as we approached the house. "Shall I get us some fish and chips for tea?"

"Sounds great. Do you want me to come with you?"

"No. I feel like being on my own for a bit, if you don't mind."

I didn't mind at all. I'd have some time to relax. Plus, I had a Skype date with Brian.

Chapter 12

I was wrapped up in a thick woollen cardigan and had settled myself on the patio with a glass of wine. Brian beamed at me through the laptop

"Hey, you!" he said. "I miss you already. When are you coming home?"

"I don't know. There was a bit of a mix up with the wedding date and Grace totally flipped out so I don't know what the plan is. I daren't ask too much."

"That doesn't sound good."

"She's so stressed out," I said. "Hopefully she'll start to relax once she's over the jet lag and gets the wedding plans back on track."

"I don't think she and James have much of a social life in New York. Imagine how crazy you would be without your friends to keep you sane." He flashed his boyish smile and I laughed at him.

"I presume that's a joke? I used to be sane before I met you and our misfit friends. Imagine how simple life would be without that crazy bunch hanging around all the time …"

"Watch who you're calling crazy!" A cushion flew past Brian's head, knocking the laptop out of his hands. I caught a glimpse of Sophie before my screen showed the ceiling. I laughed as she appeared on the screen.

"Hey, Marie! How about I put you on the table so you have a better view of all your misfit friends?"

They waved at me, totally unoffended. I'd known that they'd be in the background.

"So things aren't going well?" Linda asked. "Poor Grace. It's very stressful planning a wedding."

"I know. But she's like a different person and it's quite scary. If I get like that you can punch me!"

"Bridezilla?" Sophie asked.

"Exactly."

"I remember my aunt being the same when she got married. Best just to steer clear."

"I don't have that option, Sophie! I'm her bridesmaid. She's relying on me."

"She's really stuffed then, isn't she?" Sophie grinned and I stuck my tongue out at her.

"It doesn't sound like a lot of fun," Jake said. "Where is she anyway?"

"Gone to get fish and chips."

There was a collective groan. "Fish and chips by the sea!" Jake said. "That's not fair, I want some."

"Oh and look at this ..." I turned the laptop around to show them the garden which ran towards the cliff, overlooking the bay.

"You've got a sea view," Sophie remarked. "I'm jealous!"

"It's lovely," Linda said, as I turned the computer back to me.

"It's fantastic," I agreed. "I just wish I could relax and enjoy it a bit more. I'm walking on eggshells around Grace. You know I'm not great at walking on egg shells!"

"Bigfoot!" Brian and Sophie said at once.

"Hey!" I mock protested before changing the subject. "How's work, Linda?"

"It's fine …" She hesitated. "It's really boring in the week. It's so quiet. Jean is quite snappy at the moment too. I think she's having marital problems. Anyway she's not much fun to be around." Jean was the owner of the shop and I don't think Linda had ever been very fond of her.

"Get a new job," Sophie said.

"I can't just get a new job, Sophie!"

"Why not?"

"Loyalty, for one thing. Plus Marie worked hard to get me that job. You all did."

"Not really," I said. "You got it on your own merit."

"Yes, but you made everyone write references for me." We all smiled at the memory. Linda had been out of the workplace for so long that she didn't have any references, so we all wrote her character references and sang her praises

"What's loyalty got to do with anything?" Sophie asked. "If she wants loyalty she should make sure you're happy at work. If she's creating an unhappy working environment then it's her own fault if you leave. Life is too short to stay in a job that you don't like. Especially you, Linda. It's supposed to be more of a hobby, isn't it? George said you didn't need to work."

We all looked at Sophie. It was rare for her to be sincere but when she was, everyone listened.

"I'm really starting to hate my job, too," she added, "and there's no way I'll stick around out of loyalty. I'll be off as soon as I can. Anyway, we should find Linda a new job. I love it when we have a project."

Jack shook his head. "Let's check Linda wants a new job before we go fixing something that's not broken."

Linda shrugged and wrung her hands.

"Okay," Jake said. "Carry on, Sophie!"

Sophie beamed. "Let's all keep our eyes and ears open for anything suitable. Next week we can tailor-make some fake CVs and references to send out."

Linda's eyes were wide. "We can't do that."

"Oh, we can," Sophie said. "And we will!"

I heard the words 'unethical' and 'immoral' being thrown around amidst Sophie's laughter but I'd turned at the sound of the patio doors sliding open behind me. Grace was back with dinner.

"That smells delicious! Everyone's here …" I pointed at the laptop and Grace leaned in to wave.

"Grace, do you think it's unethical to write a fake CV and references to get a job?" Sophie asked.

"Yes," Grace said without hesitation.

"Okay, so it's unethical. But sometimes it's okay to be unethical, isn't it?"

"No," Grace replied.

"You ethical people on your high horses!" Sophie laughed. "How else will Linda get a job?"

"She'll get one," I said. "She managed it last time."

"With fake references!" Sophie said.

"They were real references. They were just character references from friends and she didn't claim they were anything else."

"Mine was fake," Sophie said. "I wrote that I

thought Linda had great fashion sense and was always up-to-date on the latest trends."

"I'm going to go and eat my fish and chips," I said, chuckling. "I'll talk to you soon."

There was some more groaning about fish and chips amidst the goodbyes and then I got a close up of Brian as he picked up the laptop.

"Call me tomorrow?"

"I will." I blew him a kiss, drawing immediate vomit noises from Sophie.

When I turned my attention to the delicious fish and chips, I had a silly little grin on my face. Brian still gave me butterflies.

Chapter 13

A woman from the hotel rang the next morning to apologise again for the mix-up and to invite us to speak to the Events' Manager the following morning. I called Brian to tell him that I'd be staying another night and then quizzed Grace about what she wanted to do for the day.

"We could have a walk around the town, I guess." She was fairly unenthusiastic. I think she was really hoping to see the Events' Manager sooner. She didn't like it when things didn't go to plan and she now seemed to think we had a wasted day, on top of everything else.

When she went to shower, I slid the patio doors open and wandered out into the back garden. It was a beautiful morning and the garden was bathed in sunshine.

"Hello!" The voice in the next garden made me jump. A little old lady was sitting at the patio table. It was all decked out with a dainty tea set. "I've got tea if you want a cup?"

"Erm …" She'd taken me by surprise and I wasn't sure what to say.

"Come on, I'd like the company." She patted the chair next to her and I squeezed through a gap in the low hedge to take a seat.

"Thanks, this is lovely."

She poured me a cup of tea. "You must be a friend of Grace?"

"Yeah, I'm Marie."

"I'm Holly," she said. "I heard about the wedding mix-up. Is it all sorted out now?"

"Not really …" I said hesitantly, not sure how she could know about it.

"It's a small town," she explained. "Not much happens here. We gossip a lot."

I laughed at her honesty as I took a sip of tea.

"That's Seth over there." She nodded down the garden. I hadn't registered the man trimming the hedge. "He'll mow the lawn next."

"Okay," I said.

"It doesn't even look like it needs doing, does it?" she mused, looking down the long narrow garden.

"No. Not really." She probably didn't see many people and had lost her social skills. Her small talk was pretty mundane.

"It's good to keep Seth busy, though." She looked at me and I struggled to read her expression. I wasn't sure I knew what she meant. Maybe Seth was desperate for money so she was finding him work to help him out. Or maybe she worried about him for some reason and wanted to keep him occupied.

"I'm going to disturb your peace, I'm afraid, ladies." The gardener's voice broke my thoughts as he wandered up the garden towards us. "Shall I wait and mow the lawn later?"

"No," Holly said. "Come and do it now. It's fine,"

He walked to an old shed at the end of the garden and reappeared a minute later wheeling an old lawn mower. He smiled up at us before pulling on the cord to bring the cumbersome looking contraption roaring to life.

Holly's voice rose over the din.

"Before my William died, he kept talking about getting a more modern lawn mower, but I always worried it would make life too easy for Seth."

I took another sip of tea and wondered how I could excuse myself from her garden and the stilted conversation.

"I guess the lawn mower won't last much longer anyway," she went on, "and then I'll have to get one of those silly little modern things."

I was puzzled by her talk of lawn mowers and wondered whether her mind was starting to go. She didn't seem to be making much sense. We watched Seth move away from us again down the garden.

"Here we go." Holly nodded towards Seth, a mischievous smile playing on her lips.

I followed her gaze as Seth came to a stop at the end of the garden. He peeled off his T-shirt, wiped his face with it and then slung it onto the wall. He waved to us before setting off with the lawn mower again.

"Act normal," Holly said out of the corner of her mouth. I took a sip of tea and tried to ignore the blush which rose in my cheeks as Seth came nearer.

"He wouldn't work up a sweat like that with one of those modern, lightweight mowers, would he?" she said as he moved away from us again.

A laugh escaped me. "Holly! You're terrible!"

She beamed at me and we went back to quietly drinking our tea when Seth got nearer again.

"It's a shame you don't have a bigger garden," I

remarked once he was out of earshot.

"Definitely!"

We stifled laughter like a pair of schoolchildren as the hunky Seth pushed the mower up and down the garden.

"Do you want to sit and have a drink with us before you get off?" Holly asked him once he'd finished.

"No time, I'm afraid, Mrs P. You ladies enjoy this sunshine though."

"This is Marie, by the way," Holly said.

"Hi, Marie!" He grinned as he pulled his T-shirt back on. He was ruggedly good-looking and his half smile and twinkly eyes made him look constantly amused.

"Marie is a friend of Grace," Holly explained.

He looked towards the house. "Grace is in town, is she?"

"Do you know her too?" I said. "She went to have a shower but I can give her a shout …"

"No, it's fine. I don't really know her, not since we were kids anyway … I better get on. Have a great day, ladies!" He flashed us a huge smile and had just turned to move down the side of the house when a frantic voice stopped him in his tracks.

"Hi, Mrs H!" Seth turned and greeted the grey-haired lady in the next garden.

"Arthur's back's playing up again. Could you do the lawn for me when you've got time?"

"No problem, Mrs H. It'll have to be tomorrow though."

"Lovely." She waved after him. "See you then."

We watched him disappear around house and then

Mrs H. turned to us. "Fingers crossed for another no T-shirt day tomorrow, ladies."

I wasn't sure how to feel as the two old dears laughed heartily. I felt somehow offended on Seth's behalf. Then I caught Holly's eye and burst into a fit of giggles. I couldn't help myself.

"There you are," Grace said when she stepped outside a few minutes later. "Hi, Mrs Perkins."

"Hello, Grace! Will you please call me Holly?"

"I couldn't do that. My mum would have a fit. Are you ready, Marie?"

"Yes." I smiled at Holly who shook her head, seeming bemused by Grace. "Thanks for the cuppa and the morning entertainment."

"You're welcome dear. Same time tomorrow if you feel like it!"

"We'll see …" I said lightly.

When I followed Grace into the house, I was overwhelmed by her bad mood. I had the distinct feeling she was annoyed with me for having a good time She walked through the house and out of the front door. I followed close behind.

"Shall we go down to the beach?" I tried to override her bad vibe by being upbeat.

"What for?"

My eyes went wide at her question and I felt like banging my head against the nearest wall. Literally. I managed to resist the urge and smiled sweetly at Grace.

"Just thought it might be nice … What do you want to do?"

"I'd like to have a look for good spots for the wedding photos. Further up on the cliff top beyond the hotel should be nice, and maybe in the memorial gardens."

"Won't you get the photos taken at the hotel?"

"Yes." She stared at me like I'd said something stupid again. "But it's nice to have some different scenery."

"Okay, lead the way." Slapping on a smile, I tried to put a spring in my step. We walked away from the town and onto the path up to the cliff top. I was trying very hard to ignore the feeling of annoyance that was stirring in me. I knew if I gave in to it, there'd be no coming back. I'd get angrier and angrier until I finally exploded and said something to her. I'm not sure why she was so determined for it to be such a miserable weekend.

We spent the morning trekking around, searching out suitable photo-shoot locations. When we headed into the town I was totally fed up and was wishing the day away.

"Let's grab some lunch," I said as we passed the pub. Grace frowned but I walked inside before she could protest.

"I don't know what the food will be like in here," she said as we entered the slightly dingy room.

"Don't be such a snob." I waltzed up to the bar to get us some wine. Surely that would help the mood.

We sat at a cosy little round table in the window and sipped our drinks. I tried to make conversation with Grace; asking her about James and New York, but she wasn't very chatty. Eventually I gave up and we ate in silence while I watched the comings and goings in the pub.

"Hello!" I called automatically when the familiar

face of the gardener walked in the door, just as the barman cleared our empty plates away.

He looked momentarily confused, but grinned at us, looking thoroughly pleased with himself. His smile was slightly unsettling after spending so much time with Grace. It was as though his soul was happy and it radiated from his face and whole demeanour.

"We met this morning at Holly's house," I reminded him. "Seth right?"

"Yes! Marie?"

I returned his smile, nodding.

"I'm just calling in for a quick drink between jobs. Is that chair free?" His huge smile was infectious and I hoped it might even cheer Grace up.

"It is! Come and join us."

"Great. I'll grab a pint and be right with you."

Grace glared at me. "What did you do that for?"

"What?"

"Invite some stranger to sit with us."

"He's not a stranger. He's Holly's gardener. Besides, he said he knew you from years back."

"I don't think so." Grace looked over at Seth. He was standing by the bar, laughing with the barman.

He rejoined us a few minutes later with a pint of beer in his hand. "You don't remember me, do you?" he said to Grace.

"I'm not sure …"

"Mrs P. used to look after me when my mum was at work. We played in the garden together sometimes when we were little."

"That was you?" Grace seemed to forget herself and laughed.

"It was indeed. After all these years I never forgot you!" I wasn't sure if he was flirting with Grace or if he just had a playful nature. Grace seemed oblivious anyway.

"You stopped coming though?" Grace looked thoughtful, as though she was trawling through her memories.

"Yes. Mum got a job in the school office so she was always home to look after me after that. We did meet again though. You must have been about thirteen or fourteen."

"And?" Grace looked at him impatiently.

"And what?" he said.

"What happened?"

"You were there." He laughed and took a swig of his beer.

"I don't remember."

His eyes sparked. "Maybe it'll come back to you."

"You can't just say that and not tell us the rest," I said. "The suspense might kill me!"

He carried on grinning and I laughed again. "Are you always so cheerful?" I asked.

"I don't know. Maybe it's just when I'm around beautiful women."

"Stop it!" I said. "I think you're a bit of a tease."

"And we're both engaged, so you're out of luck," Grace said frostily.

"Lucky fellas!" he said. "You know, I think I am always pretty cheerful. I live in this beautiful little place and my lungs are full of sea air. I have great people around me and I enjoy my job."

I nodded at him and he leaned in to whisper conspiratorially. "You know, some of the women in this town will pay just to see me take my top off."

I cracked up laughing. "You know about that?" I asked.

"They're not as subtle as they like to think."

"So you don't find it degrading? You aren't morally outraged?"

"I take it as a compliment. If it makes them happy, who am I to complain? The winter months are brutal though. I can barely scrape a living!"

"They don't invite you in to keep them warm?" I teased.

He laughed easily. "I'm careful to keep some boundaries! There's an unwritten 'look but don't touch' rule."

"That sounds like a good rule."

"What do you think of Mrs P. though? She looked after me from me being a baby and now she gets her kicks from watching me doing her gardening with no shirt on. That's a bit disturbing, isn't it?"

I nodded. "It's quite disturbing."

"So, that's what you were laughing about this morning?" Grace asked.

"Yes. You missed the morning entertainment." I finished off my wine. I'd happily have stayed in the pub for the rest of the day. The wine and Seth's easy company had lifted my mood. I didn't dare suggest another glass of wine though so I sat and chatted to Seth while I awaited instructions.

"I need to get back to work," Seth said as he emptied his glass in one long gulp. "It's been lovely chatting with you."

"Aren't you going to tell us the end of the story about when you last saw Grace? I don't want to go to my grave still wondering …"

He turned to Grace with that twinkle in his eye. After a brief hesitation he reached in his pocket and produced a handful of coins, carefully picking out one and placing it on the table in front of Grace. Then he grinned and turned to leave without another word.

"What was that?" I asked as my eyes followed him to the door. "Did he just tip you?"

"It's for the wishing well." She inspected the coin with a sly smile. "That's where we met when we were teenagers."

"Well, that's a bit romantic. You should go after him and snog him or something."

"We don't all forget our other halves at the slightest bit of attention from other men you know." She shook her head.

I gave her a puzzled look. "I was only joking."

"You were flirting with him," she said.

"No, I was just being nice. Maybe you should try it." I tried to sound light-hearted but realised I was walking a thin line. We didn't seem to be able to talk anymore without sniping at each other. It seemed like we were constantly verging on an argument.

"Let's go," Grace said with a sigh. "The jet lag is getting to me. I just want to go and relax at the house."

We called at the shops to pick up some dinner and Grace spent the rest of the afternoon lying on the couch, looking through bridal magazines. I wandered around trying to kill time. Out on the patio, I watched the sun go down over the water and was relieved when Grace put her head out of the door to say she was going up to bed. I watched TV for a while before taking myself up to bed, happy that the day was over and that I would soon be home in my own bed.

Chapter 14

The next morning, while Grace was showering, I stepped out to the patio. Holly immediately invited me to join her for a cuppa again. I did my best not to laugh as Seth shouted a greeting from the neighbouring garden. The grey-haired Mrs H. was also sipping tea with us and enjoying the view. I avoided eye contact with Seth but found the whole situation hilarious.

"I've got to go." I stood up quickly when I saw Grace look out through the patio doors. "Thanks for the tea!"

I followed Grace out of the house and up the road in the direction of the hotel.

"Is that your wishing well?" I asked as we walked through the park. The old well was hidden away in a corner.

"I thought they'd have got rid of the crumbly old thing by now."

"It's cute. Do you want to make a wish?"

She looked puzzled. "Why waste money throwing it into a hole in the ground?"

"It's not a waste," I said. "You get a wish. Anything you want!" I hurried to keep up with her, amused by how different we were.

We'd just reached the hotel when my phone started to ring.

"It's Brian," I said as I stopped to answer it.

"I missed you so much," he said without greeting. "I thought I'd drive over and have a day on the coast with you. But I'm outside the house and no one's here."

"We're at the hotel." I beamed into the phone. "Just keep driving up the road and follow the signs, you can't miss it."

Grace told me to wait for Brian while she went in to meet with the Events' Manager. Apparently she didn't really need me anyway. I just hoped she didn't turn into Bridezilla again and get herself barred from the place.

I stood in the car park and waved when Brian's car pulled in.

He looked nervous as he exited the car followed by Sophie, her boyfriend, Jeff, and Linda. A familiar car pulled up next to them and Jake climbed out followed by his partner, Michael, and nephew, Callum. I couldn't help but smile even as I wondered how Grace would react to the arrival of my friends. I had the feeling she wouldn't be too keen on my attention being divided.

"Surprise!" Brian gave me a quick peck on the cheek before Sophie nudged him out of the way and flung her arms around me.

"Fat club field trip!" she announced.

I laughed and did a round of hugs and greetings. I ruffled Callum's hair as he struggled out of my embrace. I'd become really fond of Callum. He was a cheeky twelve-year-old who was a pleasure to be around. His mum, Carol, wasn't very reliable and, being a single parent, she depended on Jake to help out with Callum.

"You don't mind, do you?" Brian whispered. The outing clearly wasn't his idea.

"I don't, but I'm not sure what Grace will make of the intrusion."

"Where is she?" he asked.

"Just having a look around the hotel, chatting things over with the Events' Manager."

"It's lovely here." Sophie inhaled dramatically. "Get a lung-full of that sea air!"

"I can see why Grace wants to get married here," Linda said. "It's beautiful."

We took in the regal hotel and its immaculately kept lawns. "Come on, I'll show you where the action happens." I took Brian's hand and set off through the gardens. There was the usual amount of banter and tussling as we walked, so I didn't notice there was a wedding taking place until we were uncomfortably close to it.

An open-sided marquee stood on the lawn and the guests were seated under it. There was a table at the front with a flower arrangement in the centre of it. A man, who I took to be the groom, was pacing nervously.

An usher hurried over to me and thrust something into my hand. I looked down to find an order of service for the marriage of Katy Sutton and Neil Wilson. "Oh no, sorry …" I began to protest.

He looked us up and down. "You are here for the wedding, aren't you?"

"Yes!" Sophie said, pushing past me. The usher looked her over, clearly not convinced. She forcefully took an order of service from him.

"We've had a nightmare with lost luggage. Katy won't mind what we're wearing though."

"Okay, sorry. Be quick! You're really late. Katy will be here any second. Sit anywhere." He nudged me forward.

When one or two of the wedding guests turned, I automatically returned their smiles and looked back to find the rest of my gang casually walking over to take seats on the back rows. I glared at Sophie who had a mischievous smile on her face.

"Should we leave?" I whispered to Brian.

"Too late now." He nodded to the hotel entrance where a wedding car was pulling up.

Linda looked slightly panicked, but the rest of our crew looked thoroughly amused. I tried my best to keep my head down for fear of being caught out, but as time ticked by I began stealing glances. It seemed that most of the wedding guests were getting twitchy as they looked back at the bride. Over at the hotel, the bride was pacing and a couple of bridesmaids tried to keep up with her.

My eyes instinctively darted to the groom who was looking increasingly nervous in front of the guests. He was deep in conversation with his best man but kept glancing at the bride. Finally, the best man took a deep breath and reluctantly headed back down the aisle in the direction of the bride.

"What's going on?" I asked Brian quietly. Murmurs arose from the wedding guests.

"I'm not sure. Can you see cameras anywhere? It feels like a scene from a soap opera …"

As I looked back, the bride took strides towards the best man and slapped him across the face. There was a collective intake of breath from the wedding guests. The bridesmaids hovered awkwardly as the best man held his hands up to the bride and appeared to try and talk her down.

She seemed to be getting more hysterical; shouting at him and pushing him back when he took a step towards her. The groom took off at a jog to get to his bride. Although at this point I wasn't entirely convinced whose bride she was.

"I can't hear anything." I leaned into Brian as we watched the drama unfold from a distance.

"My guess is there's something going on between the bride and the best man," Brian said.

Just then the best man reached out a hand to the bride. The groom punched him in the face.

A gasp went up around us. It didn't quite cover up Sophie's cheer. When several pairs of eyes landed on her, she quietly lowered the arm she'd thrown up in excitement.

A few of the guests had headed over to the scene of the drama as soon as the punch was thrown and the rest stayed in their seats unsure of what to do. Finally, the wedding party dispersed into the hotel or away in the wedding cars; it was hard to tell with all the bustle.

The remaining guests headed slowly towards the hotel, leaving only our amused group sitting dumbfounded in our seats.

We looked around at each other with amusement.

"Well that was brilliant," Sophie remarked.

My eyes were drawn to the tall woman in a grey suit at the front. She was shuffling papers around the table.

"Anyone fancy getting married?" Sophie said, following my gaze. "I hear there's been a cancellation!" She cackled with laughter and then stopped abruptly and looked at Jeff. "Should we?" Her eyes were wide, as though she'd just had a light-bulb moment.

Panic flashed across Jeff's features. He managed a half-hearted laugh, obviously hoping Sophie was joking.

"Seriously?" she said. "We could get married. Let's do it!"

"You can't just get married," I said.

"Why not?" She glared at me and I realised my mistake. Telling Sophie she couldn't do something was like waving a red rag to a bull.

"You're too young," I said. "And if anyone was going to get married on the spur of the moment it would be me and Brian, since we're already engaged."

"We won't though," Brian said. I glared at him and he withdrew back into his seat.

"It's a shame George isn't here," Linda said. "We've been talking about renewing our vows."

"You wouldn't though," Sophie said. "It's my idea. You can't hijack someone's idea."

"You're too young to get married," Jake told Sophie gently. I caught the look in his eye. The look that was boring into Michael and was clearly a question. I let out an excited gasp.

"He's proposing," I whispered to Brian with delight.

"He's not said anything!" Brian turned to look at Jake and Michael. Jake was still gazing at Michael with a silly grin on his face.

"No!" Michael finally said without looking at Jake. "Not today. Stop looking at me like that! We're not doing it. Stop!" He finally turned and put a hand over Jake's sweet, smiling face, laughing as he pushed the puppy dog eyes away from him.

"We should just do it!" Sophie said excitedly to Jeff.

"Sophie!" I said. "You're not getting married. Look at the fear in Jeff's eyes!"

"Shut up, Marie! Stick to worrying about your own relationship. Brian shot you down straight away when you mentioned it."

I let out a sigh of exasperation as I sought for a comeback. "Brian would marry me. Right here. Right now. Definitely. Wouldn't you?" I turned to look at him and then looked around the place. "It's actually a really nice place to get married …"

I felt my face fall into a sly smile as my eyes came back to Brian. "It's really nice," I said again.

He shook his head and raised his eyebrows as his cheeky smile played on his lips.

"Excuse me …" We were interrupted by the tall lady. "I couldn't help but overhear. It does seem a shame to waste a good wedding, doesn't it?" She looked around at us all. "Can I interest anyone?"

"We will." Sophie shot out of her chair. "We'll do it!"

"No. You won't." I got to my feet to look her square in the eyes. "Brian! Tell her!"

He stretched out his legs and entwined his hands behind his head, leaning back and saying nothing at all. I kicked him but he just smirked.

The suited lady let out a laugh. "Were you really serious? You really thought you could waltz up to the front and get married, just like that! You're hilarious." She turned and walked towards the hotel with a folder tucked under her arm. "You really made my day! As if it wasn't crazy enough already."

Sophie and I managed to stay straight-faced for a few seconds before we erupted with laughter. We were sitting in someone's abandoned wedding venue and creasing up with uncontrollable laughter. Brian kicked me playfully.

"You're crazy," he said as I sat beside him.

"You knew she was going to say that, didn't you?"

"Yes." He spoke slowly, with his know-it-all tone. "There's this thing you need called a marriage licence."

"Oh shut up!" I kissed him.

"This is why I always love a fat club outing," Sophie said. "We crashed a wedding and then tried to hijack it for ourselves!"

We just about had the laughter under control when Grace joined us, looking puzzled. "What's going on?"

"Erm …" I wasn't sure how to explain. "It's a long story …"

Her brow creased. "You only left me twenty minutes ago. How long can it be?"

"How was it with the Events' Manager?" Standing, I took Grace's arm and pulled her away.

"Okay, I guess. I'm not sure what we'll do. I need to talk to James. What are *they* doing here?" She nodded back toward the wedding tent.

"They fancied a day at the seaside." I shrugged. "You don't mind, do you?"

"I guess it's fine. Don't you get fed up with them? They always seem to be hanging around. And why do they always feel the need for surprises? Couldn't they ask you instead of just turning up?"

"I guess they think I might say no." I glanced back at them sitting around, chatting and laughing. "And, no, I don't get fed up with them, but don't tell them that. I like to keep up the air of indifference."

Chapter 15

On the beach, Sophie pulled off her shoes and socks. "Who's coming for a paddle?"

I didn't hesitate to abandon my shoes and socks and chase Sophie down the beach. Callum and Jeff overtook me before I reached the water's edge. I paused to roll up my trousers, then ploughed in until the water was almost up to my knees. I gasped and shivered, laughing even before Sophie and the boys started splashing me.

"It's freezing." Brian looked fairly pathetic as he dipped a toe in the water.

"Come on." I kicked water at him.

"Hey!" He rolled his trousers up and followed me into the sea. I put my arms around his neck and pulled his body into mine as I kissed him.

"I think I might be drunk on sea air." I squealed as a wave rolled in and soaked the bottom of my trousers.

We were all slightly damp when we headed back up the beach to rejoin the others. They'd rented a row of deckchairs and I dropped straight into one.

A shout drew my attention. Seth was walking along the road at the top of the beach.

"Hi!" I shouted back and gave him a wave. "Seth's there," I told Grace. She leaned forward in her deckchair to turn and wave at him.

"Enjoy the sunshine!" he called before carrying on along the road.

"I wouldn't kick him out of bed," Sophie said with a raised eyebrow.

Jeff nudged her. "I'm right here, you know?"

"Aww." She put her arms around him. "Not literally! It's just a saying. I really just meant 'phwoar!'"

"You're digging yourself a hole," Jeff said with a smile.

She chuckled. "Who is the hottie?"

"Just some local who Marie's being flirting with," Grace replied flatly.

I glared at her as I felt Brian's eyes on me.

"Oh, you were!" she said lightly. "She invited him to have a drink with us yesterday and got all giggly."

"That's not true." I shifted my gaze to Brian. "He and Grace were friends when they were kids. We had a drink with him but I wasn't flirting."

"You didn't seem to be in any hurry to tell him you were engaged," Grace said. My anger levels rose dramatically.

"I didn't have chance. You jumped in and told him before it came up."

"Hey!" Jake interrupted as he wandered over to us. I'd not even registered his absence. "I got a few things to keep Callum entertained." He held up his shopping bags and then emptied them onto the sand to reveal an array of beach toys.

"I love kites!" Sophie grabbed one and opened the packet.

Linda jumped up and took a spade. "Let's have a sandcastle competition. I used to be great at making little sand sculptures … turtles were my specialty."

I think everyone was glad of the interruption. The atmosphere had been getting increasingly awkward. Brian gave me a quick smile and looked unconcerned by Grace's comments.

Michael and Brian each grabbed a bucket and spade, and Jeff reached for a second kite. I looked up at Callum. "What would we do without you, Callum?"

He picked up a Frisbee, then grabbed my hand to pull me out of the deckchair. "You would act like kids with no excuse."

I couldn't stop smiling as I played Frisbee with Callum. We made it more fun by staying close to the rest of our party, meaning that we had to dodge kite strings and partly built sand sculptures as we ran after the Frisbee.

The wind whipped at us, and as the tide came higher, the spray lifted off the sea and landed on us like a fine mist of rain. The sun stayed out making the temperature comfortable.

"You okay?" I asked Grace when I took a break from Frisbee and slumped into the deckchair next to hers. I was still annoyed with her for her comments about Seth but she was looking pretty miserable.

"Fine." She didn't look at me. I had the sudden urge to shake her. I wished that she'd lighten up. She seemed to be looking down her nose at us. I wanted to tell her that it wouldn't hurt to let go and have some fun. I kept quiet though, mainly because after being privy to her Bridezilla moments in the past few days, I was scared that I might re-awaken the beast.

"Right, I'm done!" Brian stepped back to admire his fairly impressive sandcastle. I'd enjoyed watching him work on it with such intense concentration. He made a futile attempt to brush some sand off his jeans before declaring he was starving.

"I'm off to find fish and chips," he said. "Who wants some? My treat."

Hands flew immediately in the air accompanied by words of approval.

"Shall we all walk up?" Grace said. "There's a little restaurant in the chip shop."

Sophie sat beside me. "I'd rather just eat them on the beach."

"But everything gets covered in sand," Grace said, "and it attracts the seagulls."

"A bit of sand won't hurt." Brian grabbed a spade and dumped a mound of sand over her feet. "And I don't mind the odd bird hanging around me!" He winked at me and headed up the beach, leaving no room for discussion.

I avoided eye contact with Grace and focused on Linda who was putting the finishing touches on her sand turtle. I thought back to my time here as a child, and remembered Grace's mum always insisting we walk up to the hotel gardens to eat our picnic at lunchtime. It clearly had a lasting impact on Grace.

"Look out!" Jeff called as he ran past and dived for the Frisbee. He managed to catch it but landed heavily on Brian's sandcastle.

"Brian's going to kill me." Jeff groaned and stood up to survey the damage. "We'll have to rebuild it."

"I don't think he's going to be that bothered about a sandcastle," Grace said.

"Are we talking about the same Brian?" Sophie got up and stood next to Jeff. "I'm not sure what it looked like."

"It had turrets with sticks in the top for flag poles," Linda said.

"And a moat," Callum added.

"Help then," Jeff said as he started re-digging the moat. "He'll be back soon."

We were all sitting casually in a line on the deckchairs when Brian re-appeared ten minutes later.

"What happened?" he asked immediately.

We shrugged and tried to keep straight faces as he looked at each of us in turn. "Who ruined my castle?"

"Oh, that," Sophie said innocently. "A kid ran past and knocked it a bit. We patched it up though "

Brian took a seat in the empty deckchair, clutching a plastic bag, which was emitting the irresistible scent of fish and chips.

"I know that one of you trashed my castle," Brian said seriously. "That person won't be getting any fish and chips. Until I find out who it was, I'll assume it was all of you."

"It was Jeff!" We were all quick to confess when the fish and chips were at stake.

"Oh, come on," Jeff complained as Brian quietly handed out the paper wrapped packages of fish and chips. "It was an accident and I rebuilt it with improvements. Look, it's even got a little door now." Jeff proudly pointed out the door he'd drawn with a stick and then hovered in front of Brian. "Please," he dropped to his knees dramatically. "Don't make me cry in front of everyone!"

Brian smirked as he threw a chip in the air. When Jeff caught it in his mouth, Brian rewarded him with his portion of fish and chips.

Grace was right about the seagulls. They appeared a few at a time until there was quite a crowd of them trying their intimidation tactics on us. Grace told me off when I threw a chip into the crowd.

"Well, you've done it now," she said as the birds closed in on us.

We all threw out chips, sending the seagulls into a frenzy; squawking and fighting and flapping around us. I hurriedly ate a few more chips and once I was sure I'd had enough, I threw out the remnants to the birds. We stamped our feet when they got too close and I was amazed that Grace somehow still managed to look serious.

When the gulls were confident there was no more food to scavenge, they gradually dispersed. We were left to enjoy the peaceful beach and watch the lapping waves that crept ever nearer to us. The sun sunk low on the horizon, becoming masked by hazy clouds and leaving a chill in the air. We started to murmur thoughts of leaving for the drive home.

"We've not done races yet," Michael said. "I always used to end up in kids' clubs on my summer holidays and there were always races on the beach ... three legged, sack race, piggyback ..."

"Piggyback races!" Sophie squealed and jumped up onto Jeff's back.

"Linda, you're with me." Michael bent down in

front of her. I was amused that Linda didn't protest at all.

I turned to Grace. "You go with Brian. I'm going to judge." I pulled her out of the deckchair and she didn't for a second try to hide her disdain at our silliness.

"No chance," she said.

"Quick!" Callum clung on to Jake's back. "We're all ready."

"Go on, Grace," I said, nudging her.

"Leave her alone." Brian draped an arm around her shoulders. "She doesn't have to join in if she doesn't want to."

I was about to disagree when I saw Brian aim a discreet wink at me over Grace's head.

"Fine! On your marks. Get set. Go!" I shouted.

The moment the racers took off along the beach, Brian removed his arm from Grace's shoulder and turned to face her with a cheeky grin.

"No!" Grace stepped away from him, as she realised what he was up to. He had a mischievous twinkle in his eye.

"Get away from me …"

He took her hand and pulled her effortlessly to him, ignoring her protests as he slung her over his shoulder and took off after the others.

I couldn't help but laugh at the sight of Grace becoming more and more hysterical, hitting and kicking at Brian furiously and demanding to be put down. Brian caught up to the others and I realised we'd not defined the finish line. Jeff glanced at Brian next to him before veering to the side to give him a friendly shove. I jogged slowly after them, watching them nudging each other and getting more boisterous as they went.

Michael slowed and put Linda safely down on the sand and Jake moved a safe distance away from Brian and Jeff. They seemed to be getting competitive. As Jeff aimed an elbow at Brian he received a shove in return, sending him stumbling to the ground with Sophie cackling away as she landed in a heap beside him.

Jeff managed to get a hand to Brian's ankle as he went down and knocked him off balance. Brian stumbled for a few steps and then fell onto the sand, dropping Grace as he went.

Jake and Callum were cheering triumphantly. They made their way back for a victory lap of the losers, who were mostly sprawled out on the sand, laughing and swapping banter about who'd tripped who.

Grace was lying on her back, looking straight up at the sky so I couldn't see her expression until I was standing over her. I was surprised to find her holding her stomach and laughing uncontrollably. Brian rolled onto his side to look at her with a wicked smile on his face.

"That was your fault! If you'd gone for a piggyback instead of forcing me to give you a fireman's lift, we would have won!"

Grace could hardly catch her breath, but finally gave Brian a friendly shove. "You're an idiot."

I pulled her up with a huge smile on my face. We linked arms to walk back along the beach and she briefly leaned her head onto my shoulder.

The smile didn't leave her face.

Chapter 16

On the drive home, Grace was the most relaxed I'd seen her in a long time. We chatted and laughed about everything that sprang to mind. All the tension between us seemed to disappear. We turned the radio up when our favourite songs came on and sang along heartily.

The journey flew by and when Grace dropped me home, we arranged to meet for lunch at my mum's house the next day. Grace had always been fond of my mum and was keen to see her during her trip.

Brian was already home and was tapping away on his laptop. I went and kissed the top of his head.

"I don't know what Grace was talking about at the beach," I said. "With the guy …"

He smiled at me. "Grace is not in a happy place at the moment. Don't worry about it."

"I wasn't flirting with him though."

"You think I'm worried about you talking to some beach bum?"

"He's not a beach bum. He's a gardener …" I smiled. "And kind of a stripper!"

Brian raised his eyebrows. "Sometimes it's good to know when to stop talking."

"Sorry." I grinned. "But you have nothing to worry about."

"I know." He pulled my hand to his lips and

kissed my palm.

"I'm going to get an early night," I said. "All that sea air and flirting has worn me out!"

He gave me a cheeky slap on the bum as I moved away.

I found Brian in the exact same position when I got up the next morning. If it weren't for the fact that he was wearing different clothes, I would've sworn he'd not been to bed at all. I forced myself to sound casual when I asked if he was coming to Mum's house. As expected he said he had to get some work done. At least Grace would be there so Mum might forget to complain about Brian working too much.

Grace drove me over there, and we were hit by the mouth-watering scent of roast dinner as we walked into Mum's house together. I was happy to find Aunt Kath working away in the kitchen.

"I'm sorry I couldn't make it last week," she said, hugging me. "I'm cooking your favourite to make up for it."

"All is forgiven." I leaned over the stove and inhaled the delicious aroma.

Mum and Aunt Kath quizzed Grace about her life in New York, and James, and wedding plans.

"You might get a break from the questions while we're eating," I said lightly when we sat at the dining table.

"We haven't seen her for so long," Kath said. "Of course we've got a lot of questions."

"How long are you back for?" Mum asked.

"Actually I've decided to fly back earlier than planned," Grace said as we filled our plates with roast chicken and all the trimmings. "I just don't think there's anything I can do about the wedding now and I feel like I'm missing work for no reason."

"Can't you just enjoy a bit of holiday time?" Aunt Kath asked.

"I wish I could, but I can't relax knowing I'm missing so much at work. The longer I take off, the crazier things will be when I get back."

"That's a shame," Mum said.

I refrained from telling her it was insane, and instead remained focused on the roast chicken and veg in front of me. It was great when Aunt Kath cooked and I didn't have to worry about any untoward ingredients lurking on my plate.

"When will you leave then?" Kath asked.

"I've got a flight on Tuesday morning."

"Wow!" I couldn't hide my shock. "You only just got here."

"I've seen everyone I want to see and done everything I need to do. There's just no need to hang around. I have so little holiday time; I'd rather save some and come back for a visit at Christmas."

"It sounds very stressful," Mum said. "Sometimes you just need to switch off from work, no matter how hard it seems. I know exactly how it is. Obviously, working in a caring profession, it's very difficult for me to ever completely switch off, but you have to know when to take time for yourself, otherwise you'll end up burnt out and unable to work to your full abilities."

I smiled at Mum's evaluation of her job and supressed a giggle as I watched Grace digest the conversation.

"You still work with the dogs?" Grace, obviously thinking Mum may have retrained as a nurse or carer without Grace hearing about it.

"Yes," Mum said. "I have a day-care now; for the dogs. It's a lot of responsibility and obviously I'm constantly thinking about my little ones and their welfare."

Grace smiled tightly. I loved the fact that Mum had left her speechless. Mum had a knack of being able to redirect conversations in the most absurd ways.

"Do you think you can give me the number for your fitness friend?" Mum asked me. One day I might get used to my mum's random tangents but she still surprised me with the scatty conversations.

"Yeah," I said slowly. "Do you need a personal trainer?"

"No!" She looked at me like I'd gone mad. "I had a business idea and I thought he might like to get involved."

"The dogs need a personal trainer?" I asked, trying to follow her train of thought.

"Of course the dogs don't need a personal trainer!" Mum tutted. "They spend all day running around, why would they need a personal trainer?"

"I really don't know," I said, chuckling. "Just another of my wild ideas."

"No. I was thinking of *doggy fit*," she said. "An exercise class for dog owners but they can bring their dogs too. So it would be a combination of my dog training and Jason's exercise class. We already have the field to use, so we could start straight away. A few of my regulars said they'd be interested. I just need to speak to Jason."

"Well I can give you his number. He's very busy though, Mum, so don't get your hopes up. He may not have time." I made a mental note to call Jason later and warn him, so he could let her down gently.

"I just got the idea the other day after you were talking about Jason and his customer who always has her Chihuahua with her. People must be looking for something like this."

"I'm sure there is a demand for it," Grace said kindly. "I'm glad things are going so well for you."

I was amused by the conversation and for once I was glad that talk had turned to Mum. I really didn't understand Grace's obsession with her job and I was getting sick of hearing about it. It was a mystery to me why she was so keen to get back when she didn't even seem to enjoy it. I thought about Linda who was looking for a new job, and Sophie who was adamant she was going to change her situation.

I was lucky to be so content where I was.

Chapter 17

I was attempting to straighten out a mix up with an airline on Monday afternoon and had just hung up the phone when Grace walked into the shop carrying a bunch of flowers and a box of chocolates.

"I've just come to say goodbye." She handed over the treats. "These are to say thank you for everything. You've been amazing and I know it's not been easy."

"Thanks." I placed the flowers and chocolates on my desk and gave her a big hug. "I'm sorry things didn't go to plan but I'm sure everything will work out perfectly."

"I'll talk everything through with James and we'll decide what to do. I know I've been a bit crazy and it's been a whirlwind visit but I do appreciate everything you've done."

I hugged her again when she started to well up. "I wish you were staying longer."

"Me too."

I glanced over her shoulder to smile at the customer walking in the door.

"Marie?" The young blonde woman smiled nervously as she entered the shop. "You probably don't remember me but I'm Kelly …"

"How was the honeymoon?" I asked.

"Amazing!" She beamed. "I wanted to say thanks

for being so patient with me when we were booking it. You said I should come and tell you all about it …" She glanced at Grace. "Is this a bad time?"

"No, not at all. I was hoping you'd call in. Did you bring photos?"

"Loads!" She pulled out her phone and pressed buttons. "The sunsets were as unbelievable as you said. And you were right about the snorkelling; we saw turtles. It was unbelievable."

She held out her phone to show me a photo of her and her new husband in front of a beautiful sunset in the Maldives.

"Come and sit down," I said pulling out a chair for her. "Five minutes," I mouthed to Grace apologetically. Another customer wandered in and stood looking at the holiday brochures on the wall opposite me.

"I'll be with you in a minute," Anne said. She was finishing booking a cruise for a lovely retired couple who regularly booked holidays through us.

I glanced up again to see Jason jogging in. He sighed when he saw we were busy. "I'll come back later."

"If you must!" I said jokily, then turned to Kelly. "He's my personal trainer," I explained. Her holiday photos were stunning and she kept telling me little stories to go with them.

It was typical: the shop was often empty but when I really wanted it to be quiet, I could guarantee a stream of customers. Grace moved outside, chatting to Jason. I was glad she got to meet him. She'd been so shocked when I told her I had a personal trainer. I wasn't actually sure she believed it. I also felt like

Grace would approve of Jason; he was such a likeable character.

I turned my attention back to Kelly and asked her questions about her honeymoon. I was touched that she'd come back to tell me about her holiday, and didn't want to rush her out of the door. Eventually Grace gave up waiting for me and knocked on the window before blowing me a kiss and waving goodbye.

It was Thursday before I knew it. My favourite day of the week. Sophie was the first to arrive for fat club as usual. The three of them used to arrive together but it had become a bit of a free for all.

"How's Bridezilla?" Sophie asked as she made herself at home, flicking the kettle on. "She's not here is she?"

"No, she's gone back to the States."

"She's not exactly a barrel of laughs, is she?"

"She's just having a bad time at the moment. I feel pretty sorry for her. She sets herself ridiculous goals and is constantly stressed."

"That's all a bit deep, isn't it? I thought she needed someone to remove the stick from her arse, that's all!"

I smiled at her analysis. "She doesn't have many friends to keep her grounded like we do."

"True. She's just got you. There's no hope for her!"

"I meant in New York." I laughed, but it occurred to me I could probably be a better friend. I tended to agree with whatever Grace said and be blindly supportive of her decisions instead of telling her when I thought she was making mistakes. In our friendship there was always the assumption that Grace knew best. So, while she would freely tell me what she thought of my life and decisions, I tended to keep quiet about hers.

"What are you doing this weekend then, now you don't have to be Bridezilla's shadow? I bet shopping with Linda has never seemed so appealing!"

"You're always welcome to join us," I said.

"No thanks!" She thought my shopping trips with Linda were very amusing. "Anyway, I want to get on with reading the books for my course. They just arrived and I want to be ahead of the game. It's pretty boring though."

"So you're definitely going ahead with the course?" I'd half thought that she might change her mind.

"I'm all signed up," she told me excitedly. "It starts next week."

"That's quick."

"I know, otherwise I have to wait three months for the next course. I figured I may as well get on with it. It's four nights a week. Work weren't very happy about me not being able to stay late any evenings, but I told them I want to learn more about the business side of things so I have more to offer them. I didn't mention it's actually so I can get away from them."

"That's a bit sneaky."

She made four cups of tea, then glanced at me. "I'm presuming Brian will be late?"

"He messaged and said he won't be long." Although, that that could mean anything. "So it's four evenings a week, your course?" It suddenly dawned on me what that meant.

"Yes, but it's just eight weeks." She grimaced, obviously following my train of thought.

"So you're going to miss fat club?"

"I have to. It's Monday to Thursday. I couldn't very well ask them to change the course to accommodate my fat club. And I'm lucky to get on a course so quickly."

"That will be weird." I hated the fact that I was struggling with this information.

"I'll be finished at 9pm so I thought maybe I could come for half an hour or so. Especially when Brian's late too. He can pick me up and drive me. But I might be too tired. It's going to be hard, working all day and then going to college. Then I'll have studying to do on the weekends. Plus, I'm having to help Mum out with the morning school run now that Roy's not there. Jeff's already complaining that we're never going to see each other."

"Sounds exhausting," I said.

"It's just eight weeks." She removed the teabags from the cups. "At least that's what I keep telling myself."

"It'll all be worth it in the end."

"I hope so."

There was a knock at the door. "Perfect timing," I said, moving to answer it.

"I have some great ideas for jobs for Linda," Sophie shouted.

"I hope you've taken it seriously?"

"Oh, very!" There was a mischievous lilt to her voice.

***

When we were all settled in the living room, Sophie pulled a crumpled sheet of paper from her pocket. "Right, I'll go through my list first, since I'm sure I have better ideas than the rest of you!"

I sat on the floor in front of the armchair and leaned against Brian's legs. It was nice to have him home for the evening and not have him hidden behind his laptop.

"I'm not even sure I want a new job," Linda said.

"Shush, Linda. I've gone to a lot of effort." Sophie leaned forward, resting her elbows on her knees. "First of all, would you be open to the possibility of working from home?"

"I'm not sure," Linda replied. "It depends …"

"Because apparently there is a demand for sex hotline operators …"

"Sophie!" I couldn't quite stifle the laughter as Linda went bright red.

"No? Don't worry, I've got more …" She drew a line across the paper. "That was actually a joke, Linda! But how about a *strip-a-gran*? I hear the tips are good in that line of work."

Linda sighed. "I might've guessed you wouldn't take it seriously."

"Oh, come on," Sophie said. "Let me have a bit of fun. I guess I'll cross out the next few on the list and move straight on to … waitress? There's a 'staff wanted' sign in the Italian place down the road from our place …"

"Oh no, I couldn't do that. I don't speak a word of

Italian."

Sophie looked at Linda sceptically before noticing the twinkle in her eye and breaking into a grin. "I love it when you crack jokes, Linda! There's also a job going in the betting shop? I'm not sure you'd really fit in there, though." She crossed it off the list without looking up. "That just leaves the chip shop – they're always looking for staff – or a bookshop?"

"A bookshop might be nice." Linda smiled at Sophie's one sensible suggestion.

"Well it's actually a newsagent. They mainly sell magazines and newspapers but they have a little stand with cheap romance novels."

"Are you finished?" Jake asked. "Because I've found the perfect job for Linda."

"Go on then," Sophie said. "But if it's in a bookshop, it's technically my idea."

He shook his head. "It's in a school. A dinner lady."

We all looked at Jake and nodded our approval. I could definitely see Linda working in a school canteen.

"There's a notice up at Callum's school. Callum looked it up on the internet and printed out all the information for you. He did say to warn you that if you get the job, he can't really speak to you at school. Something about looking cool. Or uncool, I guess."

"It sounds nice." Linda scanned over the printout that Jake gave her. "It would be less hours and less money than I've been doing in the shop, but I think I might enjoy working in a school."

"It's just tidying up after the kids have eaten their

lunch, you know?" Sophie grumbled.

"It's not," Linda said as she read the job description. "They're looking for a 'school catering assistant'. I'd help with preparing and serving meals. Cleaning up is only one part of the job."

I always enjoyed it when Linda put Sophie in her place.

"The kids might be mean to you," Sophie said. "Kids can sense weakness. You'd be an easy target."

"Well I'd have Callum there to look out for me."

"He already said he's not going to talk to you …"

I leaned back against Brian's legs. "Shut up, Sophie."

"I'm only trying to be helpful," Sophie said. "This is the sort of teasing she'll have to get used to."

"I'm quite used to it." Linda looked at Sophie. "Surely they can't be any worse than you."

"I think we've bored Brian," Jake said.

I craned my neck to see Brian fast asleep in the chair. "Sorry," I said. "He's not a great host."

"So will you apply for the job?" Jake asked Linda.

"Yes, I think I might."

"You should," Sophie said. "You'll be good at it. The kids will probably even like you."

We all looked at Sophie, waiting for a punch-line that didn't come.

"I was being nice," she said. "It doesn't suit me, does it?"

"Maybe we need to find poor Brian a new job," Linda suggested. "He works too hard."

Brian was still sleeping when Linda, Sophie and Jake left. I nudged him awake once they'd gone, and found myself suddenly and irrationally annoyed with him.

"Sorry," he said sleepily. "Have they gone?"

"Yes. You should go to bed."

"I've got to finish preparing for my meeting tomorrow." He stretched his neck and rubbed at his eyes.

"Are you serious?"

"I'll just get a coffee. I'm fine."

"Just go to bed, please." I pulled him up out of the chair.

"It won't take long." He gave me a quick peck. "I'll be up soon."

Upstairs, I felt myself getting angrier as I got into my pyjamas and ready for bed. I decided Linda was right: Brian needed a new job.

Chapter 18

"Do you feel like going out tonight?" Brian asked down the phone as I left work on Friday. "I've been in meetings with Graham all day and he asked me to go for dinner. There are a few other people going too. Do you want to come?"

"I really don't like your work dinners." I'd tagged along a few times and had always been bored stiff. "I was really looking forward to the couch and a glass of wine."

"I can't get out of this one."

"It's fine, you go. I just don't think I have the energy for small talk. You don't mind me skipping it?"

"No, I don't blame you. I won't be late."

I treated myself to a frozen pizza and a large glass of wine in front of a nice romantic comedy before I happily took myself up to bed. It felt like I'd only just fallen asleep when I woke to the sound of the bedroom door crashing open.

"Shhhh!" Brian said, laughing.

"Hi," I mumbled.

"Shhh! Don't wake up!"

I flicked on my bedside lamp and squinted into the light to find Brian struggling to get undressed with a silly smile on his face.

"You're drunk," I said.

"Just a little bit." He waved his thumb and index finger around near his eye and grinned at me. "Shhhh!"

"If you were trying to be quiet you're not doing the best job."

"Shhh!" He giggled and fell into bed beside me. "I missed you."

I laughed at the sight of his drowsy eyes and wonky smile. "It's a good job you're a cute drunk."

"You should have come out with me," he said, pouting.

"I don't like going out with your colleagues." My eyes were blurry and I was only half awake.

"Neither do I," he said. "That's why you should come with me. It would have been more fun with you there."

"It looks like you managed to have fun without me."

"No, there was no fun." He was slurring his words. "I love you." He draped an arm over me, trapping me under his dead weight as he passed out.

"Thanks!" I said, wriggling to get away from him.

"You're amazing," Brian said when I handed him a bacon sandwich and a coffee in the living room the next morning. "I feel like death."

"You look like it," I replied as I looked him up and down. "What happened?"

"We went to a bar after dinner and someone started ordering shots." He took a bite of his greasy sandwich. "I'm getting too old for partying."

"I hope everyone was as drunk as you were."

"Fingers crossed," he replied, then groaned dramatically.

"What?"

"I got a taxi home with your friend, Dave …"

"Aww! I love taxi Dave." He was the favourite of my regular drivers.

"I think I told him he should refuse to drive you anywhere so you would finally learn to drive … I said it was all his fault that you can't drive."

I laughed at Brian. He looked mortified by the memory. "Dave won't care. I think he's used to driving drunk people around. He's taken me home enough times after a night out."

"I feel like crawling back into bed." Brian looked fairly pitiful as he finished his sandwich and set the plate down on the coffee table in front of him.

"Why don't you?" I suggested. "I'm going out with Linda soon."

"I need to get some work done," he said. I felt my eyes roll automatically. "I promised your mum I'd go to her place with you tomorrow, so I really need to get something done today. I got an earful from her for not going last week."

I shrugged. "Sorry."

"I was in the middle of a meeting and couldn't get her off the phone."

"Sorry," I said again. I felt like I spent half my life apologising for my mum.

***

"How's Paul?" Mum, quite predictably asked about Brian's dad as we sat down to lunch on Sunday. She always asked about Brian's dad.

"He's fine," Brian replied as he handed his plate to Kath. She was serving up lasagne. There was garlic bread and salad to go with it and it looked and smelled delicious.

"He's not been to visit for a while, has he?" Mum asked.

Brian piled salad onto his plate beside the lasagne. "He might be down next weekend."

"That'll be nice," Mum said.

"What day is he coming?" I asked. This was the first I'd heard of Paul's plans to visit. Although, it wasn't unusual. He lived in Scotland and travelled a lot for his job so would visit once a month or so when he was anywhere nearby for business. He'd take us out for dinner and he and Brian would talk about work while I people-watched in the restaurant. Paul was nice enough but I always found the atmosphere strained.

"I don't know," Brian said. "You know what he's like. It'll be a last-minute thing as usual."

"Is he bringing his wife?" Mum asked, as she usually did.

"No, he's just around on business."

"It's a shame she can never make it," Mum said. "What about your sister? Have you spoken to her recently?"

"Half-sister," Brian corrected her. "I've not spoken to her for a while." He tucked into his dinner, clearly hoping for a change of subject. I'd never met his stepmum or little sister. Brian got cagey at the mention of them. He said he'd never had much contact with them.

"How old is she now?" Mum asked.

"Twelve," Brian said hesitantly. "Thirteen maybe."

"Guess what?" Mum said, suddenly changing the subject. "I spoke to Jason and he's excited about my business idea."

"Fitness Jason?" Brian asked, looking slightly puzzled.

"Yes. He and Mum are going into business together."

I'd completely forgotten I'd given Mum his number until I'd gone for my session with Jason on Tuesday. He'd been really excited about Mum's phone call. He genuinely seemed to think it was a brilliant idea and was even a bit miffed he'd not thought of it himself. He was also gobsmacked by the revelation that my mum was 'Ellie the dog whisperer'. I'd never really told him anything about Mum, but apparently he often goes jogging by her allotment and knew exactly who she was.

"What kind of business would that be then?" Brian asked with a smile.

"An exercise class for dog owners and their dogs," Mum told him proudly. "We're calling it 'Doggy Fit'."

Brian coughed and put a hand to his mouth in his attempt not to laugh. "Doggy Fit?"

Mum nodded enthusiastically.

"Jason said he was trying to think up a different name," I told Mum gently.

"Fit Dog?" Brian suggested. I squeezed his thigh under the table to encourage him to be nice. He laughed and shoved my hand away. "Workout Walkies?" I rolled my eyes as I watched his brain

whirring with ideas. "Poochie Fitness? No, wait …
Fitness Unleashed!"

I slapped his arm. "Don't make fun."

"Fitness Unleashed is a good name," he said.
"Everyone likes a play on words."

"I quite like it," Mum said. "I'll suggest it to
Jason. We're meeting soon to discuss the routine for
the first class."

"Please let me know when you're up and running,
Ellie," Brian said. "I'd love to come and check it
out."

I squeezed his thigh again, making him wince and
wriggle away.

"I'll let you know," Mum said before returning
her attention to her lunch.

I shook my head at Brian who couldn't keep the
grin from his face. He raised his eyebrows and
shrugged. I suppose it was fairly amusing.

Chapter 19

"Well this is a bit weird, isn't it?" Jake said. There was definitely an awkward atmosphere at fat club on Thursday evening.

"Very," Linda agreed.

Brian was still at work and Sophie was at her business course, so it was just the three of us, drinking tea in the living room.

"It's fine." I tried to be positive. "It's great that Sophie's doing this course. I think it will be really good for her."

"You're probably right," Linda agreed.

"It's a shame she has to do it on a Thursday though," Jake said.

"It's four nights a week." I blew on my tea. "She can't pick and choose when."

"Should we have fat club on Friday nights instead?" Linda suggested.

"No!" Jake and I said immediately.

I used to laugh about the fact that my fat club friends were resistant to change, but it seemed like I'd become guilty of the same. There wasn't really a good reason why we shouldn't change the day to Friday, other than the fact that we've always met on a Thursday. The world wouldn't make sense if we met on Fridays.

I also found it strange not having Sophie with us,

but I was trying to be upbeat about the situation.

"It might be quite fun, just the three of us," I said. "We can hardly get a word in when Sophie's here."

Linda's shoulders drooped. "She's a lot of fun though."

"She always has us laughing, doesn't she?" Jake said.

"And she's very kind," Linda said. I nearly spat my tea out.

"She makes a great cup of tea too." Jake lifted his cup and raised his eyebrows.

"What's wrong with my tea?" I demanded. They glanced at each other and didn't comment. "And let's not forget that as well as being fun, she is also obnoxious, annoying and quite mean!"

"Don't say things like that," Linda said, tutting.

I placed my mug on the table. "Let's not pretend she's perfect just because she's not here."

"It just won't be so much fun," Jake said. "That's all we're saying …"

"*I'm* fun," I declared.

Linda cocked her head to the side. "Not really."

"What?" I crossed my arms across my chest, wondering whether I should kick the pair of them out and hit the wine.

"You see!" Linda broke into a grin. "Sophie would've realised that was one of my jokes. Wouldn't she, Jake?"

"Without a doubt. She always knows when Linda's joking around."

"Okay," I said. "It's definitely better when Sophie's here. Stop picking on me!"

"I've got some news actually," Linda said, turning

serious. "It feels a bit wrong to tell you without Sophie though."

"Can we shut up about Sophie?" I blurted out.

Linda shifted in her seat and re-crossed her legs. "I got the job at the school, that's all."

Jake grinned. I got the impression that he already knew.

"That's amazing," I said. "I thought you only applied for it last week?"

"Yes. I went for an interview yesterday, and they offered me the job there and then. I start on Monday."

"That's brilliant. Well done."

"Callum's very excited about it," Jake said. "Plus he's taking all the credit for finding the job so he's very proud of himself."

"I'm a bit nervous, but I can't wait. I met the cook and he seemed lovely. Everyone I met seemed really nice. I think I'm going to like it there."

"I bet you'll be great at it," I said.

We spent the next hour chatting and drinking tea until Brian finally wandered in looking exhausted.

"I thought you were picking Sophie up?" I said.

"I did but she was exhausted so I dropped her home." Brian draped his jacket over the back of the couch and loosened his tie as he perched on the arm of my chair. "Everyone okay?" he asked.

"Linda got a new job," I told him excitedly. "She's going to be a dinner lady at Callum's school."

"Congratulations!" he said.

"Thanks," Linda said. "You look tired, Brian. I think we'll leave you to it."

"I'm fine," Brian protested half-heartedly as Linda and Jake got up to leave.

"We were only really hanging on to see Sophie anyway," Jake said.

Brian laughed. "Thanks a lot!"

"You know what I mean," Jake said, chuckling.

I stood at the front door with Brian and waved them off.

"I really missed Sophie," I said as we moved back inside.

"She'll be back annoying everyone before we know it." Brian rubbed the back of his neck.

"Do you want a beer?" I asked.

"No. I want to go to bed."

"It's only just gone nine." I glanced at my watch. "Are you that tired?"

He smiled cheekily as he took my hand and pulled me towards the stairs. "No, not really."

Chapter 20

Work seemed to drag on forever on Friday. Anne talked non-stop. It seemed like she didn't even pause to take a breath. I felt a definite sense of relief whenever customers walked in, giving me a break from her incessant chatter.

I was looking forward to an evening on the couch with a glass of wine. I planned on messaging Sophie to see if she'd come over. Not having her there on Thursday had left a strange absence in my life. I'd sent her a text asking how she was but hadn't had a reply. I was eager to know how the course was going.

When Brian called, I answered the phone while simultaneously tapping away on the computer. He didn't even bother with saying hello, which was a sure sign he was in a bad mood.

"My dad's taking us for dinner tonight," he said.

"He never gives much warning, does he?" Apparently I wouldn't be lounging in my pyjamas by 7 p.m., as I'd planned. "Where's he taking us?"

"I said we'd go over and eat at their hotel. He's got his wife and daughter with him. He waited until I'd agreed to dinner before he mentioned that bit."

"Really?" That explained the bad mood. Brian was never particularly excited about his dad, Paul, arriving for a visit but it didn't put him in a bad mood. The stepmother and sister were another matter; the smallest mention of them seemed to make his blood boil. I'd never met them and had mixed feelings about them.

On the one hand I'm naturally curious, so it would be interesting to see what they were like, but on the other hand I already had them pegged as pretty stuck-up and slightly evil, so I wasn't keen to spend too much time with them. Paul had once let slip that the little girl had a pony. I'd made a lot of assumptions based on that fact alone.

"Julie, is it? And Abigail?" It suddenly felt weird that I wasn't even sure of their names.

"Yeah. I said we'd meet at 7 p.m. We can eat and make a quick getaway. They just wanted to meet you before the wedding."

"Did you tell them there's no rush?" I laughed but Brian clearly wasn't in the mood for jokes.

"I'll pick you up at home."

I sighed. He was so weird about his family. "I was supposed to go for a jog with Jason but I won't have time. I'll call and cancel. That's one good thing."

"Okay. See you later." He sounded miserable as he hung up.

"What was that about?" Anne asked as soon as I was off the phone.

"Brian's dad's in town with his wife and daughter. We're meeting them for dinner tonight."

"Ooh! The evil stepmother?"

I smiled at her. "It could be an interesting evening. Oh! I need to cancel on Jason …" I reached for the phone and tried calling him but he didn't answer.

"He probably guessed you're cancelling and chose

to ignore it," Anne said.

"Probably."

I tried calling a few more times over the course of the afternoon but Jason was definitely ignoring his phone.

He jogged in at five o'clock looking his usual chirpy self.

"I've been trying to call you all afternoon," I said. "I'm having dinner with Brian's family. I need to go straight home to get ready."

"Fine. A sprint it is then … come on!"

"I don't have time. Why weren't you answering your phone?"

"I thought you'd be trying to cancel with some flimsy excuse. By the time you get to the bus stop and wait for a bus, it's no quicker than running home. Get your running shoes on and let's go."

"I was actually planning on a taxi." I'd already admitted defeat and was heading to the toilet to get changed into my jogging gear. I could sense both Anne and Jason rolling their eyes at my mention of a taxi. I'd like to find someone else in the world with my appreciation for taxis.

"I've not got time for all that warming up and cooling down business either," I called behind me.

I turned at the sound of laughter and found Jason slapping his thigh in fake mirth. I raised a lone eyebrow at him.

"Sorry, Marie. It's just not particularly effective the way you do it anyway. We can skip it this once."

"I met your mum yesterday," Jason said cheerfully as we set off through town. "She's a hoot."

"She is indeed."

"We've planned out the first trial session for Fitness Unleashed and we've already got six people signed up."

"So you're definitely going through with it?"

"Of course. I think it's really going to take off. Your mum's a genius."

I couldn't help but laugh. Of all the words to describe my mum, I never thought genius would be one.

"Seriously," he said. "I think it's going to be a real money spinner."

"I hope it does well," I said. "Maybe you could sell tickets for spectators too?"

"It's a very serious business," he said. "You really shouldn't mock."

"Sorry. But it sounds ridiculous. Maybe you could pitch the idea for a TV show ..."

I veered to the side as Jason swiped at me.

"Hey! Personal trainers should not attack their clients."

"Clients shouldn't tease their personal trainers," he said with a grin. "Let's up the pace a bit."

"I'd rather not." I matched his pace regardless. We jogged in silence the rest of the way home. I rested on my knees outside the house and waited for my breathing to return to normal.

"From one torture to the next," I said, smiling at Jason.

"Don't you get on with the in-laws?"

"I've only met his dad. I'm meeting his stepmum and half-sister tonight. I'm not really in the mood for polite conversation."

"Drink a lot. You'll be fine."

"As my personal trainer, is that really the sort of advice you should be dishing out?"

"When have you ever listened to me anyway?" He jogged a circle around me. "Let me know how it goes!"

HANNAH ELLIS

Chapter 21

I waved at Paul as we walked across the restaurant. "Sorry, we're a bit late."

"Don't worry. The girls were still getting ready so I said I'd come down and wait for you." He stood and kissed me on the cheek before moving to shake Brian's hand.

A woman appeared at the table accompanied by a young girl. "I thought you'd be waiting for us – Abby was having a wardrobe dilemma. Anyway it looks like perfect timing. You must be Marie?"

She pulled me in for a hug.

"I'm Julie. I'm so glad we're finally getting to meet you." Her voice was warm and she beckoned her daughter over as she moved to hug Brian.

"You must be Abigail," I said as the girl moved towards me. "The wardrobe dilemma can't have been too bad. You look lovely."

"Thanks," she replied. "It's Abby. Nobody calls me Abigail. Except for Brian. He knows I hate it."

Her smile flicked on and off her face. I looked over at Brian, certain he'd be sticking his tongue out at her or pulling a face. Instead, he ignored the comment and pulled out the chair next to his dad.

Paul ordered champagne for us, and an orange juice for Abby.

"How was your journey?" I asked, searching for

something to say.

"Easy," Julie said. "We cheated this time and hopped on a plane. It's much nicer than driving. We have to be back tomorrow night so the drive would've been too much. We've been dying to meet you, so we thought we'd tag along with Paul."

I smiled, unsure of what to say. I took a big gulp of champagne. If Brian was going to leave me to carry the conversation along, I'd have to do as Jason suggested and drink a lot.

"How's work?" Paul asked Brian. The two of them ambled into the most boring conversation on earth.

I glanced at Abby and rolled my eyes. She gave a snort of laughter and her hand shot to her mouth. It lightened the atmosphere. I turned towards Abby and Julie.

"Your dad said you've got a pony …" I regretted the line of conversation as soon as the words left my mouth, but it was the only thing I really knew about her.

Abby sighed heavily and shook her head. "He always tells people I've got a pony. It's actually a horse. It makes me sound like a spoiled little princess when he says he bought me a pony."

I chuckled. "Horse sounds loads better!" My eyes went wide at my sarcastic tone. "I'm sorry … that came out wrong."

Abby glanced up at her mum and then snorted with laughter again. Her hand went to her mouth once more as she blushed bright red.

The corners of Julie's mouth started to twitch and I relaxed, laughing. Abby gave in to her bout of giggles and the men looked on at us bewildered.

It took us a few minutes to regain our composure and I had to take a few deep breaths and a few gulps of champagne before I managed to get myself under control. The ice had been broken and the conversation flowed easily. Abby eagerly told me about her love of horse riding and then moved on to talk about her school and friends.

I felt an immediate attachment to Abby. She had an awkwardness about her that was endearing. It seemed like she didn't quite fit in her body; her limbs were long and seemed to be just slightly out of control. Her laugh was loud and infectious. I was mesmerised by her.

By the time we'd finished the main course, I felt like I had two new best friends. It occurred to me that they'd soon be my family and we'd be connected forever. It was a lovely thought.

I glanced at Brian. His brow was furrowed and he looked older. He was like a completely different person. For a moment, I found myself wishing he wasn't there. I was having such a lovely time but whenever I looked at him I felt deflated. This was a whole new side to him and I didn't like it.

"There's a garden on the roof of the hotel," Abby said. "Do you want to come and see it?"

"I'd love to."

Julie and I followed Abby across the restaurant as Brian and Paul ordered more drinks.

We stepped out of the lift at the top floor. A set of double doors led to a beautiful rooftop garden. A mix of ornate conifers and rose covered trellises separated a variety of seating areas.

I looked around in awe. "I've always lived near here and I never knew this existed."

"I guess there's never any need to stay in hotels in your hometown," Julie mused. We moved through the peaceful rooftop garden to take in the view across the city.

Paul worked as a quality assurance manager for a hotel chain, and spent time travelling around the hotels. There were three hotels pretty close to us and he always stayed in one of them when he was here. I'd been to all of them but this was the first time I'd been up to the roof.

"Why are you marrying Brian?" Abby asked.

I smiled at her, waiting for her to crack a joke but she looked up at me seriously. Julie hissed her name to chastise her.

My smile slipped. "Because I love him." I'm not sure what sort of answer she was expecting.

"You just seem like an odd couple. I didn't think you'd be so nice–" Abby stopped abruptly, catching a fierce look from her mum.

"Can I bring you up a drink?" A waiter asked, interrupting us.

"No thanks," Julie said. "I think we'll go back down. It's a bit chilly up here."

I reluctantly moved towards the door with a sudden urge to quiz Julie and Abby about their relationship with Brian. Since Brian never wanted to talk about them, it would be nice to get their side of the story. There must be a reason why he was so detached from them. The moment had passed though and I wasn't sure how to broach the subject again.

We skipped dessert and ordered coffees when we

rejoined the men in the restaurant. The atmosphere felt a little strained after Abby's comment on the roof. Brian at least managed to acknowledge Abby's presence and asked her a couple of questions about school.

"You should come to our house one day," Abby suggested.

"We'd love to," I said automatically.

She looked surprised. "Really? You'll come?"

"Yes, of course."

She clapped her hands together. "When?"

"Work's busy at the moment," Brian said. "I can't take time off." He seemed determined to dampen the mood.

I glared at him. "We could go for a weekend." He shrugged and I caught the disappointment on Abby's face. "Or I can just come for a girls trip."

"Even better!" Abby said, making me laugh. "We can go shopping. There's a wedding dress shop near us. Do you have a dress yet? We could go wedding dress shopping." She talked fast with bright eyes. Her enthusiasm was charming.

"Slow down," Julie said, patting her arm.

"Do you have a dress, though?" Abby asked.

"No, not yet. We've not set a date. We don't even know where we'll get married."

"That doesn't matter. It'll be fun."

"Actually, I'd love to go dress shopping with you," I said. "But my friends want to go with me and they'll be upset if I leave them out. We could definitely go shopping, just maybe not for a wedding dress."

"Bring your friends!" Abby's eyes lit up even

more. "We could have a hen night for you! Can we mum?"

"I'm not sure you can have a hen night before we've even set a date for the wedding," Brian said, shaking his head.

"Plus you're not old enough to go on a hen night," Paul added.

Abby ignored the men's comments entirely and looked to her mum with questioning eyes.

"You're definitely welcome to bring your friends," Julie told me kindly. "There is a lovely bridal shop. A few in the area actually."

"I'd feel like I was intruding, bringing my friends. I only just met you."

"You're going to be my sister soon though," Abby said.

"She's right. You're pretty much family. Our home is your home. Bring whoever you want."

I was touched by Julie's warmth and generosity. A trip to Scotland was very appealing. "It does sound like fun. If you're sure?"

"Definitely," Julie said. "We'll look forward to it."

At the end of the evening, Julie told me again how welcome I was to visit and as Abby squeezed me tightly she made me promise I'd make it soon.

I felt such warmth as I hugged them both goodbye. I was excited about being part of their family and getting to know them better. A little trip to visit them in Scotland would be lovely and I was sure Linda and Sophie would be excited by the idea too.

Chapter 22

On Saturday I went out for lunch with Linda. I relayed the whole of the previous evening to her and gave her my glowing reports on my new family members. I couldn't stop thinking about Julie and Abby and what a lovely evening it had been.

When Linda dropped me home, Brian was in the living room, sitting on the couch with his laptop on his knees. I sat beside him and gave him a quick kiss on the cheek.

"I really liked Julie and Abby," I said.

"You've mentioned that a few times now," Brian glanced briefly up from his laptop.

"They're really lovely, though. Why do you have a problem with them?"

"I don't," he said without looking up.

I hesitated, wondering if I dare ask more. I'd wanted to quiz him the previous evening, but he'd gone straight to bed in a foul mood.

"But you hardly see them. I can't believe I've only just met them." I got nothing more than a shrug so I pushed my luck a bit further. "Why are you so weird around them?"

"I'm not." Finally, he looked me in the eyes. "I've got loads of work to do …"

"Sorry." Apparently I'd delved far enough for one day. "Callum's coming over later." I moved towards the door. "Jake was asked to cover for someone at work so I said Callum could come here."

"Okay. Where's his mum?"

"Working. You don't mind do you?"

"No," he mumbled.

***

"Can we have a Nerf war?" Callum asked a few minutes after Jake had dropped him off.

I agreed enthusiastically. I'd bought the Nerf guns as a joke for Brian at Christmas but Callum and I had spent many hours chasing each other around the house, firing foam pellets at each other. We had the routine well figured out by now. We divided up the guns and pellets and then Callum waited in the upstairs bathroom while I went and found a hiding place. Then we'd creep around until we found each other and went crazy firing at each other and ducking and hiding. We'd retreat to different rooms of the house to catch our breath and then repeat the process.

"Do you wanna play?" I asked Brian. He was sitting on the couch, reading through some papers with a pen in his hand.

"No, thanks." He looked annoyed and I felt suddenly silly walking around with a brightly coloured toy gun. The two holsters full of foam pellets also felt fairly ridiculous. There was one draped across my shoulder and one around my waist. What on earth was I doing?

"Coming!" Callum called.

I shot into action, moving out of the living room

and through the dining room, sliding into place behind the island in the middle of the kitchen. It was a good spot, providing good cover. I kept peeking out until I saw Callum's legs come into view. Slowly, I moved around so he wouldn't see me. Quickly, I made my move: standing and firing off as many pellets as I could before ducking down again.

Callum moved to attack me and I made a run for the stairs, laughing loudly as he chased me.

I froze on the first step when Brian shouted at us to stop. He was standing in the hallway rubbing his brow. "I'm trying to work," he snapped.

"Sorry," I mumbled. "We'll be quiet."

He walked heavily back into the living room and I felt like a naughty child.

"Let's play something else," I said. Callum nodded his agreement.

"Is Brian really angry at me?" he asked as we put the Nerf guns away in the box in the spare room.

"No," I said lightly. Callum was such a good kid; I don't think he was used to getting shouted at. "He's just stressed with work. We weren't doing anything wrong."

With hindsight, I should probably have realised that us running around the house shouting and screaming wouldn't go down well.

"Let's collect up the rest of the pellets and play cards," I suggested.

We played quietly at the dining room table and both tensed when Brian wandered into the kitchen an hour or so later.

"Anyone want a drink?" he asked.

We politely declined and carried on with the

game. The silence was broken by the sound of Brian running the tap. Then he came and stood over us.

"What are you playing?"

"Uno," I replied, although he could clearly see that.

"Do you want to play?" Callum asked politely.

Brian looked at Callum sadly and ignored the question. "Sorry for shouting."

Callum shrugged. "It's okay."

"We can play Nerf now if you want?" Brian said.

"No, it's fine."

"I can just stand against the wall and you can take free shots at me?" Brian smiled sheepishly. "I think I deserve it."

"It's okay," Callum said. "Can I play on the Playstation?"

"Yeah. Go for it." Brian would clearly agree to anything that would get him back in Callum's good books. Callum passed me his remaining cards and headed for the living room.

Brian crouched down beside me and sighed heavily, resting his head on my thigh. "I'm a horrible person, aren't I? Do you think I've scarred him for life?"

"I think he'll survive." I ran a hand through his hair. "Go and play your silly computer games with him and I'll make us some dinner."

He did as he was told and I got to work in the kitchen. When I brought dinner through to eat on our laps, I was relieved to find that the laptop was nowhere in sight and Brian had joined Callum in playing the computer game. They were both shouting at the little men on the screen and it took a while before they noticed I was there.

I would've happily watched mindless reality TV shows for the evening, but since I was outnumbered by the boys, it ended up being some action movie with high speed car chases that made me dizzy trying to keep up with what was going on. It was marginally preferable to watching them play on the Playstation all evening.

When Michael came to pick Callum up, Brian was already asleep on the couch. I left him there as I made my way up to bed.

Chapter 23

"How's the new job?" Sophie asked Linda on Thursday evening. I'd already spent a couple of hours chatting with Linda and Jake when Brian arrived with Sophie. It seemed like we were about to have the same conversation all over again.

"I love it," Linda said. "The women I work with are great. They're so chatty. Actually, they're a bit gossipy, but it's a lot of fun. The kids are good too."

"You're not getting bullied then?" Sophie asked.

"Not yet," Linda said, chuckling. "It's such a great, lively atmosphere. So much nicer than working in the shop. I'll be glad when I finish there."

"You're working two jobs?" Sophie asked.

"Yes, I had to give two weeks' notice. It'll soon be over."

"How's the course going, Sophie?" I'd sent her a load of messages but she'd been pretty vague in her replies.

"It's good. I'm pretty tired, but it's not for long."

"So you still think you'll be able to set up your own business?" Jake asked.

"Yes," she said impatiently. "I'm learning lots on the course and I think I'll be able to set up on my own sooner than I thought."

"That's brilliant," Linda said. "It's all so

169

exciting."

"It's a lot of hard work actually." Sophie looked stressed as she sank back into the couch. I caught Brian's eye and he gave me a reassuring smile. I was unnerved by Sophie's lack of enthusiasm. She was usually jumping around like a crazy thing but it seemed like she'd lost her spark. I'd been looking forward to catching up with her but it didn't seem like we were going to get much conversation out of her.

"Can you make me a cup of tea please, Brian?" Sophie asked.

"I'll get it," Linda said.

"No, you make terrible tea," Sophie grumbled. "Let Brian get it."

Brian did as he was told and moved to the kitchen as the rest of us shouted our drink orders at him.

Linda looked upset. "What's wrong with my tea?"

"Nothing. I just wanted to get rid of Brian." Sophie turned to me. "How was it with the evil stepmother?"

I'd forgotten I'd not seen Sophie since my evening with Julie and Abby. "It was okay," I said, glancing nervously at the door.

"Are they really horrible?" Sophie asked.

"They're lovely. But Brian was in a bad mood for days after we saw them. I don't know what his problem is."

"So he doesn't get on with them?" Jake asked.

"No. He's polite to them, but it's like he can't relax around them. He wasn't himself at all. Although he's always a bit weird with his dad too. They seem to only talk business to each other. It's all a bit formal and stuffy."

"Have you talked to him about it?" Linda asked.

"I tried, but he doesn't tell me much, just that they've never been close."

"It will probably all become clear the more you get to know them," Linda said. "Perhaps, they're not as nice as you think. They might just know how to make a good first impression. They'll make you trust them and then turn evil."

"Linda!" I said, laughing. "You sound like Sophie."

"I do, don't I? I was only joking."

"Leave the jokes to me," Sophie said. "Although Linda might have a point …" She glanced at the door and lowered her voice before continuing. "But maybe it's Brian who's evil. They might be really nice but don't get on with Brian because they know what he's really like. He might not have shown us his true colours yet."

I laughed at her theory. That was the Sophie I knew and loved.

"Well, you hear about it all the time," she said. "People fall in love and everything is fine, then they get married and, bam, suddenly there's a psycho in the relationship."

"Where do you hear about this stuff?" I asked.

"I don't know. I just hear it." She shrugged. "It happens though."

"Actually his family invited me to visit them in Scotland for a girls' weekend," I said. "They said I could bring friends."

"It sounds wonderful," Linda said, "and I won't be working weekends anymore so that will be perfect."

"Excellent." Sophie rubbed her hands together. "I can get to the bottom of things for you. I like a mystery."

"What's a mystery?" Brian appeared with drinks.

"It's a mystery how I'm still awake," Sophie said without hesitation. "Can you give me a lift home, Linda?"

"I just made drinks," Brian said.

"Thank you!" She smiled sweetly at him. "I'm just so tired all of a sudden. I can hardly keep my eyes open."

"Fine. Go home then," he said.

Linda and Jake moved into the hallway to find their coats and Sophie pulled me to the other side of the living room.

"Do you think it's safe for us to leave you alone with him?" She glanced at Brian who was chatting to Jake in the hallway.

"Sophie!" I gave her a playful shove.

"But did you see how upset he got about me not drinking the tea? His eyes went a bit crazy. He may flip out at any time." She went cross-eyed as she gave me her best crazy face.

I shoved her again and she cackled with laughter.

"I thought you were tired?" Brian shot at her from the doorway.

"Exhausted!" She bounded over to give him a hug before following Linda and Jake out of the front door.

"What was going on with Sophie?" Brian asked as I headed back to the couch and picked up a cup of tea from the coffee table.

"Nothing much. She just thinks you might be a crazed psychopath."

He grinned. "Is that all?"

"She's always good for a laugh."

"And what's going on with Jake?" Brian asked.

"I don't know." I was slightly puzzled by the question. "What do you mean?"

"He's just been a bit quiet lately. I'm not sure. He seems a bit stressed. I thought you'd know." He shrugged. "Maybe I'm imagining it."

"I think he's fine. I hope he's fine because if there are any problems in Jake's life, it's usually something to do with his sister and I thought everything was settled with Carol at the moment." Carol had previously had problems with drinking and her terrible choice of men. It always put a lot of stress on Jake as he tried to keep things on an even keel for Callum.

"I probably just imagined it," Brian said.

"I need to call Grace," I said, suddenly remembering. "We keep missing each other's calls." I reached for my phone and listened as it rang once and went to voicemail. I'd only managed a quick chat with her since she flew back to America. It was hard with the time difference and our busy schedules.

"I'll try her again tomorrow," I said and shuffled along to cuddle up to Brian on the couch. I closed my eyes for a minute and woke an hour later with my head on his chest. I watched him sleeping for a few minutes before nudging him awake and encouraging him upstairs to bed.

Chapter 24

I couldn't get used to Sophie not being at fat club. After joining us that one evening after her course, she'd been completely absent for three weeks. It wasn't the same without her there. I chatted to her on the phone a couple of times a week and I'd usually see her at some point at the weekends. She seemed worn out and I was starting to worry that the business course had been a really bad idea. Brian argued that if she couldn't cope with the course, she'd never hack it with her own business.

Spring hit with full force and the unusually warm weather lifted my spirits. I was managing to completely deny that fact that Brian was turning into more of a workaholic with each passing day.

There'd been no talk of weddings and I'd happily decided that we were destined to live in sin forever. Grace and I barely spoke anymore and when we did speak, I struggled to find anything to say to her. She'd decided to postpone their wedding until the hotel was available and it seemed like she'd put wedding planning out of her mind and thrown herself back into work.

I was focussing on the positives in my life. Work was good and I enjoyed my Saturdays with Linda who seemed to be invigorated by her new job. My mum was probably the happiest I'd ever known her.

The 'Fitness Unleashed' class had really taken off and had even been noticed by the local paper who'd written a short article about it. Mum and Jason had been invited onto a local radio show to chat about their new venture.

I'd been chatting to Julie and Abby regularly. They'd call sometimes in the evenings and I'd sneak out of Brian's hearing to chat to them. Abby would tell me all about school and her friends, and ask me a string of random questions about my life. Julie would always politely ask about Brian but I was no closer to figuring out what the situation between them really was. I didn't feel I could ask. I liked talking to them and was really pleased that they wanted to be in contact with me. I'd spoken to them some more about going up to visit them but we hadn't managed to finalise a date yet.

It was a beautiful Saturday morning and I'd been determined to ignore the fact that Brian was, once again, giving his laptop his undivided attention and neglecting me.

"Do you want to come and watch Callum's football game?" I asked. "Jake called to say he and Michael are both working. They're worried Carol might not turn up and there'll be no one there to cheer him on. Linda's coming."

"I've got some work I need to do …" He paused and looked up at me. "I guess I can do it this evening."

The smile spread quickly over my face. It would be fun with Brian there and Callum would be excited to have Brian watching him. "I'm going to jump in the shower," I said.

I was getting dressed when I heard Brian chatting on the phone.

"Who was that?" I asked, walking back into the living room.

He frowned. "Graham Clifford."

"And now you can't come?" I knew that a call from Graham tended to send Brian running in the direction of the office.

"He's meeting clients for a round of golf and asked me to join."

"It's Saturday," I snapped. "Couldn't you have said no?"

"Not really." He narrowed his eyes and I wanted to punch him. "I can come and meet you later."

"You'll miss Callum's game though." I shook my head and walked away. Arguing with him about it was pointless.

"Do you want me to drop you off on my way?" he called after me.

"No, I'll get the bus." I was doubly annoyed now that I'd told Linda she didn't need to pick me up. "I'll see you later," I shouted as I pushed my feet into my shoes and made for the front door.

"Don't be angry with me." Brian appeared behind me.

"Of course I'm angry," I said. "You don't *have* to work today. You're choosing to work instead of spending time with me and our friends."

"It's not as straightforward as that." He sighed heavily. "I would love to spend the day with you but it's a crucial time for the project and I need to make sure everything goes smoothly. It's stressful enough without you giving me a guilt trip."

I stared at him, feeling like I might explode but knowing I didn't have the energy to argue. "I'm going," I said. "I don't want to be late for Callum's game."

He moved to kiss me and I forced myself to give him a peck on the cheek before turning and rushing out of the door.

***

I felt slightly out of place as we arrived at the school. All the other adults had kids running around their legs and everyone seemed to know each other. Fortunately, I quickly found Linda waiting for me in the car park.

"This way." She proudly directed me to follow the crowd. As we walked she waved to a few people and some of the kids shouted unintelligible greetings at her.

"You're like a celebrity," I remarked. She beamed and seemed to walk taller.

We found a spot on the side-lines and Linda spread out a blanket for us to sit on. I automatically checked my phone for messages. I half expected an apology from Brian but I'd overestimated him. I'd also messaged Sophie to tell her where we were but hadn't heard anything back from her. I scanned the field until I saw Callum warming up with his teammates at the opposite side of the pitch. I waved frantically until he managed a discreet wave back at me.

"Don't embarrass him, Marie. Be cool." Linda

was unpacking her shopping bag and offered me a bottle of Coke.

I took the bottle from her. "Did you just tell me to be cool?"

"Yes. The poor boy has enough to deal with. Don't show him up."

"I only waved," I said.

"I know but they're at a funny age these kids. It's all about being cool. Kids get picked on for all sorts of things, and Callum's such a sensitive boy."

"He's not getting bullied is he?" I felt sick at the thought.

"No, but he's easily embarrassed. He knows we're here, that's what matters. Let's not draw anymore attention to ourselves."

I was unsure how to feel about getting a lesson from Linda on how to be cool in the schoolyard. Sipping my drink, I tried not to dwell on it.

Carol appeared beside us just as the match started.

"Hi!" I tried to hide my surprise. I'd come to expect the worst of her and didn't think she'd show up.

"I'm a bit late," she said. "I had to work last night and only just got up in time."

Carol worked in a bar and was fairly notorious for drinking after work and not managing to get up the next day.

"The game's only just started," Linda said. "You haven't missed anything."

"Here, do you want to sit with us?" I shuffled over to make room for her on the blanket.

"Thanks. I guess Jake didn't trust me to turn up so he called in the back-up?"

"No, Jake said you'd be here." I like to think my lie was convincing. "I just kept telling Callum that I wanted to come and watch him play and since it's such a lovely day …"

"Thanks," she said, smiling before turning her attention to the game.

The first half went by fairly uneventfully. There was no score at half time when Callum ran over to say a quick hello to us.

"Couldn't Brian come?" he asked.

"No, he had to work." I got the distinct impression that having three women watching him play football was not quite the audience he would've liked. "Aren't we good enough for you?" I asked, ruffling his hair.

"You'll do!" He laughed and ran off across the pitch to rejoin his teammates.

In the second half there was some excitement when Callum quickly and casually moved in for a tackle, effortlessly manoeuvring the ball away from his opponent and taking off down the pitch. I jumped up and moved to the side-line, as did the rest of the spectators.

"Go on, Callum!" I called out. Linda gave me a gentle nudge. I laughed and nudged her back. A boy almost twice Callum's size moved over and nudged him off the ball.

"Hey!" I shouted.

"What was that?" Carol screamed from my side.

The referee issued a free kick just as the other parents turned to glare at us.

"I should think so!" Carol muttered of the referee's decision. When she turned to glare at the other parents on the side-lines, they quickly looked away.

We watched as Callum took the free kick, crossing the ball to the striker who tapped it into the back of the net. Carol and I cheered wildly, completely ignoring Linda's instructions. I was so proud of Callum and I was glad that Carol had turned up to watch him play. I felt a strange camaraderie with her as we both stood and cheered Callum on.

Callum's team won the game 1-0 and we waited as he ran in with his team to get changed after the game.

"Does anyone want to go out for lunch?" Linda asked. "My treat," she added, obviously sensing that Carol wouldn't have money.

"I'm starving." Callum appeared beside us, making us all laugh.

"Okay," Carol said. "Lunch sounds good."

"Does anyone feel like a picnic?" I asked as a thought occurred to me. "I know somewhere fun."

We stopped at the shop and filled a bag with sandwiches, snacks and drinks, and from there I directed Linda to my mum's house.

"I'll warn you, this might be crazy." We walked through the trees at the end of the road, which led to the hills and fields beyond.

As we emerged from the trees at the top of the hill, we stopped and stared. Callum started laughing first and the rest of us joined in pretty quickly.

It was about as funny as I'd expected. Jason couldn't be missed in his fluorescent leggings and tight T-shirt. He'd decided on a sweatband to keep the hair out of his eyes today and he looked ridiculous.

My mum was at his side, bouncing away next to him. It was quite a sight. There must've been about ten people with their dogs, all doing an aerobic workout while holding a lead with their dog beside them. Jason had a portable stereo, which made him look like he'd wandered straight out of the eighties. A Madonna track drifted on the wind.

"We'll have to stay up here, at a safe distance," I said. "We don't want to get roped into that!"

"Is that Jason?" Callum asked, having heard all about him.

"Yep!"

I helped Linda spread out the picnic blanket. Callum and Carol were unable to take their eyes off the entertainment at the bottom of the hill.

"It looks like your mum's business is going well," Linda commented.

"That's her little garden down there." I pointed down the hill. "With the caravan on it."

"What are they doing?" Callum asked with wide eyes as we watched the dog owners follow Jason into a press-up position. My mum then went around attempting to get the dogs to jump onto the owners' backs.

I got the giggles and couldn't stop. I tried to stay quiet, worrying that we might be heard. It was really hilarious though. I caught sight of Little Miss Chihuahua with her pooch perched on her back.

"Poor Alsatian lady!" I said and snorted with laughter.

We sat and ate our picnic, occasionally getting the

giggles as Jason instructed some strange fitness/dance move involving the dogs. My mum alternated between standing beside Jason and weaving her way through the group, apparently offering additional instruction where needed.

"I recognise the woman with the tiny dog," Carol said. "She's been on TV hasn't she? One of those talent shows."

"I have no idea," I said. "It's possible." Maybe Jason really did have celebrity clients. For some reason I tended not to believe him.

"Yeah, she ended up dating a footballer. I'm sure that's her."

I was surprised when Brian rang to ask where we were and said he'd come and join us. He arrived shortly after and Callum immediately complained to him about missing his game.

"Sorry," Brian said. "Did you win?"

"Yeah, of course. I set the striker up for the goal."

"I'll need a replay." Brian held out the shiny new football he was carrying. He gave me a kiss and said a quick hello to Carol and Linda. Then he grabbed a sandwich and took off with Callum to kick the ball around.

"Do you want to come and say hello to my mum?" I asked Linda and Carol once the sporty dog owners had dispersed. Jason gave me a wave and then joined the boys playing football. We packed up the picnic things and wandered down the hill.

"I thought it was you up there," Mum said. "Did you watch the class?"

"Yeah, it looked like fun," I said.

"Come and sit down," she said. "I've got tea."

"No biscuits today I hope?"

"I baked a cake yesterday, but it's at home. Shall I run up and get it?"

"No, it's fine, we just ate."

We settled ourselves on the picnic bench under the tree.

"It's a nice little spot, you've got." Linda said. "Seems like business is booming?"

"It's going great. And I'm really enjoying working with Jason. He's such a wonderful guy. Maybe you should ask him out, Marie."

"Brian might not be too happy if I did that." I wasn't at all surprised by her random suggestions anymore.

"Oh I forgot about Brian," she said. "He never answers my calls anymore."

I rolled my eyes and there was an awkward silence while Mum poured us all tea from a flask.

"You know, he doesn't answer my calls these days either." Carol shot me a wink.

"Or mine," Linda said.

"Does he answer yours, Marie?" Carol asked.

"Rarely, now I come to think of it …"

"So it's not just me?" Mum asked.

"I think it's a problem with his phone," Carol said.

"That could be it, couldn't it?" Mum said. "Don't ask Jason out then, Marie."

"I won't, Mum." I laughed and took a sip of my tea.

"I think I'm going to join in the game," Carol said when she finished her tea. "Anyone coming?"

"Go on then," Linda said. I loved that she'd join in with anything.

I moved over to sit on the wall to watch the game and waved when I saw Jake and Michael arrive. Sophie and Jeff had arrived at some point and were also chasing the ball around on the field.

I handed Brian a bottle of water when he jogged over to me with beads of sweat gleaming on his hairline.

He leaned against the wall and took long gulps. "Sorry about this morning."

I didn't say anything – not wanting to get in another argument - but put my arm around him and kissed the side of his head, not caring about the salty taste of sweat. It was nice to see him so relaxed.

"You're right about Jake," I said, resting my head against his.

"What about him?"

"Something's bothering him." I'd been noticing little things since Brian mentioned it weeks ago. Jake definitely had something on his mind. He was quiet and sometimes he seemed to be in his own little world, not listening to conversations at all.

"Who are you talking about?" Sophie ran over and took the bottle of water from Brian.

"Jake," I said. "Do you think he's acting weird?"

"I've hardly seen him recently." She hopped up to sit beside me on the wall. "But I did notice Michael keeps giving him funny looks. Like he's expecting him to burst into tears any minute."

"Everything seems fine with Carol," Brian remarked.

"Yeah, I don't think it's Carol," I agreed. "She seems better than I've ever known her. I had fun with her today."

185

We watched quietly as they ran around after the ball. It was fun to sit and watch everyone enjoying themselves.

"Look …" Sophie nodded towards Jake as Michael ran over and patted him affectionately on the arm. Jake had been standing at the edge of the game, occasionally cheering at whoever had the ball. He looked tense and it seemed like Michael was keeping a close eye on him.

We didn't speculate any further, but I could almost feel the worry that emanated from the three of us as we sat on the wall. The more I looked at Jake, the more convinced I was that something was wrong.

"It's a shame you couldn't make it to Callum's football game," I said to Sophie in a bid to change the subject.

"I wanted to come but I had to work this morning and then I had some studying to catch up on. How was it?"

"No rest for the wicked," I said, smiling at her. "The game was great. Callum was a star!"

"I'll come next time."

"You could reply to my messages next time as well," I said.

"Sorry. I'm just so busy. Don't get stressed with me. I've got enough to deal with."

I leaned into her affectionately. "I'll be glad when your course is over and done with."

She sighed. "You and me both."

Chapter 25

It was a strange Fat Club on Thursday. I made tea when Jake and Linda arrived and we sat around in the living room as usual. I waited for Linda to finish telling us anecdotes about the school canteen before I casually questioned Jake to try to get to the bottom of what was going on with him.

"How's work for you, Jake?" I asked, moving the conversation seamlessly from Linda to him.

"It's good. It's probably not that much different from Linda's job sometimes. Old people can be quite childlike. Some of them are quite mischievous. They get bored, I think, and try to have a bit of fun. Usually at the expense of the carers, but it keeps us on our toes."

"And your job is really secure?" If he was happy with his job, maybe he was worried about losing it. "You've been there a long time, haven't you?"

"I wouldn't want to work anywhere else. It's a private place and I feel like I have good job security. The owners are nice people."

"And Michael likes it there too?"

"Loves it."

"He's looking really well at the moment. He seemed to be really enjoying the football game at the weekend …" I'd say this was about the point in the conversation where Jake started to grow suspicious of my questioning.

"He's fine. Same old Michael," he said vaguely. I wondered how to dig discreetly further into his life.

"And Carol seems to be doing well too?"

"She is, yes." He glanced at Linda. "And Callum's fine. So is my mum … Anything else you want to know about?"

I'd been rumbled but it didn't deter me. I decided to dive in with the direct approach. "I've just been worried about you. You seem a bit down. Like there's something on your mind …"

He shifted in his chair and looked uncomfortable. I knew I was right.

"Really?" he asked.

"You seem distracted. If there's anything we can help with, you just need to say." I hoped that would coax him into spilling the beans.

"You're very observant." He smiled at me. "I guess I have been a bit worried recently. It's nothing though. Honestly." He went quiet and I thought the suspense might kill me. I'd come this far. He wasn't getting away now without baring his soul.

"What is it?" Linda asked, seemingly as on edge as I was.

He waved a hand in front of him. "It's hardly even worth talking about."

"But we're your friends," I said. "Whatever it is, you can tell us." I absolutely needed to know now. My concern had been overshadowed by curiosity.

"I've been worrying about my weight again," he finally said.

"Really?" What a let down. I was expecting some drama.

He patted his stomach. "I was doing so well, but I feel like I've fallen off the wagon." Linda and I sat quietly and I wondered how I could make myself sound concerned and caring on this subject.

"Is it the fried breakfasts again?" I asked automatically.

"I'm afraid so." He made a sad face and suddenly it clicked with me. He was making this up. There was a problem that he couldn't talk about but he needed to say something so I'd stop asking questions.

Linda looked sympathetic. "The odd fry up isn't so bad."

"But I've been lying to Michael." There was a slightly dramatic tone to his voice and it made me angry. This was utter nonsense he was spouting and he was expecting us to believe it and offer him support and comfort on the matter. He was mocking us.

"He thinks I eat healthily, but whenever he's at work, I'm gobbling down grease and junk. Then of course I'm hiding the evidence. I feel terrible about it."

"Well that's not good for your relationship," Linda said. I'm glad Linda was keeping up the conversation because all I wanted to do was jump up and shout, "Liar!"

"So this is your big problem?" I asked unsympathetically.

"Yes." He looked at me and I stared him out, making sure he knew I'd not been fooled.

"Maybe you should start getting weighed again each week?" Linda suggested. We'd done this in the early days of fat club; weighed Jake each week in order to shame him into losing weight.

"Maybe," he said.

"Shall we have another cup of tea?" I looked at Linda, knowing she'd take the bait and go and make it.

"I'll do it," she said as she collected up mugs.

"Give me some credit," I said once Linda was out of the room.

"What do you mean?" Jake drummed his fingers on the arm of the chair.

"I didn't buy that for one minute. All that stuff about your weight; nonsense!"

"Well, I'm sorry my problems aren't serious enough for you." He was playing games with me now, but if the weight really was his problem I was being very insensitive.

"And I'm sorry you're a rubbish liar!" I decided to continue on my course and see if he'd crack. "Just tell me what's really going on."

We stared at each other silently before he admitted defeat. "Alright Sherlock! The fry-ups were a cover up. I can't tell you the truth though."

"You have to," I said. "We don't have secrets."

"It's sensitive. I will tell you, just not now. And don't say anything to anyone else."

"Fine," I finally agreed. It didn't seem like I'd get any further with him today. I knew when to back down.

"Promise you won't say anything," he whispered as we heard Linda on her way back from the kitchen.

"I tell Brian everything." I pulled my legs under me. "But he doesn't always listen so you're probably safe."

Sophie's voice rang through from the hallway just as Linda set the tea down on the coffee table. I hadn't expected to see her so it was a pleasant surprise when she wandered in with Brian. Jake looked relieved that the conversation moved away from him.

"How is everyone?" Sophie asked cheerfully as she took a seat and helped herself to my cup of tea. She didn't wait for a reply, just kept talking. "It's great to see you all. I'm really missing my Thursdays with you. It's made me appreciate you so much more."

"What do you want?" I asked.

"What makes you think I want something?" she asked innocently.

"Because I know you."

"Okay, now that you mention it, I do have a small favour to ask you. Just something tiny ,,," She grinned at us and I waited to see what we were about to get roped into. It wasn't just Brian that had trouble saying no to Sophie. "It's my mum's birthday at the weekend and she's going down to visit Roy. She's farming the kids off between friends and relatives so I was thinking it would be really great to tidy up the house a bit as a surprise for her birthday."

"That's a nice idea," Linda said. "She'll love it."

"So can you help me?" she asked.

"Of course." Linda was far too keen. I think she was even excited by the idea.

"Marie?" Sophie turned to me.

"Saturday?"

"Yes. And I know all you ever do on Saturdays is hang out with Linda so you need to think fast if you want to get out of it."

My brain whirred as I desperately searched for a way to avoid spending Saturday cleaning someone else's house. "I would but Brian and I have plans."

"Brian said he's working." Sophie flashed me a knowing smile.

I glared at Brian. "I guess I'm in then!"

"Jake?" Sophie asked.

"I promised Callum I'd take him to the cinema."

"Don't look smug," I said. "You had longer to think of a excuse than me"

"It's true." His eyes were full of amusement. "Ask Callum!"

"Don't worry, I will." I grinned at him.

"Okay, Jake is excused," Sophie said. "Linda can you drive me home now? My work here is done!"

Chapter 26

Julie called me on Friday evening to say that Paul had a last minute meeting at a hotel near us on Saturday and they'd decided to come with him for a visit. I briefly thought about cancelling on Sophie's big clean-up operation before deciding I wasn't that brave. I told Julie I'd try and get away early so I could spend the afternoon with them and go for dinner together.

"Brian?" I gave him the big eyes on Saturday morning and he looked immediately suspicious. I should have had this conversation with him the previous evening but I just couldn't face an argument on Friday night. At least I was going out soon if it ended in a shouting match.

"What?"

"I promised Sophie I'd help her with her mum's house, but Julie and Abby are coming down for the day. I said I'd meet them for dinner later but could you entertain them for a bit today? Maybe take them out for lunch? I don't want them to be hanging around waiting for me all day. Please …"

"I said *yes*." I realised I'd spoken over him, sure it wouldn't be that easy. It hadn't even occurred to me that he might just agree.

"Oh, great." I gave a tentative smile but he'd gone back to the documents he'd been reading. "Thanks.

They'll be really pleased. And it means I don't have to dash off too early. Sophie's so excited about cleaning up the house."

"That's good. Her mum will be happy."

"I hope so. I was worried she might be offended by people coming in to clean her house for her. Like we're saying she's incapable of keeping her house clean."

"She's got a house full of kids. I think she's completely incapable of keeping it clean! I'm sure she'll love it."

"That's what Sophie says." I paused for a moment, wondering whether he really was okay about spending the day with Julie and Abby. "Shall I tell Julie they should come straight here? They're getting the train down. Your dad's working somewhere nearby. He'll meet us this evening."

"I'll call Julie and arrange something," he said hesitantly. "I just need to finish reading through these." He indicated the papers in front of him.

"Okay, I'll leave you to it." I kissed him before bouncing into the living room. I was relieved that he'd agreed to spend time with Julie and Abby. I hoped that it would help to ease the tension between them.

I called Julie and told her the plan. She was sceptical and wanted to know what I'd bribed him with. She didn't believe he'd agreed to it of his own free will. I told her I'd call as soon as I'd finished helping Sophie and hoped that they'd have a nice time with Brian until then.

Linda picked me up and drove me to Sophie's

house. Sophie was looking out of the window for us and immediately ushered us through all the rooms in the house, excitedly telling us her plans. Apparently she'd had the great idea of painting a couple of rooms, as well as the big clean up, so she'd sent Jeff out to buy paint.

"This sounds like a lot for one day," Linda said. "Are you sure it's not a bit ambitious?"

"No, we can do it. We'll just have to work hard." She smiled at us as she led us into the kitchen where she had buckets lined up next to an array of cleaning products. "I wanted to tidy up the garden too but I crossed that off the list. See? I'm being realistic."

"Let's stop wasting time them." I said. It was futile to argue with Sophie. The wisest approach was to just get on with it and hope we could leave sometime in the near future. "I'll start in the kitchen," I announced as I picked up a pair of rubber gloves and a bottle of multi purpose spray.

"I'll do the living room." Linda rummaged through the various cleaning products.

"You guys are the best!" Sophie said.

Jeff arrived back with the paint an hour later but it seemed like the more we cleaned, the more there was that needed cleaning. I made tea late in the morning and delivered cups to Linda, Sophie and Jeff in their various rooms of the house. I sat at the kitchen table to drink mine and typed a quick message to Brian, complaining about how much Sophie wanted us to get done. I was starting to worry Sophie would realise she'd been over ambitious and be upset when we didn't finish it all.

I went back to work, wiping down the doors of the

kitchen cupboards and then got the mop out for the floor. I was busy cleaning windows and wondering how to broach the subject of lunch when Callum's voice drifted through to me.

In the hallway, I was over the moon to see Jake, Michael and Callum.

"We brought food for the workers." Jake held up a bulging shopping bag.

"And apparently we have to help," Michael said.

"But I'm supposed to tell you we were planning on going to the cinema!" Callum laughed and Jake gave him a friendly nudge.

"I love you guys," Sophie shouted from the top of the stairs.

"Brian called and said you needed a hand." Jake moved into the kitchen with the food. "So we cancelled our plans to go to the cinema." I followed them and got out plates for the sandwiches and emptied crisps into a bowl.

"Hello?" Brian's voice drifted from the front door and I moved back into the hallway.

"Hey!" I smiled. Julie and Abby were standing behind him. "What are you doing here?"

"Brian told us what you were doing," Julie said. "We volunteered to help."

Brian cleared his throat. "I wanted to take them for a nice lunch. It was all their idea."

"It's okay. I believe you." I kissed his cheek. "Plus, I'm exhausted already and there's still loads to do. We need all the help we can get."

I did quick introductions and then Linda whisked Julie and Abby off to start painting.

"Brian?" Sophie said sweetly as she sidled up to

him.

"Where do you want me?"

"Can you make the garden look pretty? I'd crossed it off the list but since there's so many of us now, maybe we can get that done too."

"I'll help," Callum said.

"You two start tidying it up," Michael said. "I'll nip out and get some plants and things."

"It's going to be so amazing," Sophie said. "Thanks so much." She gave Michael a big kiss on the cheek before running out to answer Linda's questions about paint.

Sophie arrived back in the kitchen five minutes later and Jeff jumped up out of the seat. He'd been cheerfully finishing off the lunch things and chatting to me as I worked.

"Get to work, will you," she said.

"Yes boss!" He saluted her and stopped to give her a kiss before hurrying out of the room

"You two seem happy," I remarked once he'd left.

"We are," she said. I was glad. I liked Jeff a lot and it was nice to see that Sophie had at least one part of her life under control.

The afternoon whizzed by. I had so much fun. Sophie turned the radio on and we were singing and dancing as we worked. Having so many of us there made it more of a party than a chore and I kept finding more things I wanted to do to make it special for Sophie's mum. I kept an eye on Jake too, but both he and Michael seemed relaxed and happy. I hoped whatever was going on was nothing serious.

Sophie was over the moon with everything when we finally geared up to leave. "I can't wait to see

Mum's face," she said. "She won't recognise the place. Do you want to stay for a drink?"

"We need to go and find Brian's dad," I told her. "And I think we need to take Julie and Abby out for dinner to thank them. I don't think this was how they anticipated spending their day."

"I had a great time," Abby said.

"Me too," Julie agreed. "Your mum's a lucky lady, Sophie. What an amazing gift."

"Thanks so much for helping." Sophie looked around at us all in the pristine living room. She looked exhausted and emotional as Jeff appeared behind her and wrapped his arms around her.

"Right, we're going, Sophie, before you start blubbing. Tell your mum we said Happy Birthday! and have a great time with her."

"Thanks!" She gave me a hug and there was a round of goodbyes as we all headed in our separate directions.

We drove Julie and Abby back to their hotel and headed home to shower and change before jumping in a taxi back to the hotel to have dinner with them.

Paul smiled when we greeted him in the hotel lobby. He'd just arrived from his business meeting and seemed more relaxed than usual.

"I hear you treated my girls to a fun-filled day?" he said to Brian.

"They volunteered." Brian held his hands up. "I would've taken them out for lunch."

"It was a really lovely day though," I said. "They had fun, didn't they?"

"Yes. They couldn't stop talking about it. It seems

like your friends made a big impression on them."

"We have interesting friends."

"It sounds like it," he said.

The maître-de appeared and directed us to our table. Julie and Abby arrived just as we were sitting down.

"I've got blisters and I can't get all the paint off." Abby excitedly held out her hands for me to inspect.

"Me too." I put my hands beside hers to compare.

"No war wounds, Brian?" Paul asked.

"He was just lazing around in the garden," Abby said lightly.

"I got in a fight with a thorn bush actually." Brian rolled up a sleeve to reveal a long red scratch.

"I'd love to see Sophie's mum's face," Julie said.

"Me too." Brian pushed his shirtsleeve down again. "She deserves it. She's lovely."

"It looked amazing," Abby said. "Can we make-over our house?"

"What's wrong with our house?" Julie asked.

"Nothing. It was just so much fun. I want to do it again!"

"Maybe when you have your girls' weekend," Brian suggested with a cheeky grin.

"No!" Julie and I said.

"That's going to be a relaxing weekend," I added. We'd discussed it more over the day and Linda and Sophie were keen on the idea. I felt better about it now everyone had met.

It was wonderful to relax with a glass of wine after working so hard all day. My arms ached from the painting and my hands throbbed slightly where blisters had formed from gripping the paintbrush.

There was a definite feeling of satisfaction though, and it was lovely to spend the evening with Paul, Julie and Abby. Brian edged his chair closer to mine and rested his arm along the back of my chair. He was in a great mood and the conversation flowed effortlessly. We told stories and laughed as we ate. The evening flew by and I was exhausted and light-headed from the wine as we said our goodbyes.

I promised to call Julie and arrange a weekend to visit them. I was increasingly excited by the prospect and was keen to spend more time with Julie and Abby.

Chapter 27

I had a session with Jason after work on Monday and was surprised to find Brian lying on the couch when I got home. I registered his jeans and T-shirt. "How long have you been here?"

He rubbed at his eyes. "A while."

"I'm going to jump in the shower. Your phone's ringing." I pointed to it as it buzzed around the table.

When I returned ten minutes later, the phone was still vibrating its way around the table. Brian was lying in the exact same position.

I nudged him and he slowly opened his eyes. "What's wrong?" I asked.

"Nothing. I'm tired." He pushed himself up on his arm to make space for me and then lowered his head into my lap.

"Sophie called and said her mum was over the moon with the house. She said it was the best present she'd ever had."

"That's good," Brian mumbled into my lap.

"Are you ill?"

"No, I'm okay." The phone began to move around the table again. "I'm ignoring it." He stretched as he slowly stood up. "Do you want a drink?"

"Tea, please." He headed for the kitchen.

There were twenty-three missed calls showing on Brian's phone when I picked it up and slipped it under a cushion to muffle the vibrations. My phone rang with a call from Grace. I was happy she was actually getting around to calling me.

"Brian's not answering his phone," she said hastily. "Is he with you?"

"Yeah he's here. He's just making tea."

"Tea?" She laughed. "I thought he'd be on champagne. Are you going out to celebrate? I'm surprised he's not out partying with the rest of the firm."

"Yeah." I pretended I knew what she was talking about. "I'm sure we'll get to the alcohol later."

"Everything okay?" she asked.

"Yes. I think all the hard work has just caught up with him. He looks exhausted."

"I'm not surprised. It was a critical deal for the firm and Brian was the one to push it through. He'll probably be up for promotion now."

"I know. It's amazing."

"I've got to run. Tell him I said congratulations!"

"I'll tell him," I said. "Talk soon."

When Brian placed a cup of tea on the table in front of me, I was perched on the edge of the couch, ignoring the hum of the phone coming from beneath the cushion.

"Grace has been trying to get hold of you," I said, as he flopped down beside me. "She wanted to say congratulations."

"Oh, yeah," he murmured. "The deal went through."

"Were you going to share the good news with me?"

"Yes." He stretched out on the couch again. "I

was just about to."

"That explains why you're so popular anyway." I pulled out his phone and handed it to him.

"I guess I'm supposed to be out celebrating."

"You don't seem very excited." His lack of enthusiasm was starting to worry me.

"I'm too tired to be excited. I just wanted to come home."

"And drink tea?" I picked up my mug and raised it to him.

"Exactly."

I set my tea down and shuffled down to lie next to him. "Congratulations."

"Thanks."

"Do you want to go out and celebrate?"

"Not really."

It wasn't long before his body relaxed and he fell fast asleep in my arms.

Chapter 28

"I thought work might slow down a bit now," I said to Brian on Saturday, trying hard not to sound irritated. After the big news on Monday I'd hardly seen him. My week had dragged and even fat club hadn't lifted my spirits.

"It will." He closed his laptop and stood to wrap his arms around me. "Some stuff came up but things should settle down again now."

"Okay." I wasn't at all convinced.

"I might even take you for a night out," he said, tickling me.

I laughed and wriggled away from him. "I won't hold my breath!"

A loud knock at the front door startled me.

"I thought Linda wasn't coming until later?" Brian said.

"She's not." At one time she would have been on my doorstep at 9am but I'd gradually trained her to make it later. It was a surprise to find Sophie on the doorstep. I was used to my friends turning up at random times but on the occasions that Sophie wasn't working on Saturday mornings she wouldn't generally be persuaded out of her bed before midday.

"What's wrong?" I asked when I registered her tears.

She barged past me. "Where's Brian?"

"In the kitchen," I said, following her.

She slammed a bunch of papers on the counter in front of Brian "It was a total waste of time and money," she shouted, barely coherent as she paced and cried. Brian didn't react as he reached for the papers.

"I can't do it. I can't do anything," she said. "Now I can't pay you back and I'll never be able to."

"What are you talking about?" Brian asked.

"The stupid business course," she spat back at him. "I get everything wrong. I don't understand it. I kept trying and I thought I had it figured out in my head but now the bank won't lend me any money so it was all a big waste of time. I can't do anything."

She sobbed and moved into the dining room to sink into a chair and lay her head on the table. "I'm just stupid," she cried, more vulnerable than I'd ever known her.

Brian looked at me and took a deep breath before picking up the papers and following her. Pulling up a chair next to her, I squeezed her arm.

"You've been to the bank today?" Brian asked.

"Yeah," she said, sniffing.

"And this is your business plan?"

"Yeah."

Brian sighed as he flicked through the papers. He shook his head and Sophie started crying even more.

"Is it really bad?" she asked.

He looked frustrated as he put her business proposal to one side and rubbed his eyes with his palms. "Why didn't you show me this before you went? I could've helped you."

"I didn't want to bother you," she said. "You already paid for the course and I wanted to show you

206

I could do it. But I don't understand what he's talking about in class and everyone else just seems to understand, so I feel like I'm asking stupid questions. I thought that if I talked to someone at the bank they would see that I've got lots of experience. I thought I could convince them that I can do it."

"It doesn't work like that," he said softly.

"I know that now," she snapped. "But I don't know how to pay you the money back." Fresh tears appeared and Brian pulled her off her chair and into a big hug.

"I don't care about the money," he said gently.

I went to put the kettle on and when I returned a few minutes later with three cups of tea, Sophie looked calmer.

Brian looked through her business proposal again, before looking up at her with a smile. "It's very annoying that you bother me with all the trivial little details of your life but when it's something important, that I would actually like to hear about, you suddenly decide to keep quiet."

Sophie managed a pathetic laugh and then cupped her hands around her steaming tea, blowing on it before taking a sip.

"So what can we do?" I asked.

Brian raised his eyebrows at me. We both knew I wasn't going to be much help but I had a sneaky suspicion he'd have a plan.

"Drink your tea," Brian said as Sophie looked at him hopefully. "I'll drive you home and you can pick up everything from your course; all your notes and papers, coursework … whatever you have. We can bring it back here and I'll go through it with you and see what we can figure out."

"But the man at the bank said it wasn't a viable business and that I'd never make any profit."

"That's just one guy's opinion," Brian said.

"But what's the point now? The bank already said they won't give me any money."

"There are lots of banks," Brian said. "You just need a bit of help that's all."

***

That evening, I flicked through the TV channels while Brian stared at his laptop. He looked tired and stressed.

"You okay?" I asked.

"Yeah." He frowned. "I just spent so much time going through things with Sophie today. It set me back a bit. I've got a lot to get done for Monday. I hoped I'd get it all done today but it looks like I'll be working tomorrow too."

"It's okay, I'll explain to Mum, she'll understand." I was fairly sure she wouldn't understand but I was concerned about how much pressure Brian was under and didn't want to add to his stress levels.

"I would much rather go to your mum's than do this," he said with a sigh.

"How was it with Sophie?"

He exhaled loudly. "Her business plan was a joke. A lot of what she'd written didn't even make sense."

"So you don't think she can set up on her own?"

"I don't know. When she talks about what she envisions, she seems to understand the fundamentals, and she's really driven. She's a hard worker so she's got that going for her. But if she can't get a grasp of book-keeping and managing people, she's got no chance." He paused, deep in thought. "She could do really well. But she needs a lot of help and someone with a lot more patience than the idiot who's teaching her business course."

"Like you?"

He put his laptop aside. "I was thinking maybe I could find some time in the next couple of weeks to help her through her course."

"That would be good." I wasn't sure why my eyes filled with tears.

He put a tentative hand on my knee. "Sorry."

"It's really nice of you." I tried to fight the tears but I didn't seem to have much control over them. "Honestly, I think you should help Sophie." I managed a pathetic laugh. "I don't know why I'm crying."

He put his arms around me and I buried my head in his shoulder. "I know why," he said. "If anyone deserves more of my time, it's you."

"I didn't say that." I pulled away and wiped at my eyes. "I want you to help Sophie."

"But I don't want you to think I'm making time for Sophie and not you." He stroked circles on the back of my hand with his thumb. "I want to have more time for you too. I can try and cut down on work somehow …"

"I doesn't matter." I wiped furiously at my cheeks. "I'm just tired. I'm going to bed."

I left the room before he could say anything else. He *did* work too much and I was angry that he never had time for me, but I refused to be a nagging wife, telling him how to live his life. He needed to figure things out for himself.

Chapter 29

A small miracle occurred in that I messaged Jason and arranged a workout with him for Monday morning. I worried about my sanity even as I typed out the message on Sunday evening. I was irrationally upset about Brian's intentions to help Sophie. It was stupid. If he hadn't suggested it, I would've done. Unfortunately, my emotions seemed to be getting the better of me.

"Did you and Brian have an argument?" Jason asked. The sun was just rising as we jogged around the park, and the grass shimmered with dewdrops.

"No." I followed his lead, stopping for a set of star jumps.

He stood still and didn't take his eyes off me. "Are you okay?"

"Is it really so worrying that I volunteered for exercise on a Monday morning?"

"Yes." His eyebrows drew together. "I'm worried about you. You don't seem yourself."

"I'm fine." I stopped my star jumps, puffing as I caught my breath. "I'm just feeling a bit crappy. Stop staring at me." I turned and continued jogging along the path. "Come on. You're worrying me now. I've never seen you stay still for so long."

He broke into a grin and followed me.

"How's the dog business going?" I asked in an attempt to lighten the atmosphere.

"It's brilliant. The classes are getting bigger each week. The newspaper article gave us a massive boost and we've got the radio interview next week. We may even need to offer a second class if things carry on as they are."

"That's great. Maybe you should think about making a video so people can do the routine in the comfort of their own home. I especially like the push-up move."

"That one is hilarious," Jason said. "I tried to cut it out, but I got requests for it so we have to do it every time now. I'll be honest though, I think it's probably a health hazard."

"It definitely is for poor Alsatian lady!"

"I tell them to only do what they feel comfortable with but they get really into it. They love it."

"Nutters!" we said at once.

"Your mum tried to poison me, by the way," Jason said amid the easy laughter.

"Oh no! I forgot to tell you not to accept food from her. What was it?"

"Chocolate and stilton muffins! I nearly gagged."

"There's a logic to that. If you can have chocolate cheese cake, why not chocolate cheese muffins?"

"Stilton?"

"Cheese is cheese!" I said. "Just don't accept food from her again. No matter how good it looks, don't be tempted. Always say you've just eaten."

We stopped outside the house and did some stretches before I headed in for a quick shower. Brian had already left so I had to brave the bus to get to work. It was fairly painless; just some old guy across the aisle who was eating yoghurt like it was a can of Coke. I couldn't figure out what it was about buses that always brought out bizarre, antisocial behaviour in people. I don't think I've ever travelled by bus and not ended up worrying about the state of the human race.

"Morning, Anne!" I smiled as I walked into work and then stopped to do a double take. It seemed like I'd walked into work like a little ray of sunshine while Anne was looking decidedly troubled. Something was not right with the world.

"Everything okay?" I hung up my coat and shoved my bag into my drawer. Anne moved straight into position, perching on the edge of my desk.

"You just missed Jason," she said.

"Is he okay?" I asked. "Because I saw him an hour ago and he was fine then."

"It's not Jason I'm worried about. It's you."

I sighed. "Is this because I volunteered for a workout session on a Monday morning? I'm a bit worried about that myself!"

"Not just that. Jason said you seemed a bit fed up. I've noticed that you've been a bit down too."

"Really?" I used to dismiss about ninety-nine per cent of everything Anne said but recently I'd started to realise she was usually spot on with her observations about me. "Maybe," I conceded.

"What's bothering you?"

"I don't know," I said honestly.

"Are you pregnant?" she asked with big eyes.

"No." I laughed and she raised her eyebrows. "I'm not! I'm fine. Now back off and let me do some work."

A knocking on the window distracted her and she went to try and convince the two grey-haired old dears that we weren't open yet. They ended up talking their way in and left an hour later with a stack of holiday brochures. I'm fairly sure they were only killing time until the hairdresser opened.

I was taken aback by the sound of Grace's voice when I rang her. I'd gotten so used to her voicemail that it was a shock to hear her answer the phone. It would be the early hours of the morning in New York but I didn't like to ask why she was still up, knowing the answer would be work.

"Nice to finally get hold of you," I said, smiling into the phone.

"I know, I'm sorry. I'm a terrible friend."

"Don't worry about it. Everything okay with you?"

"Yes, work's hectic as ever."

"How's James?"

"He's fine. Same old James. What's going on with you? Did Brian get round to some celebrating?"

"No, he didn't have time. He's working more than ever."

"That's normal," she said. "Things should ease off soon. At least until the next big project comes along."

"So this is how life will be?" I tried to keep my voice light but didn't quite manage it.

"Not forever. Brian's at a high point in his career. He's worked hard to get where he is. It's great that he's doing so well."

"I guess. It'd just be nice to see him a bit more."

"Get him to take a holiday. He probably needs a break too. You could come and visit us."

"A holiday would be good." I sighed. "Sorry, I better get back to work."

The quick chat with Grace cheered me up a bit. It was nice to talk to her; it felt like how things used to be with us. I got back to work and the day went surprisingly quickly.

My mood nosedived as I spent yet another evening alone. Brian walked in late with Sophie in tow and they parked themselves in the dining room for an hour while I sat on the couch, listening to them talk and wishing I didn't care.

The week went painfully slowly after that. I did a great job of acting normal around Brian. Not that it was difficult given how little I saw of him.

Sophie didn't make it to fat club on Thursday so it was another quiet evening with Jake and Linda. Jake seemed a bit happier so I hoped whatever was going on with him had sorted itself out. I decided he'd tell me in his own time and I would just live with the torture of not knowing until then.

"How's it going with Sophie?" I asked Brian on Friday evening when he actually came home at a reasonable time, and without Sophie.

"Pretty good." He put an arm around me on the couch. "I think she's starting to understand things. Her course finishes next week and I think she'll have managed to get to grips with everything by then."

"That's good." I suddenly felt bad for my negativity all week. I was glad Sophie was getting some help. It would totally knock her confidence to finish the course feeling it was a waste of time.

"I told her she could come over tomorrow afternoon and go over some more stuff. Do you mind?"

"No, it's fine. I'll be out with Linda anyway."

"That's what I thought." He paused for a minute, looking thoughtful. "It's actually quite nice, helping Sophie."

"Yeah?"

"It makes me feel really knowledgeable."

"That's a bit mean!"

"I didn't mean it like that," he said, nudging me. "I just feel useful. It feels like I'm making a difference."

I smiled but felt a definite pang of jealousy. The pesky goblin in my head whispered that it would make a difference to our relationship if he spent more time with me too.

My feelings about the Sophie situation annoyed me. I wanted to be a happy-go-lucky girlfriend who was constantly cheerful and supportive. In reality, I wanted to get a frying pan and smack him round the head with it while shouting at him that this is not okay. I didn't want to be waiting around for him to have time for me, and begging him for attention.

It wasn't what I wanted for our relationship, or for my life.

Chapter 30

"I did it!" Sophie's voice sang around the room before she bounded in on Thursday with a huge grin on her face. "It's all over and I survived it!"

"I've got champagne." Brian followed her in. We all cheered as he popped the cork.

"Speech!" Jake looked to Sophie as we raised our glasses.

"Sod that," she said. "I've earned a drink!" She took a long sip and then sank into the couch.

"So you're all ready to set up shop now, are you?" Linda asked.

"No. Definitely not!" Sophie laughed and we all looked at her in confusion.

"I thought the course went well…" I said.

"Well I got through it. But Brian made me realise I was probably setting my sights too high."

I glared at Brian. "What did you do?"

"Nothing." He sat beside Sophie. "I think you can definitely run your own business. I thought we'd discussed everything–"

"Don't look so worried," Sophie said, cutting him off. "I've got a new plan!"

"Well don't keep us in suspense," Jake said.

"I'm going to set up a mobile beauty salon," Sophie said. "I don't need a lot of money up front. I'll need to buy some equipment and a second-hand car, but I won't have any bills to pay. It will take a bit of time to build it up, but I think it will work, and if it doesn't, at least I've given it a go without losing anything."

"We need more champagne." Brian blinked rapidly and left the room.

"Did Brian just get a bit choked up?" Sophie asked.

"Well I'm very proud of you," Linda said as she fished her hanky out of her sleeve and dabbed at her eyes.

"Me too," I added.

"Me three! I think it's a brilliant idea," Jake said.

"Who needs a top up?" Brian asked. Sophie and I held our glasses out to him.

"And," Sophie said, "I've entered the nailympics!"

"The what?" Jake asked.

"The nailympics!" Sophie laughed. "It's a huge nail art competition. Very prestigious in the nail world. If I won it, it would be a massive boost for my career."

"That sounds exciting," Linda said.

"It is. But I'll warn you, I'll need to practice on you all!"

Jake looked at his nails. "That'll be the day."

"You too, Brian," Sophie said.

"Sure, why not?" He smiled at her. "I don't know why I didn't think of a mobile business."

"I'm glad you didn't," Sophie said. "I needed to figure it out for myself and you helped me do that." She stood and gave him a big hug before turning to me. "Got any chocolate?"

"I'll look." I stood up and went into the kitchen.

"Are you still angry with me?" Sophie's voice made me jump as she followed me into the kitchen.

"What?"

"You were really angry with me, weren't you?" she asked.

"No. Why would I be?"

"Because I've taken up all of Brian's time and I've been a bit annoying." She grinned. "But I have a plan for you too."

"What do you mean?" I asked slowly.

"Well, since I figured out my own life, I'm now moving on to yours."

I rolled my eyes. "You think my life needs fixing?"

"Yep." She looked smug and it made me nervous.

"How are you going to do that then?"

"You'll see." Her eyes twinkled as they lingered on me.

I called out to her as she made to leave the kitchen. I raised my eyebrows questioningly.

"Let's just say that I may have put some wheels in motion … and if they move the way they should, you'll be thanking me in no time."

"Well that's made everything crystal clear," I said. "What have you done?"

"All will be revealed." She laughed loudly, then left me alone in the kitchen, wondering what she was up to this time.

Chapter 31

It didn't happen very often but Sophie joined Linda and me for our shopping trip that Saturday. We had a great time wandering round the shops and trying on random outfits that we picked out for each other. There was a lot of laughter and I was totally relaxed. We had a long lunch together in a cute little Italian restaurant.

Sophie decided she'd earned a treat after all the work she'd put into her business course in the past couple of months and suggested we make plans to go up to Scotland for our girls' weekend. I messaged Julie while we were still at lunch and she called me immediately and invited us to come up the following weekend. I could hear Abby squealing with delight in the background. I smiled as I hung up the phone and we spent the rest of lunch planning our little getaway.

The week went quickly and Brian seemed to be making an effort to be home earlier in the evenings. I still couldn't quite shake my feelings of annoyance towards him but I decided if I ignored it for long enough it would sort itself out.

It was nice to have Sophie back at fat club. She was the first to arrive and went to work in the kitchen, making tea.

"I've messaged Brian," she said. "Told him he

needs to be a good boyfriend and come home early since he won't see you all weekend."

"Well he knows I'm away all weekend. If he wants to see me, he should be able to get home on time without you nagging him."

I was annoyed the moment I saw the smirk on Sophie's face.

"You're an idiot," she said. "He's a man. He needs to be nagged. If he didn't want anyone nagging him he would've stayed single, wouldn't he?"

I perched myself on a stool. "I don't like nagging."

"You need to start. It's not fair to Brian. You're messing with his head." She poured water over the teabags and turned to smile at me. "You can't get mad at him for working too much unless you've complained to him about it. Nag him a bit and then he knows where he stands."

I tapped my fingers on the countertop. "Or I can just leave him to work, if that's what he wants."

"Yes, but then you're not allowed to get angry about it!"

"I'm not angry," I said.

She laughed as she dropped the teabags into the bin. "Anyway, I've nagged Brian to come home early today. When he walks through the door in the next five minutes I'll have proved my point."

"You didn't make him a cuppa so you can't be that confident."

"I did actually. Jake's not coming tonight."

"Really?" Jake never missed fat club.

"He rang me earlier to say he couldn't make it. He

222

sounded a bit weird on the phone. Did you find out what was going on with him?"

"No. I spoke to him but he said everything was fine." I turned at the sound of a key in the lock. "I hate you!" I hissed at Sophie.

"I made my point! Nag him more." She looked irritatingly smug.

"How do we know he hadn't already planned on coming home early to see me?"

Brian appeared in the kitchen.

"You're home early," I remarked.

"Sophie told me I had to be here." He smiled and moved over to her. "Just in time, too," he said, picking up a cup of tea.

Sophie grinned at me as she leaned casually against the counter. I glared back at her without a word.

"What?" Brian asked as he moved over to me.

"Nothing. I just thought you'd come home early to see me."

His eyes went wide. "Yes. That's what I meant. Isn't that what I said?"

"Nope," Sophie said. "You said you came home early because–"

"Sophie!" Brian snapped. "Shut up and get out of the kitchen."

She reached for a cup of tea and scuttled away.

"I did come home to see you," Brian said. He set his cup down and took my face in his hands as he kissed me.

I ran a hand through his hair. "You think you can get round me that easy?"

"Come on, that was unfair." He pulled up a stool

close to mine. "You two ganged up on me. It was a trap."

"And you walked straight into it!"

"I guess so. I do want to spend more time with you though. Things are starting to calm down again at work."

"I know," I said.

"Don't look at me like that!"

I was relieved when Linda knocked at the front door.

"Jake's not coming," Linda said as she settled herself in the armchair.

"I know," Sophie said. "He sounded weird when I spoke to him."

Brian sat beside me on the couch and put his arm around me, squeezing my shoulder lightly. I relaxed into him. Staying angry at him was too much effort.

"I'm a bit worried about him." Linda sat and smoothed out her skirt. "He seemed upset the other week, didn't he, Marie?"

"Huh?" I'd only been half listening. "What?"

"When he was saying about his weight problems cropping up again and how it's affecting his relationship with Michael. He seemed really down about it. I thought it would all blow over but he sounded stressed on the phone. And he didn't even say why he couldn't make it."

"He told me he thought he was getting a cold," Sophie said, as she eyed me suspiciously. "I forgot to put sugar in my tea."

"Since when do you have sugar in your tea?" I asked.

"I just feel like it …"

"I'll get it for you." Linda took Sophie's mug and heading for the kitchen.

"Thanks," Sophie called after her, before shuffling along the couch and glaring at Brian. "Go on," she said. "Biscuits or whatever. Go."

He sighed. "You're really annoying."

"Quickly, please!" she snapped.

"Can't you just talk in front of me?" he asked.

"No! Otherwise I wouldn't be trying so hard to get rid of you. Linda will need help anyway. None of us ever have sugar. She won't know where it is."

"Where's the sugar?" Linda's voice drifted in from the kitchen.

"See?" Sophie got up and pulled Brian out of his seat before slipping into it herself.

He gave in and headed for the kitchen.

"What's going on with Jake?" Sophie asked me.

I shrugged. "I don't know."

"You lied to me," she whispered "You said he was fine and never mentioned he'd been complaining about his weight and stuff."

"I just didn't think it was that much of an issue," I said, avoiding eye contact with her.

"You're a terrible liar," she said. "You didn't mention it because you knew it wasn't true. Something else is going on and I want to know what."

"I honestly don't know." I decided it was pointless to try and fool Sophie. "Something is bothering him but he said he can't talk about it. He made up the stuff about his weight so we'd stop asking questions."

"Okay. Don't lie to me again." She moved out of

Brian's place as he and Linda came back in.

"Tea with sugar!" Brian handed her cup back to her.

Sophie smiled sweetly at Linda and Brian, then winced when she took a sip. "It's horrible," she said. "Brian you take this one with the sugar and give me yours …"

He didn't even bother to argue, just handed over his mug and leaned back into the couch. I couldn't help but smile. I had no idea how she managed to be so obnoxious and still have everyone wrapped around her little finger.

Chapter 32

On Friday I was only working a half-day. I was leaving work early for our trip to Scotland. Jake took me by surprise when he wandered into the shop just before lunchtime.

"I don't suppose you've got your lunch break coming up?" he asked.

"Arrgh, Jake!" I grimaced. "It's terrible timing. I'm leaving early today, so I can't take a lunch break."

I felt bad. He looked miserable and it was rare for him to show up at work to see me. Something clearly wasn't right and he had me worried.

"I'm so sorry," I said. "Can I call you later?"

"It's fine." His lips tightened in a thin smile. "I just fancied a chat."

Anne appeared in front of me. "Just go, Marie."

"Oh no, I couldn't." I already felt like I did the least amount of work around the shop and leaving three hours after I arrived seemed bad even for me.

"It's fine," Anne said. "I can hold the fort, and if it gets busy, Greg can come out."

Jake looked at Anne. "I didn't mean to be any trouble."

"You're not." She patted his arm affectionately. "But you look like you need a shoulder to cry on. Go on, Marie."

"I'll have to check with Greg first," I said.

Anne picked up my phone and pressed the button for Greg's office. "Marie's having a family crisis. She needs to take some personal time. It's okay if she leaves now, isn't it?" She paused and rolled her eyes at us. "Of course it's urgent or I wouldn't be asking, would I? Good, I'll tell her." She hung up and turned to me. "Yes, it's fine. Off you go!"

"You're amazing." I pulled my bag out of the drawer. "Thanks so much, Anne."

"Have a great weekend," she said. "I hope everything's okay, Jake."

He smiled and waved at her as we hurried away. "What's wrong?" I asked when Jake linked his arm through mine and ushered me down the street.

"Everything," he said. "It's my day off and Michael is working. I thought I was going to go mad, sitting at home on my own."

"Why?" I asked. "What's going on? Why weren't you at fat club last night?"

"I had an appointment …" He trailed off. "I'm so sorry, I can't tell you about it. Please don't ask."

"Okay." I squeezed his arm. "What can I do?"

"Distract me. Tell me all your problems so I forget about my own."

"I can do that," I said. "But you're definitely not worried about your weight?"

"No, why?"

"So we can go and get burgers for lunch?"

He seemed to perk up at the mention of burgers. "Let's do it!"

I steered him in the direction of the American-themed place and spent the entire lunch telling him anything that popped into my head. I complained about Brian and his job, and talked about how worried I'd been about my friendship with Grace. Then I chatted about my mum, and Jason. I even told him all about Brian's family and how strange it was that Brian was so distant from them.

It almost felt like a therapy session. There was something cathartic about spilling my guts so freely. Jake seemed interested too. I was pleased I'd distracted him effectively.

"Will you be okay?" I asked once we'd paid the bill and were standing back on the street.

"I'll be fine," he said. "I'm picking Callum up from school so he'll keep me occupied until Michael gets home."

"I wish you'd tell me what was going on. Maybe I could help?"

"You have helped." He gave me a big hug. "I wish I could tell you, but I just need to keep it to myself for now, just until everything is a bit clearer. I don't mean to be so secretive."

"It's fine. I'm just worried."

"I'll tell you everything as soon as I can. You better go or you'll be in trouble with Sophie and Linda."

I gave him another hug and then flagged down a passing taxi and gave the driver my address.

At home, I walked straight into Brian. "What are you doing here?" I asked.

"I wanted to see you before you left." He pulled me into the dining room. "Linda and Sophie are already here waiting for you."

"I had lunch with Jake and lost track of time …

Why aren't you at work?"

"I'm working from home this afternoon." He put his hands on my waist and pulled me close to him. "I wanted to catch you before you left."

"Why? What's wrong?" I couldn't really cope with any more problems to deal with.

"Nothing. I just won't see you all weekend."

"It won't be much different to any other weekend," I said.

Sophie shouted from the living room, asking me if I was ready.

"Just a minute," I called back. "Sorry," I said to Brian. "I didn't really mean it to come out like that."

He didn't say anything but he felt tense as he pulled me in for hug. "How about I take a weekend off and we go away somewhere?"

"That sounds great." I planted a kiss on his lips. There was a slightly awkward moment. Because I didn't actually believe he would take a weekend off, and I had the distinct feeling that he could read that in my face.

"I better go." I put my arms around his neck. "Are you okay?"

"Yes." He pulled me closer and touched his forehead to mine. "I'll see you on Sunday."

"Come on, Marie. We'll miss the train if you don't hurry up." I turned to Sophie and was surprised to see Linda's husband George with them too.

"George is going to drive us to the station instead of getting a taxi," Linda said. "He wanted to see me off."

"Come on," Sophie said impatiently.

"I'm ready!" I moved to pick up my bag from the hallway and gave Brian another kiss before I followed them out of the door.

Chapter 33

We'd decided on getting the train to Scotland as Linda wasn't keen on driving so far. Linda and I had brought books for the journey but that turned out to be slightly optimistic. Sophie didn't stop talking long enough for us to concentrate. After reading the same page about seven times, I gave up and shoved the book back in my bag.

We took it in turns to fetch coffees and snacks and the time whizzed by. Linda told us tales of the school kids and her new friends at work. She was obviously really happy in her new job and it seemed to have been a great confidence boost for her.

The sun streamed in the window of our train carriage and I felt myself relax in the company of my friends. I smiled as we finally pulled into the station and saw Julie waiting for us on the platform.

"Abby didn't come with you?" I asked as I embraced Julie.

"No! It was a big drama." She turned to greet Linda and Sophie. "I told her she had to stay at home and get all her homework done so she has the rest of the weekend free. But apparently that makes me the worst mother in the world. Hopefully she'll be talking to me again by the time we get back."

We followed Julie to her car and drove out of town and away from civilisation. The scenery was beautiful; a rugged green landscape of rolling fields broken by dry stone walls. We meandered through the countryside, passing various small towns and villages until we drove over a small bridge and up a hill into a tiny village that Julie declared to be theirs. At the other side of the village, we turned up a narrow lane and eventually into the driveway of a picturesque house with a smoking chimney. A dog ambled out of the way as Julie pulled up. Abby appeared at the front door.

She bounded over to give me a big hug as soon as I was out of the car and then turned to greet Sophie and Linda. People who were constantly cheerful usually drove me crazy but Abby was so adorable. I could just sit and watch her bounce around all day. She even managed to make Sophie look calm which was some feat.

"Come on in! Dad's going out for the evening and Mum's got wine in the fridge for you!" She grinned at Julie. Clearly all was forgiven.

Paul appeared in the doorway. "Come in. Thank goodness you're here. I thought Abby was going to explode!"

I introduced him to Linda and Sophie before he excused himself, saying he was going out to meet a friend and leave us to a girls' night. Julie led us through to the kitchen. It was surprisingly old fashioned with a huge, cast-iron stove in the corner. Linda's eyes went wide at the size of it and she moved over to hover beside it as though she'd made a new friend.

Abby sidled over and leaned against me for a moment before her next wave of excitement hit her.

"Shall I show you your rooms? I can give you a tour of the house!"

"Abby!" Julie gave her a look. "Calm down and let them catch their breath. Maybe they want a drink or something to eat before you start dragging them around the place? Tea, coffee? Or I've got wine chilled and ready to go …"

"Just a tea for now thanks." I ignored the goblin in my head that was screaming for wine. I wanted to try and look respectable in front of my future in-laws at least for five minutes.

"She's being polite. She really wants wine." My goblin had apparently jumped into Sophie's head and made her speak for him. I tilted my head and gave her a look.

"It's true," Linda agreed. "She'd love wine!"

"Hey! Just because you two are a pair of alcoholics … don't drag me into it."

"Okay then," Sophie said. "A cup of tea for Marie. I'll take a wine, please."

"Ooh, I'll have wine too," Linda said.

Julie looked at me. "Tea?"

I sighed. "If everyone else is having wine, I won't put you to the trouble of making tea. Not just for me. I'm not a big drinker though usually … am I?" I glared at Linda and Sophie with my best serious face.

"Ooh, no. Hardly ever drinks." Linda played along with a cheeky smile.

"No, not much at all really," Sophie said. "At the weekend she has a very strict limit. What is it these days? A couple of bottles of wine and four shots of tequila?"

"Is that all?" Julie laughed as she handed me a glass. "You're on holiday now though, so all limits are out of the window."

"I was trying to make a good impression," I said.

Julie clinked her glass against mine. "You already did."

When we finished our wine, Abby gave us a tour of the house while Julie got dinner ready.

We sat around the beautiful, solid oak table in the kitchen to eat and chatted easily. Sophie, Linda and I broke into huge grins when Julie asked how we knew each other.

It occurred to me that this was probably not quite what Julie had been expecting in my friends. She was probably expecting old school friends and was likely intrigued by my random group of friends.

"Seems like there's a story there?" she said.

"Tell us!" Abby demanded, cradling her lemonade and grinning away.

"We met at … a club … for people with weight issues," Linda began.

Sophie grinned. "Fat club!"

"What?" Julie's eyes darted around us.

"It was called 'Emily's Encouragement'." I smiled at the memory. "Emily sort of encouraged people to lose weight. People would sit and talk about food and discuss how they were trying to lose weight."

"And there was meditation," Sophie said quickly. "Don't forget that. That's really the key to the weight loss if you ask me!"

"Did you all used to be fat?" Abby asked cautiously.

"No." I laughed. "None of us were. I was going

speed dating and was sent into the wrong room."

"She sat at fat club for ages before she realised she was in the wrong place." Sophie roared with laughter. "I don't know what she thought speed dating would be like! Anyway she got in a huge argument with the lady running it and when she stormed out, we followed her."

"They've turned up at my house every Thursday evening since, and I don't know what to do about it."

"It sounds like a restraining order might be an idea," Julie suggested.

"You might be right!"

"No. She may pretend she's too cool for us." Sophie tried to look serious. "But she secretly loves us."

I grinned and took a sip of my wine.

"How did you meet Brian?" Abby asked.

I took a deep breath and looked to the ceiling as I pondered how to answer that one.

"If she didn't sound crazy already, she will now!" Sophie said.

I shook my head and sighed. "I was late to meet friends for drinks and I ended up hitching a ride on the back of his bike." I lowered my eyes at my somewhat embarrassing story.

"A bicycle?" Julie stared at me and I nodded in response. She raised her eyebrows. "Brian rides a bike?"

"Nope! Just that once."

"That's not even the whole story," Linda said. "They may never have met again after that …" She looked to me to continue the story.

"What happened?" Abby asked.

"It turns out that he was a friend of my best friend, Grace, and he turned up at her place that night because he'd lost his keys. I was staying at her place …"

"And Marie called the police on him!" Sophie said, quickly.

"I did. I thought he was a stalker. I'm still not sure to be honest!"

Abby leaned forward, resting her elbows on the table. "And then you just fell in love?"

"Not really, no. I didn't like him for a while."

"I can understand that," Abby said. We all laughed as Julie's eyes bored into her. "What? He's annoying!"

I smiled at the memories. "He started turning up on Thursday evenings for our little fat club meetings."

"A sure sign that he liked her," Linda added.

"We got to know each other better," I said. "And he surprised me with a weekend in New York for Grace's engagement party." I smiled at the memory. "And *then* we fell in love."

"Well, she missed out a load of drama," Sophie said. "But, yeah, eventually they got together and they've been annoyingly happy ever since."

As I laughed, I realised I was feeling a bit flushed. Julie had been topping up our wine glasses as we sat and told stories and I was suddenly feeling tipsy. I was glad everyone was so relaxed and the atmosphere was so light. I'd been slightly nervous about how the weekend would turn out but at that moment my fears evaporated into a hazy alcohol-fuelled glow.

"Can we go shopping for your wedding dress tomorrow?" Abby asked excitedly.

It had sounded fun when we'd spoken of it previously but it seemed like a silly idea now that we were no closer to making any wedding plans.

"I don't know if we're even going to get married," I said idly and was immediately met with a lot of worried looks. "I don't mean that we're going to split up or anything. It's just that we never even talk about the wedding anymore. We always seem to be too busy with other things. At least Brian's always too busy and I don't want to plan it on my own."

"We can help you plan it," Abby said.

"Thanks. But I guess I want Brian to be a bit more interested."

"He's a man," Julie said. "It's normal that he's not volunteering to help with wedding planning. You just have to tell him what's happening."

"I already said you should take control and tell Brian what you want," Sophie said. "Let's try on dresses and then maybe you'll be more motivated to make plans."

"And it'll be fun!" Abby said, looking at me with big eyes.

"Okay," I agreed. I was feeling a bit tipsy and emotional and suddenly felt the need to talk to Brian. Leaving them to chat, I headed up to the bedroom to call him.

"I'm going to buy a wedding dress tomorrow," I said, frowning into the phone.

"Great." He sounded hesitant, as though he was worried about saying the wrong thing.

"And then we need to plan the wedding," I said.

"Okay."

"And you need to take an interest in it." I could hear just how passive aggressive I sounded.

"I *am* interested," he replied.

"It doesn't seem like it. You never mention the wedding unless I bring it up and you never make any suggestions. You just wait for me to make all the decisions."

"I didn't know that's how you felt," he said. "I can help. We can plan the wedding."

"Good."

"Just find a dress tomorrow and then we'll figure out the rest."

"Okay." I sniffed.

"Are you all right?"

"Yeah. I guess so." I wished he was there to give me one of his big hugs.

"Just have a fun weekend, okay?"

"I miss you," I said.

"Miss you, too."

I sat on the bed for a minute after we'd hung up. I felt a bit pathetic and decided I probably shouldn't drink anymore wine.

Chapter 34

When I woke Sophie was gently snoring in the twin bed beside mine. The sun streamed in through a gap in the curtains and I pulled them aside to look out at the garden and the rolling hills beyond.

The dog was lying near the backdoor and seemed to sense me looking at him. He stood and began barking loudly. I took a step back and he quietened, settling back into his spot beside the door.

Sophie stirred and pulled herself up to sitting. "I might have had too much wine."

"Me too," I said. "It was fun though."

"Yeah. They're really nice." She rubbed her eyes and yawned. "What's the plan for today?"

"Shopping I think."

"Oh," she said flatly. "The wedding dress."

"Don't sound too enthusiastic, will you?"

"I'm not going to be enthusiastic about much until I get some coffee in me."

We took it in turns to shower and then headed downstairs together.

Linda was sitting in the kitchen. An array of breakfast foods lay on the table in front of her.

"Julie and Abby have gone to the stables to feed the horse," Linda said. "They said they won't be long."

We helped ourselves to coffee and toast. I stood

up when Paul walked through the backdoor with the dog by his side.

"Hello!" I bent to stroke the beautiful chocolate Labrador who sniffed me and wagged his tail.

"That's Clark," Paul said, rubbing him affectionately behind the ear. "Abby was obsessed with Superman when we got him and Clark was a compromise. I refused to wander the hills calling for Superman!"

"It's a great name." I smiled and patted the dog. "You're a good boy aren't you, Clark? Yes you are? You're gorgeous!" He wagged his tail excitedly and rolled on the floor for me to rub his belly. "Yes you're a good dog," I said with a silly, singsong voice. "Such a good doggy."

I looked up to find Linda and Sophie smirking. I smiled at them and moved away from Clark to pick up my coffee.

"What?" I laughed. "He's a nice dog! Aww, look at him …" He regarded me with big eyes and when I patted my thigh he came over to me. "You are a good doggy, aren't you?" I ignored Linda and Sophie and went back to my baby voice. "You're the best!" I knelt down and he licked my face before lying down for more tummy rubbing.

"Someone's made a new friend," Paul said.

We moved into the living room and I was playing on the carpet with Clark when Julie came in and shouted at him.

"He's not allowed on the carpet," she said. "And he knows it!" He looked at me with his big eyes and I jumped to his defence.

"It was my fault. I kept playing with him."

"He already has Paul and Abby spoiling him. It's always me that's the bad guy… Go on, Clark. Out!"

He wandered past her with his head down and I looked sheepish as I apologised. Julie shook her head and sighed with a smile.

"Who's ready for some shopping?" she asked.

"Me!" Abby answered excitedly and beamed at me. "I can't wait to see you in a wedding dress."

We moved to get ready and all crammed into Julie's car ten minutes later.

***

"I love it." I sashayed around the shop, swinging my hips to make the bottom of the dress swing like a church bell. It had a fitted bodice with intricate lace detail. The full skirt billowed from my waist. "This is it."

Linda tilted her head to one side and smiled contentedly. "It is beautiful."

"This isn't how it works," Julie said. "You can't try on one dress and decide that's the one you want. This is supposed to be a half-day event at least."

"I love it though." I swayed from side to side in front of the mirror. Abby stood behind me, looking up at me with her goofy smile.

"You should try some more on," Linda said.

"Okay. This is the dress though." I winked at Abby and she let out her awkward laugh that she seemed to have absolutely no control over. It was always followed by a blush.

"Can I try a wedding dress on?" Sophie asked. "Just so I can send Jeff a photo and freak him out?"

"No," I said. "You torture him enough. Let him enjoy his weekend off!"

"Hey! He'll have no idea what to do without me around to organise him."

"I'm sure he'll manage," I said. "You could try on bridesmaids' dresses if you want."

"What colour do you want me in?" she asked as she surveyed the rail of dresses.

"Baby pink."

She turned her nose up. "Are you serious?"

"No," I replied. "Whatever colour you want."

"I thought you were supposed to make me look ridiculous to make you look good?"

"I look good enough!" I said, still admiring my reflection in the mirror.

"I quite like this navy one," she said, holding it up.

"Try it," I said, before turning to look at Abby. "What about you? Any preference?"

She stared back at me without a word.

"You will be a bridesmaid, won't you?" I asked and then watched her eyes widen.

"Really?" She clapped her hands together and squealed.

"Don't hug me in the dress." I waved her away as she moved towards me. "Go and find yourself one!"

She moved over to Sophie who high-fived her. I caught Julie's eye in the mirror and returned her smile.

"Come on then, Linda," I said. "Choose some more dresses for me to try on."

I dutifully tried on a few more dresses and was on cloud nine as I watched Sophie and Abby look for dresses. It was much more fun than I'd expected. I think the experience of shopping with Grace still lingered in my mind. I was enjoying every moment with my little gang though. I should probably have been more aware of the absence of my best friend but it was only when my phone rang and Grace's name flashed up on the display that I thought about her at all.

"Hi!" I smiled into the phone.

"Hey." She sounded breathless. "I tried to get you at home but Brian said you're wedding dress shopping in Scotland?"

"Yeah. It was a bit of a random last-minute thing," I said, defensively. "Brian's stepmum and sister invited me up for a girls' weekend and we just thought it would be fun to look around some bridal shops."

"And Linda and Sophie are with you too?" Her voice was clipped.

"Yeah. It's funny, I was just thinking about you when you rang." That was a complete lie. "I wish you were here too!"

"You're not actually going to buy your dress this weekend though, are you? I thought we would go shopping together. I am your bridesmaid after all …"

"I was just having a look around. I wasn't sure when you'd be able to make it over again so … I just didn't know."

"You shouldn't buy your dress before you have a date anyway. Knowing you, you'll only change your mind nearer the time."

I looked up at the beautiful dress hanging on the

back of the changing room door and was suddenly annoyed at Grace for ruining my good mood. I had a head full of things I wanted to say to her. Like how I definitely wouldn't change my mind, and how I didn't want to have to wait for her to be here before I went shopping. If she was missing out it was her own fault and I wasn't going to plan my wedding around her schedule.

"Yeah you might be right," I said weakly. "It's really a shame you're not here."

"How are you getting on with the evil step family?" she asked.

"Oh, they're not evil at all." I lowered my voice as I moved away from them. "I don't know why Brian let us think that. They're amazing. Abby is going to be a bridesmaid too." I smiled at Julie as I spoke about them.

"Really? But you hardly know her. You're so impulsive, Marie."

I took a deep breath as I debated telling her to stop being so negative, and that *she* was the one who I might end up regretting having in the wedding party. I didn't understand why she couldn't just be happy for me.

"It'll be fine, Grace. Stop worrying so much."

"Someone has to worry, Marie. The 'it'll be fine' attitude to life won't always work out you know."

"I have to go." I moved my phone from my ear to look at the display. "Brian's calling me. This will be costing you a fortune anyway."

"It's fine, I'm calling from the office, but I better get on as well."

"You're in the office on a Saturday? And isn't it

like six o'clock in the morning over there?"

"Just picking up some documents I forgot. I have to read them before Monday. I'll talk to you soon."

I pressed a button on my phone to switch to Brian's call. "You just saved me from Grace," I said.

"Sorry! I was calling to warn you. I might have put my foot in it. She was not a happy bunny when I got off the phone to her."

"And she's still not a happy bunny now," I said. "Anyway, I found a dress! But don't tell Grace."

"Well that's good … maybe we will actually get married sometime!"

"Oh, we might manage it!"

"How's everyone getting on?"

"Brilliantly. We're having a great time. It's just Grace trying to put a damper on things for me."

"She'll get over it. She's just jealous."

"Of me?" I laughed. "That'll be the day."

"You're the girl who's got it all those days, you know?"

"Well I'm not sure Grace thinks so. She still thinks I can't manage without her holding my hand for every decision in my life."

"It'll all be fine," he said.

"That's what I keep saying! I need to get back to my shopping." I promised to call him later before ending the call.

Sophie did a twirl in a pale blue dress. "What do you think?"

"I liked the navy one better."

"Me too," she agreed. "I'm going to try it on again."

She reappeared a few minutes later in the

beautiful satin evening gown. It was strapless with a smattering of sequins along the bust. Abby had found a white dress with big navy blue flowers covering it. It had a blue sash around the waist, which tied and hung down the back. It suited her personality and looked really cute.

"I might need you both in pink," I said with a grin. "Everyone's going to be looking at you!"

I made a sudden decision and turned to the sales woman. "Do you have another dress like this in a size ten?" I asked, indicating Sophie's dress. "I have another bridesmaid who can't be here today."

Chapter 35

Julie arranged to pick the dresses up later and the five of us squeezed into the car to spend the day exploring the surrounding area. We had a nice walk around some castle ruins and stopped off for lunch in a quaint country pub. Julie showed us round the nearby towns and villages and pointed out all the places of interest.

"This is our local pub," she said, as we drove back through their little village late in the afternoon. There was the pub and a post office, and a few houses lining what seemed to be the main street.

"We're lucky," Julie said. "The pub does excellent food and it's always a good atmosphere in there. We can have a walk down and get a drink later if you want."

We uttered our approval as Julie drove out the other side of the village.

"I need to take Abby up to the stables to feed Jasper, but I can drop you at the house if you want to chill out for a bit?"

"No, come with us." Abby's eyes pleaded with me. "I want to show you Jasper."

"I'll come." I couldn't resist her big brown eyes.

"You really don't have to," Julie said.

"It's fine, I want to."

Linda and Sophie agreed they wanted to come too.

It wasn't quite the grand stables I was expecting. Definitely not what I'd envisioned when I learned that Abby had a pony. I'd thought it would be some sort of fancy pony club where posh people came to show off. It couldn't have been farther from it.

A few basic stables stood next to a little cottage. Instead of the neat, pebbled paths I'd expected, there were just muddy tracks. At the back of the stables was a field surrounded by a stone wall. Beyond that were a lot of green rolling hills.

Julie parked in front of the cottage. An old guy pushing a wheelbarrow stopped to wave, before disappearing around the side of the house.

"Come on," Abby said as we all piled out of the car. "Follow me!"

She tramped over the uneven, muddy ground towards the stables and we followed behind her.

"Can I have a quick ride?" Abby gave her mum the big eyes until she relented.

"Just a quick one," Julie said. "We don't want to be hanging around the stables for hours on end. Besides, I'm getting peckish."

As Abby began to brush and saddle Jasper, Julie directed us outside and showed us to a crumbly old picnic bench standing under a big old oak tree.

"I've spent far too much time on this bench," Julie said as we waited for Abby and Jasper.

"It's not a bad place to be though," Linda said.

We looked out over the fields with the late afternoon sun making everything glow. She was right; it wasn't a bad spot at all.

"That's true," Julie murmured, "and I love to watch her ride. She's so happy when she's riding."

"Is she ever not happy?" I asked, just as Abby appeared on Jasper. She rode him out of the back of the stables and into the fields.

"She has her moments," Julie said. "And I guess things are about to get worse as she hits her teenage years."

We spent a nice half hour chatting on the old picnic bench while we watched Abby move around the field on Jasper. It was quite hypnotic watching her: the rhythmic movements and the pure joy on her face as she rode.

As the sun went down we got back into the car and drove to the house. Julie decided she didn't want to cook so we had a walk into the village and ate at the pub. Paul met us there and ate with us, before taking Abby back home. We stayed for a few more drinks and then started the walk up the hill.

"It's really lovely having you here," Julie said as we dropped back and let Sophie and Linda lead the way up the winding road to the house. "I'm glad you came."

"I'm having a great time. Thanks for inviting us."

"I like your friends," she said once Sophie and Linda were far enough ahead of us.

"Not what you were expecting, I bet?"

"No, not at all. They're really lovely though." She paused. "Hopefully you can get Brian to come up sometime."

"I can try." My alcohol levels had just about reached the point where I felt I could ask a few questions. "I take it he's not been up here much?"

"No." She paused again. "It's been a difficult relationship. I'm not sure what he's told you …"

"Nothing really. He doesn't speak about you. He never says anything bad, he just doesn't say anything. I knew you existed but that was about it. I expected you to be horrible if I'm honest."

"That sounds about right. I tried really hard at first to get him to like me, but he just wasn't interested and the more I tried to force it, the more he seemed to hate me. Eventually I gave up."

I nodded under the dim glow of the streetlights, unsure of what to say.

"It was frustrating," she said. "I really wanted to help him. He was always angry but also really sad and vulnerable. He never wanted anything to do with me. When Abby came along, things got worse for a while. Then we just settled into a routine. The few times he visited, he spent time with Paul while politely ignoring Abby and me."

"It doesn't sound like my Brian."

"No." I heard the smile in her voice. "He's different with you. I see that. I guess he's different with everyone else. He blamed me, I think, for his dad moving away. I guess he never really got over it."

"Things will change," I said.

"I won't hold my breath." Julie sighed. "Although I was surprised you managed to get him to spend time alone with us on our last visit."

"I only suggested it. He agreed straight away."

"Hurry up, you two!" Sophie shouted at us. I could make out her silhouette in front of the porch light. We moved a bit quicker and were greeted by Sophie grumbling as usual.

"I'm freezing. I don't think you could've walked

any slower if you'd tried."

Linda shivered on the doorstep as Julie moved between them. "The door's open you know. You could've gone in."

"Linda!" Sophie said. "Why didn't you try the door?"

"Oh Sophie!" Linda tutted. "Shut up and go to bed, will you?"

Sophie headed for the stairs. "I will actually. Goodnight."

"I'm going up too," Linda said.

I went into the kitchen to get a glass of water and jumped when I saw Paul sitting at the table.

"Did you have a nice evening?" he asked.

"Yes, it was good thanks."

"Not too wild for you in our little pub?"

I bent to stroke Clark who was lying by Paul's feet. "It was good enough!"

"How's Brian?" Paul asked.

I wasn't sure if he was asking if he was okay at home alone for the weekend or if the question ran deeper. "He's good," I said. "Working hard no doubt. At least he can work all weekend with no complaints for once."

"He's done well at his job," Paul said. "You're right though, he probably works too much. I was always the same."

"I need to convince him to come up here with me one weekend. It's such a beautiful place."

"He doesn't visit much. I'd like him to come up more."

I moved from Clark and got myself a glass of water.

"I'm glad he met you," Paul said. "He seems happier now. And you've got a big fan in Abby. She adores you."

"She's great." I moved toward the door, yawning. "I'm glad I finally met her. And Julie. I'm having a great weekend. Oh, and I got a wedding dress."

"Abby told me all about it." He grinned. "She said you look amazing in it."

I smiled shyly and was about to move to go to bed when he called me back. "Thanks for asking Abby to be a bridesmaid," he said. "It means a lot to her."

"You're welcome," I said quietly before heading upstairs.

Chapter 36

It was mid-morning by the time I managed to drag myself out of bed. The house was quiet as I showered and got dressed in jeans and a jumper. Sophie was still sleeping when I went in search of breakfast.

"Brian!" I felt the smile spread over my face when I saw him peering into his laptop at the kitchen table. He jumped up and closed the computer as though he'd been caught out.

"What are you doing here?" I wrapped my arms around his waist and nestled my head under his chin. I lingered there and felt tears spring to my eyes. It was as though I'd not seen him for a month.

"I missed you. I thought I'd come and drive you home." He pulled out of the embrace and looked at me intently. "Let's go for a walk …"

"I need coffee." I groaned.

He handed me his cup of lukewarm coffee and ushered me towards the door once I'd taken a few gulps.

I slipped into my trainers and pulled on a random fleece that was hanging on a hook on the back door.

"You've made yourself at home," Brian remarked.

"I feel really at home here," I said as we stepped out into the fresh air to be greeted by Clark. "Hello, my gorgeous boy!" I bent down to him. "How's my best boy? You're such a good doggy! You are. Yes you are! You're the best dog in the whole world!"

"I see I've got some competition for your affections?" Brian said, amused.

He led the way down the garden and through a gap in the hedge into the field beyond. He whistled for Clark who wagged his tail and bounded ahead of us. We ascended the hill in silence and kept a good pace as we marched down the other side. After walking through a patch of trees we were faced with another hill.

"Do you know your way around here?" I asked breathlessly.

"I know there's a bench at the top of this hill."

"That's all I need to know," I said.

When we made it up the hill, I slumped onto the bench and took in the view across the valley. "How can fields and trees and a few houses be so breathtaking?"

"It's pretty amazing, isn't it?"

I turned to look behind us and only then noticed the little church. It was just a little further over the hill, at the end of a dirt track. "Wow." I stood and walked towards it. "This place is beautiful."

Standing in front of the wooden doors I looked up at the stunning little building. It looked ancient and solid and perfect.

"Do you think they do weddings?" I blurted out.

"I happen to know that they do." Brian stood beside me, staring up at the place. "Dad and Julie got married here."

"Wow. I bet it was amazing."

"I don't know," he said quietly as he walked

around the side of the church. "I didn't go."

I trailed behind him. "You didn't go to your dad's wedding?"

"No."

"Why not?"

"I was pissed off," he said flatly. "Although that wasn't my official excuse."

We wandered around the church looking up at the stained glass windows. I didn't say anything until we were seated on the bench again.

"Is it a major problem that I really like Julie and Abby?"

"No." He laughed. "I knew you'd like them. They're nice."

"I asked Abby to be a bridesmaid."

"She told me."

I nodded slowly. "You should be nicer to her."

"I am nice to her," he snapped.

"No, you're polite to her. There's a huge difference. I don't understand why you don't want anything to do with them. It would be much easier if you made a bit of effort. They're your family, whether you like it or not."

He stared out across the valley. "I know."

"You're supposed to be the rational one in this relationship, remember?"

"I've never managed to be rational when it comes to them." He inhaled a deep breath. "But in my defence, I was a messed up teenager who lost his mum and then my dad ran off and got a new family and left me alone. It pissed me off quite a lot."

I opened my mouth to speak but he cut me off. "I know that's not really how it was, but that's how it felt."

"And you never forgave him?" I asked.

"Yes, I did. But by then I'd spent so long ignoring Julie and Abby – to get back at him – that it felt too hard to change things. Things just seemed to settle as they were. Everyone expected me to be indifferent so it seemed easier to carry on as things were."

I leaned into him. "Well, that's a bit sad."

"Yes. I suppose it is." He turned to look at the church again.

"I'd like to marry you there," I said. I'd known as soon as I saw the place. It looked so quaint and idyllic, and I loved the fact that it was close to Paul and Julie's house. I felt connected to it.

"I thought you might say that."

"Really?"

"Yeah."

"That's why you brought me up here?"

"Yeah." He gazed at the church. "It's pretty. I knew you'd fall in love with it, just like I knew you'd love Julie and Abby."

"You're a bit of a know-it-all, aren't you?"

"Yes." He grinned at me. "And you're causing a lot of confusion in my life. How am I supposed to tell Dad and Julie that we want to get married in the church where I bailed on their wedding? It's slightly awkward."

"It'll all be fine! Don't worry about it."

"We're definitely not going to Mauritius then?" Brian said.

"Obviously, I'll have to check out the reviews, but I think this is the place." I snuggled into him, looking quietly out at the view for a few more minutes.

"Do you have to do some work today?" I asked as we walked back toward the house along the dirt track. "You brought your laptop …"

He squeezed my hand. "Is that your subtle way of bringing up the subject of me working too much?"

"I worry about you," I said. "And I don't have a problem if you want to work long hours. I understand you want to do well and get ahead. If I thought you were happy, I wouldn't say anything. But it doesn't seem like it's making you happy."

"I just feel like I'm being pulled in all directions and I barely have time to sleep."

"Exactly," I said. "It's not healthy. Work hard, if that's what you want, but you need to figure out how to get some balance. You need to have a life outside of work and I would really like it if you'd find more time for me. Time when you're not thinking about work."

"I know," he said wearily.

I decided to change the subject. "Has Sophie been scheming with you about the wedding?" I asked.

"No, why?"

"I just thought maybe she'd been encouraging you to help me make plans. She's up to something, I'm just not sure what."

"I've no idea. I've given up on trying to keep track of Sophie and her crazy ideas."

We wandered back down the dirt track with the sun on our faces. Clark ran happily in and out of the fields at either side of us, coming back regularly to check on us before bounding off again.

When we arrived back at the house Julie was cooking a big brunch for us all. My mouth started watering as soon as I stepped into the house and the smell of bacon hit my nostrils. I was starving.

"We went for a walk up to the little chapel on the hill," I told Julie as I took a bite of my bacon sandwich. "Brian said you got married there. It's beautiful."

"Yeah I love it up there. I often wander up with Clark."

"Is the church still in use?" I asked hopefully.

"Just for weddings. They stopped using it for regular church services years back. The road up there is a nightmare. It's only single track and it becomes a river in the rain. They couldn't afford to re-do the road so they transferred the church services down to the village hall and just use the chapel for weddings." She paused before smiling at me. "Why are you so interested?"

"Do you think we could get married up there?" I was suddenly so excited, I felt like jumping up and down. I knew that was where we would get married and I couldn't wait.

"Yeah," she answered far too hesitantly. "It's really bad timing though. They're about to start renovating it; it needs a new roof. I don't know when it will be open again and it's usually booked up quite far in advance. I can call and ask but don't get your hopes up for it being available anytime soon."

Chapter 37

I don't know why it upset me so much when Julie told me that the church wouldn't be available anytime soon. They currently weren't taking any wedding bookings as they weren't sure how long the renovations would take. Brian was right; I'd fallen in love with the place and was really deflated. We'd all driven home together on Sunday afternoon and I barely spoke the whole journey. I smiled and nodded along with Linda and Sophie as they chatted, but my mind was elsewhere.

"We'll find somewhere else," Brian said, trying to console me once we were alone that evening. I'd nodded my agreement and carried on as though everything was fine.

On Monday morning, I told Anne about it. She looked suitably devastated as she perched on my desk. "That's terrible."

For once I was happy about her being slightly dramatic about everything. Most people wouldn't understand my feelings about losing out on a wedding venue that I'd only seen once and from the outside, but it had really got me down. I even started to see why Grace was so upset about having to wait another year for her wedding. Sometimes you just get your heart set on something.

"It's annoying." I frowned at Anne. "That's life

261

though isn't it?"

"You'll just have to wait, won't you?" she said. "If that's the place then that's the place. How long can it take to renovate a little church anyway?"

"I don't know. It just seemed like it wasn't an option."

"And you're going to give up that easily?" She tutted as she moved away from my desk. "Sometimes in life you have to fight for what you want."

"That was like a motivational speech, Anne," I said after a pause.

"Did it work?" she asked with a grin.

"Maybe," I said. "I guess it can't hurt to ask again."

"Make a nuisance of yourself! Find out who you need to annoy and annoy them until they agree to put you top of the waiting list just to shut you up. And if you can't manage that, then give me their number and I will annoy them on your behalf."

I smiled at her before turning to get on with some work. She'd managed to cheer me up and I was feeling slightly more positive.

The day went quickly and I was dancing away in the kitchen when Brian got home. It was the only way I could cook; with the radio blaring and having a sing and a dance as I went.

He laughed at me. "You seem cheerful."

"I am," I said. "I had an idea about the wedding."

"You do still want to get married at my dad's place, don't you?" He snaked his arms around my waist. "Because I've been annoying Julie on the phone all afternoon trying to figure something out."

"Really?" I beamed at him. "I was going to say we should still get married there. Even if it means waiting a while. I don't mind."

"Julie spoke to a few people this afternoon and there was a suggestion that maybe they could let us have the wedding before they start the renovations … The place wouldn't be perfect and if it rains the roof might drip a bit but I said you probably wouldn't mind that?"

"No, I don't care!"

"The only trouble is, it could be quite short notice. They're trying to get the builders to confirm when the work will start. Julie thought about six weeks ..."

I grinned. "Really?"

"Don't get too excited yet," he warned. "Julie's still trying to talk to the right people and see if it could work out. She'll call when she knows more."

The week went so slowly. Julie called to say they were having problems tying the building company down to a start date for the work.

On Thursday evening I was intent on spending fat club complaining about it all, but predictably my friends had other plans.

"I'm going to win the nailympics!" Sophie told us excitedly before I could get a word in. "I've been practising and I'm really good. I've decided I can win it. It's all about attitude, isn't it?"

"I guess so." I was fairly sure it was about talent but I didn't like to say so. I knew better than to contradict Sophie.

"Jake said he was definitely coming?" I asked Linda.

"Yes, he just said he'd be a bit late."

I was slouched on the couch and pulled Brian's arm around me. "Did he sound okay on the phone?"

Linda sipped at her tea. "Yes, I think so."

"Did he sound stressed?" I asked.

"I don't think so. He just said he'd be a bit late but would see us later."

"Did he say how late?"

"Who cares how late?" Sophie asked. "I was talking about the nailympics and you rudely interrupted me."

"No I didn't," I said. "You'd stopped talking."

Brian sighed. "I see it's going to be one of those nights."

"What's that supposed to mean?" Sophie shot at him.

He ignored her and kissed the side of my head.

I smiled sweetly. "I'm very sorry I interrupted you, Sophie, please tell us more about the nailympics. I'm dying to hear …" I did nothing to hide the sarcasm and I braced for an argument with Sophie.

Brian jumped up at the sound of the doorknocker.

We sat in silence and I focussed on my tea to avoid looking at Sophie who was glaring at me.

"Michael's here too," Sophie said as the voices drifted through.

"That's weird." I turned towards the door and caught sight of Jake. I searched his face but couldn't read his expression. We waited as he moved over and stood in front of the TV. Michael wandered in and greeted us cheerfully.

"Michael!" Jake said impatiently, beckoning him

over to stand next to him and clutching his hand.

"What's going on?" Brian asked as he cuddled up next to me again.

Jake glanced at Michael.

"Just tell them!" Michael said, grinning.

There was another pause and Jake looked like he was about to burst. "We're going to have a baby!" he squealed.

There was a stunned silence before I sat up and shuffled forward on the couch.

"What?" I looked at Jake as I tried to digest the information.

"We've been approved by the adoption agency. We're on the waiting list for a baby." His face crumpled and he dissolved into tears.

"Oh my God." I covered my face as I started to cry too. "You had me so worried." I got up and slapped Jake on the arm before giving him a big hug. I sniffed as I looked up. "Congratulations!" I moved to hug Michael as Linda and Sophie excitedly went to hug Jake.

"You're not supposed to cry," Michael said, laughing at me.

"They're happy tears." I took a tissue from Linda and wiped my eyes.

"Then you need a happy face," he said.

"I need alcohol," I replied.

Michael beamed and headed to the kitchen. "I've got champagne."

Brian wrapped his arms around me and I tried to get the tears under control.

"Are you okay?" Linda asked and I felt her hand on my arm.

"Yes." I looked over at Jake who was looking really concerned by my outburst. "I thought you were ill or something."

I felt Sophie put her arms around me and when I looked up, Jake and Linda had joined the little group hug too.

"Sorry," Jake said. "I just wanted to keep it a secret until we knew for definite. I was so scared we wouldn't get approved."

I laughed. "I'm so happy. I can't believe you're going to have a baby!"

"I can't believe it either," Jake said, beaming.

"What have I told you about getting too excited?" Michael said to Jake as he returned with a tray of champagne glasses. "We might have a long wait."

"I know." Jake took a glass of bubbly. "But it's just so amazing!"

"I'm so happy for you," Linda said.

Jake looked at Sophie. "You're quiet. Don't tell me I've managed to leave you speechless again?"

She'd been similarly lost for words when Jake had announced that he was interested in men and not women. Sophie had a smirk on her face as she took a sip of champagne.

"I saw this coming a mile off," she said with a sly smile. "I don't know why nobody else guessed. I think you're all a bit slow."

"You had no idea!" Brian said.

She laughed and raised her glass. "To the best daddies any baby could wish for!"

Chapter 38

By the time the weekend came around I was emotionally drained. I was lazing on the couch with Brian on Saturday when the home phone rang.

"Let's just ignore it." I was sure it wouldn't be good news.

"Good plan," Brian agreed. Although I doubt it had occurred to him to answer it anyway. He was sprawled out across the couch with his feet in my lap.

My mobile started to buzz around the coffee table almost as soon as the landline stopped ringing.

"It's Julie." I raised my eyebrows as I answered the phone.

"Marie." Julie sounded breathless. "I'm sorry it's taken so long to get back to you."

"Don't worry." I slumped back on the couch. "Thanks for trying."

"Hang on. I haven't said anything yet!"

Brian stared at me as I sat upright. My heart started to race at the thought of getting married in the stunning little chapel. I smiled nervously at Brian who was eyeing me questioningly.

"It could work with the church," Julie said slowly.

"But?"

"Well they're going to start the renovations soon."

"How soon?"

She paused. "The wedding would have to be next week."

I sighed and let out a short laugh. I'd very nearly let myself get excited.

"But you could definitely organise a wedding in a week," Julie said. "I could help you."

"You could at least try to sound convincing, Julie!"

"I already spoke to the vicar and she's agreed to perform the ceremony next Saturday. I think we could do it …" She still sounded unsure.

"I think you're even more crazy than I am! Sorry, I've got to go. Brian needs me." Someone needed to end the ridiculous conversation.

"Just think about it," Julie said.

"Thanks for trying." I hung up and felt deflated. "Julie says the chapel is available next Saturday if we want to get married then." I rolled my eyes as I relayed the message to Brian.

"That's soon …"

"Yes! It's a week. We could never organise a wedding in a week."

"I guess not."

I reached for the remote and unmuted the TV before sinking back into the couch.

Brian nudged me with his foot a couple of minutes later.

"What?" I hissed.

"You already have a dress."

I stared at him. "There's no way we can get married next week."

"I know," he agreed. "It's a ridiculous."

"Totally ridiculous."

I returned my attention to the TV and tried to ignore Brian's eyes on me.

"Why are you staring at me?" I finally asked.

"I was just thinking about how many crazy things you've done since I met you. Really ridiculous things."

I laughed and muted the TV.

Brian sat up. "You really want to get married in that chapel don't you?"

"Yes." I sighed. "I really love the chapel. And I like the idea of getting married where your family live. Somewhere we're connected to and we'll go back to. It has some significance and isn't just a random place that we've picked based on some pictures in a brochure." I looked at him with wide eyes. "But we can't organise a wedding in a week."

"Would you rather wait a couple of years until the chapel is fixed and there's a date free?"

I grimaced and shook my head.

"I think we could do it in a week." Brian had his serious face on as he tapped his fingers against his leg. "It's a lot to organise. We'd have to find caterers and ... I don't even know. They'll be loads to do."

I bit my lip as excitement bubbled inside me. "I don't even care about the details. We can order pizzas if it comes to it. I just want to marry you ... in that beautiful little chapel on the hill ... next Saturday!"

He put a hand on my cheek as he kissed me. "Let's get organising then."

I beamed for a moment before panic set in. I nudged Brian. "You call Julie back and tell her we're doing it. I'm going to call Linda."

I felt better at the sound of Linda's voice. She was calm and said she'd come over and help me. In the meantime I just needed to write a list of guests and start inviting people.

I had a very short conversation with my mum, while Brian wandered into the kitchen to chat to Julie. Mum didn't think it was strange at all, although she was thoughtful about having to cancel her dog training and leave Jason alone for *Fitness Unleashed.*

"Should I invite Jason?" I asked Brian when he glanced at my fairly short guest list.

"You want to invite your personal trainer?" He looked surprised at the suggestion.

"He's also my friend," I said hesitantly.

"Really?"

"Yes! I think so …" I gave Brian a look to tell him he wasn't being helpful.

"Sorry. I just thought he only hung out with you when you paid him to."

"Brian! Don't say that." Annoyingly, I realised that he might have a point. "He comes in the shop a lot too. I'm not paying him then."

"I don't know. Invite him if you want."

"Well I don't know now. Will he think it's weird if I invite him?"

"I'm officially not a fan of wedding planning." Brian grinned at me.

I wrote Jason's name on the list and then crossed it off. Since the wedding was in Scotland, I decided it was a bit much to ask him to go to so much effort and at such short notice.

"What about Grace?" I looked at Brian, and felt another round of panic hit me.

"Call her now," he said. "She'll have to fly back for the weekend. It's fine. She'll be there."

His smile put me at ease and I realised he was right. If it were the other way around, I'd drop everything and get on a plane.

"I'll put the kettle on," Brian said as I scrolled to Grace's number and pressed dial.

I paced the living room and was relieved to hear her voice and not the voicemail.

"Did I wake you?" I tried to calculate the time difference but my brain wasn't working very fast.

"No, I'm on my way to the gym. Actually I'm almost there. Can I call you back later?"

"We're going to get married next weekend," I blurted out. "On Saturday!" I hoped that my enthusiasm would carry over to her. The line went quiet. "Can you come?" I asked. It sounded pathetic, like I was inviting her out for a drink or something totally unimportant.

"Next Saturday?" she asked.

"Yes! In Scotland. At Brian's dad's house."

"Are you serious?" The enthusiasm definitely hadn't made its way to her yet.

"It's the only date they have free in the foreseeable future. I know it's a bit crazy but–"

"A bit crazy? This is insane, even for you." She sounded annoyed, as though I was interrupting her with something stupid.

"Yes, it's slightly insane," I half-heartedly agreed with her, "but it will be amazing. We're really excited. I need you to be there."

"This is so typical of you." She let out a frustrated sigh.

"Can't you just be happy for me?"

"It's hard to be happy for you when you're being crazy. Can't you be sensible for once in your life? It's your wedding. Take it a bit seriously."

"I am taking it seriously," I yelled at her. "And I am sensible. Why can't you be a good friend for once? Why do you constantly feel the need to belittle me and everything I do? I don't need your approval, Grace. I am getting married next week whether you're there or not."

"Well I *won't* be there," she said calmly. "I have a life. I can't just drop everything."

"You're my best friend," I said with tears in my eyes. "And you're supposed to be a bridesmaid. Can't you just do this for me?"

"How can I be your bridesmaid? I wouldn't even have a dress because you forgot to factor shopping into your plans."

"I got you a dress," I said quickly, as though this might smooth things over.

"What?"

"When I got mine. Sophie and Abby chose theirs and I found one for you too."

"Wow." Her voice oozed sarcasm. "Thanks for that!"

"Can you please just come? We really want you to be there."

"No, I'm sorry. Did you honestly think I could hop on a plane, just like that?"

"Yes, I did." I lowered myself onto the couch with tears in my eyes.

"I have to go. Good luck with planning everything."

I sat staring at the phone and wondering who I'd just spoken to. Grace didn't used to be so cold. I couldn't believe how condescending she was. She made me feel like I was doing something impulsive and stupid. It was impulsive but surely not stupid.

"What's wrong?" Brian asked.

Tears streamed down my face. "Grace said I'm being crazy and she can't come."

He groaned but didn't seem overly surprised. "She's having a hard time. Don't take it personally. I'll call her tomorrow and have a chat with her. You probably just caught her at a bad time."

"What if she's right? It's not really fair to ask people to come with just a week's notice, is it?"

He draped his arm around my shoulders and pulled me to him. "The important people will find a way to be there."

"Grace won't."

"She might change her mind when she's had time to think about it. And if not, it won't be the worst thing in the world."

"But she's my oldest friend. She has to be there."

We were disturbed by a knock at the door and Brian got up to let Linda in. She rushed in and gave me a big hug, notepad in hand.

"This is so exciting." She pulled her pen from the spiral of her notepad. "Let's start planning."

"You can take your coat off," I said. "If you want."

She laughed as she wriggled out of her coat. "Did you start inviting people?"

"I asked my mum, who reacted as though I'd invited her for dinner. She's free and will be there. Then I spoke to Grace who thinks it's a stupid idea and won't come." I wiped the remaining tears from my cheeks.

"Oh don't worry. Not everyone will be able to make it at such short notice but that doesn't matter. I spoke to Sophie; she's on her way over. She had that competition next weekend but she said she'll cancel it …"

I dropped my head into my hands. "The nailympics are next weekend?"

"It's fine." She patted my hand. "Don't worry."

"I don't think we should do it." I looked up at Brian. "If Grace and Sophie can't come, maybe it's better we wait and organise something properly. Grace is right, it's a bad idea."

A few minutes later I was all set to give up on the idea of a last minute wedding. Then Sophie arrived.

"I will do your hair and make-up," she said, bursting into the living room. "So don't worry about that. What else can I do?"

"What about the nailympics?" I asked tearfully.

She shrugged. "I dropped out."

"You can't just drop out. It's important for you; for your career."

"Well if you're getting married, I think that's slightly more important. I can do other competitions. I'm not missing your wedding. Although, I will let Brian give me the hundred quid entry fee which I just lost." She turned and grinned at Brian.

My tears turned to laughter.

"So we're really doing this?" I looked at Brian

and then Linda.

"Yes!" Sophie practically shouted. "I already pulled out of the competition so you have to get married on Saturday now. Oh, and I spoke to Jake. He said Michael is pretty handy with a camera if you're short of a photographer."

"Brilliant. Write that down, Linda. Michael's our photographer."

"We could try and find a professional first," Linda suggested.

"Let's just save some stress and jump straight to Michael. He'll be great. Write it down."

Linda did as she was told and started scribbling away. "What about the ceremony?" she said. "That will be the most important thing. Let's make sure you've got someone who can marry you?"

"Julie said she'd already spoken to the vicar. I'll have to check with Julie about what we need to do." I reached for my phone and said a quick hello to Julie. Then Linda took the phone from me. I listened as she chatted away with Julie, occasionally writing things down on her notepad.

"Everything is under control," she said when she hung up the phone. "Julie is going to make some phone calls and see what she can organise. She'll call you back this evening or tomorrow. It sounds like it will all fall into place though; she's going to call in some favours." Linda sat back and smiled.

I looked over at Brian. "That's easy then!"

Chapter 39

"Yes, Anne! This Saturday!"

"*This* Saturday?" She scuttled over to perch on the edge of my desk. "You're getting married on Saturday? Actually on Saturday?"

"Yes! I know it's hard to believe."

"It's amazing." She clapped her hands together. "You must be so excited!"

"I am. It's just a bit manic trying to organise everything."

"Oh no …" The look on her face was of complete panic and she genuinely had me worried.

"What?"

"I can't make it." She looked really distressed and I felt bad that I hadn't put her on the guest list. I'd had the same dilemma that I'd had with Jason and didn't know whether I should invite her or not. I'd assumed it was too much to ask of people, so we'd decided to stick to family and our closest friends.

Anne reached for my hand. "I'm so sorry. We're picking Millie up from university this weekend. She's coming home for the summer. It's such bad timing."

"Don't worry." I squeezed her hand. "It can't be helped. It's the only weekend we can use the church and we knew that everyone wouldn't be able to make it at such short notice. Grace can't come either

…" I thought she might feel better about being compared to Grace.

"Oh my goodness, Marie. Why can't Grace make it?"

"It's just not enough notice for her to fly back."

"Nonsense! It's plenty of time. What's the real reason?"

"What do you mean?"

"She's your best friend and this is your wedding. Short notice isn't a good enough excuse."

"She can't get time off work … I don't know, she's pretty stressed. We had an argument."

"She's jealous," Anne said, pursing her lips together.

"I don't think she's jealous, Anne. She thinks the wedding will be a shambles – which it may well be. I really don't think she's jealous."

"Not jealous of your wedding; jealous of your life. You're so happy. It must be hard for her, seeing you so happy when she's not."

"I think she's happy," I replied. "She's got everything she wants … James and her job … living in New York …"

"So she has everything she wants but she's still not happy? Poor love."

"Do you think so?" I wondered whether Anne might have a point. Grace had found the man of her dreams but she barely mentioned James to me these days. And she had the job of her dreams but she just seemed stressed out by it. She was tense all the time.

"Definitely. She's your best friend and there's no excuse for her to miss your wedding. If you give me her number I can ring and talk some sense into her."

I looked at Anne and realised she was serious with her offer.

"I think Brian's going to talk to her. He'll make her see sense, I'm sure."

***

"I'm getting married in the morning," Jason sang as he danced his way into the shop. "Ding dong the bells are going to chime!"

"Hi, Jason!" I was just gearing up to leave. "The wedding's not tomorrow by the way."

"I know but I'm only a few days off. How's our blushing bride?"

"Fine," I said. "Apart from the fact that I presume you're about to make me go running?"

"I am indeed. Get changed."

In the bathroom, I put my running gear on. Then I shoved my work clothes into my backpack and was out the door with Jason in no time.

"Your mum's excited about the wedding," Jason told me as we jogged through town.

"Is she?" I was quite surprised. She didn't get excited about much that wasn't dog related.

"Yes. She was asking my advice on what to wear."

"Oh no!" I hadn't even thought about that. "She's not planning on any kind of costume is she?"

"Well I talked her out of a white dress. I'm not sure what she's moved on to next."

"Thanks!"

"She asked me to take over all her dog work for the weekend," he said with a sigh.

"You can always say no if you can't manage it."

"I'll be fine." He paused. "How hard can it be?"

When he suddenly increased his pace, I struggled to keep up with him. By the time we reached the park, I was in desperate need of a break.

"Are you trying to kill me?" I asked as I struggled to catch my breath.

"Just want to make sure you look good on your wedding day!"

He went on to torture me with a variety of squats and lunges before we continued the jog home.

"I'm going to be really busy this week," he said as we lingered on the front steps at home. "I have to reschedule some clients so that I'm free to take over for your mum at the weekend."

"Are you telling me you won't have time to torment me this week?"

"Call it an early wedding present if you want." He stood for a moment and gave me an awkward smile. "I hope everything is perfect for you at the weekend."

"Thank you," I called, but he was already jogging away.

Chapter 40

"Everything okay?" I asked when I walked in to find Brian sitting in front of the TV.

He pulled me down next to him on the couch and kissed me. "Everything is great."

"You're worrying me," I said.

"Did you get the time off work?"

"Yes. Anne and Greg can cover on Friday and they'll get a temp in next week. Not a problem. And you?"

"Thursday, Friday and all of next week …"

"Hey! You took Thursday off too? That's not fair!"

"My days as a free man are limited, I thought I'd make the most of them."

I punched him lightly on the arm, "You really think you're free now?" I laughed. "So what big plans do you have for your last days of freedom?"

"Thought I might buy myself a new suit."

"Any excuse," I said.

"I'm not allowed a new suit to get married in?"

"Since you're a free man you can do what you want. But you have so many suits!"

"You've got a few dresses but you've bought a new one for the occasion," he said, laughing.

"Yeah, but my dress is a bit different to any others in my wardrobe," I reasoned.

"Maybe my suit will be different."

"Will it?"

"No." He smirked. "But I'm still getting a new one."

"Okay. Did you decide anything about your stag night?"

"I'm not going to bother. Not if you're not having a hen night."

"You should have one," I said. "I don't want you complaining about this for the rest of our lives!"

"I don't see the fun in a night out without you."

"That's a good point."

He relaxed into the couch, turning to put his feet up and trapping me under the weight of his legs. "My dad's coming over, by the way."

"When?"

"Tonight." He glanced at his watch. "Any time now. He's bringing the paperwork for the wedding."

"Couldn't he have emailed it or something?"

"I guess he could have done."

"So why is he bringing it in person?"

He shrugged. "No idea,"

"And he's coming here?"

"Yep."

I tried to remember if Paul had ever been to the house before. It suddenly seemed a bit odd. "Why doesn't he ever come to the house?"

Brian moved his feet off me and sat up. "Once upon a time, I may have told him he wasn't welcome here."

I glared at him for a moment while his words sank in. "You've got issues you know?"

"Maybe." He rolled his head on his shoulders.

"Well," I said. "Why did you tell him he's not welcome in your house?"

He sat up straighter and fiddled with his watch strap. "I inherited some money when Mum died, and when Dad left I used it to buy the house." I nodded. I already knew that much. "Dad wanted to bring Julie here for a visit and I said no. He said if she wasn't welcome then neither was he. I said okay, so be it."

I sighed and closed my eyes briefly, not quite sure what to say.

"I know." He turned and looked me in the eyes. "It's crazy and I can't explain it. But the house felt like Mum's last gift to me and I couldn't stand the thought of Julie being here. I hated her."

"But she's lovely," I said, feeling a need to defend her.

"I know that. I always knew how irrational it was, I thought she was nice and I wanted Dad to be happy. I knew I should be happy for him. But I just hated her."

"And now?"

"I don't hate her." He shrugged. "I just never got around to swallowing my pride and apologising."

We sat in silence on the couch. It seemed a bit senseless of me to tell him to fix things with his family. I kept my advice to myself. I thought about my mum. Suddenly my upbringing, which I'd thought of as pretty unconventional, seemed entirely sane and functional.

"Did you speak to Grace?" I asked, changing the subject.

"Yeah."

"And?"

"She still says she can't make it."

I got the impression he was leaving a lot unsaid. "She thinks I'm impulsive and ridiculous?"

"Not just you," he said. "Me too!"

"Do you think she'll come around?"

He shrugged, suddenly unable to look at me.

"What aren't you telling me?" I asked.

"I told her she wasn't welcome anymore, even if she did change her mind."

"Brian!" I snapped. "Why did you say that?"

"Because she pushed me that far."

My whole body tensed. "You can't tell my best friend she's not welcome at our wedding."

"She's my friend too," he said. "At least she used to be."

"What are we going to do?" I asked weakly.

"Get married," he replied. "If she can't be happy for us, then maybe it's better she's not there."

I'd expected Brian to talk Grace around. He could be such a charmer and was usually good at talking people around to his way of thinking. I knew Grace had a soft spot for him and would listen to what he said. Apparently not this time though.

Paul arrived five minutes later, so I didn't have much time to dwell on it.

"Sorry, I'm a bit sweaty," I said in way of greeting. I realised I'd not managed to shower after my jog. I led him into the kitchen where Brian was busy making coffee.

In an attempt to lighten the atmosphere, I talked incessantly about anything and everything; trying desperately to fill the silence. The conversation was decidedly polite and the atmosphere was frosty. The Connor men were stubborn. I felt like banging their heads together and telling them to move on.

We sat at the dining table and went through all the paperwork for the wedding. Once everything was filled in and signed, I suggested going out for dinner. Really I just felt like a drink; being around Paul and Brian was hard work.

"I've got something else for you." Paul ignored my suggestion and went into the hallway. When he returned he placed two ring boxes on the table before us. I reached for them instinctively and opened them to reveal matching gold rings. Simple and beautiful.

My hand shot to my mouth and I gasped. "I didn't even think about rings." I vaguely wondered what I else I'd forgotten.

"They belonged to Brian's mum and me," Paul said. "If you don't want them, it's fine. I just thought you might like to have them."

I turned to Brian with a big smile on my face but he was already walking away. I heard his footsteps on the stairs.

"I can take them back," Paul said quickly. "I knew I shouldn't have come. Julie persuaded me it was a good idea."

"I'll talk to him," I said quietly.

"I'm going to go."

"Don't. Just wait while I talk to him."

"It doesn't matter what I do, it's always wrong,"

"Just sit down," I said fiercely. "Do not take the rings. Do not leave. Just give me five minutes."

I took the stairs two at a time and then paused

with my hand on the bedroom door, unsure of what I was about to walk into.

Pushing the door, I poked my head tentatively inside. Brian was sitting on the floor under the window, his head pushed back against the wall. I knelt beside him and took his hand in mine.

He attempted a smile but looked like he had the weight of the world on his shoulders.

"We don't need to take the rings," I said.

"It's not the rings." He drew me to him and I rested my forehead against his.

"You just don't want to marry me?" I asked.

He managed a short laugh. "I definitely want to marry you." He took a deep breath. "I just wish …"

I searched his face as I watched him try to get the words out.

"You wish your mum was here?" I asked.

"Yes." His voice was barely audible. "I wish she could be at the wedding. I wish she could meet you."

"Me too," I whispered, kissing the side of his head and hugging him to me. I ran my fingers through his hair as he cried.

"You need to talk to your dad," I said, finally.

"He's not easy to talk to." He wiped tears from his eyes. "He doesn't like to talk about her."

"Maybe he thinks the same about you."

"Maybe," he said. "Is he still here?"

"I'm not sure. I told him to wait."

"Can you tell him we want the rings?"

"You tell him."

He turned to kiss me before pulling himself off the floor and perching on the edge of the bed. He took a deep breath. "Just give me a few minutes."

***

"Why don't people listen to me?" I growled to myself when I went downstairs to find the house deserted. I stopped in the living room and peered out of the window. Paul was sitting on the wall outside and I hurriedly went out to him before he had chance to go any further.

"We'd really like the rings," I said as I walked out of the front door.

"That's good." He didn't turn around.

"Will you come back inside?"

"I think I'll just go." His voice was raw with emotion and I hovered on the steps behind him, trying to avoid the awkwardness of seeing the tears that I was sure were in his eyes. "I kept thinking one day he'd grow up and get over it and everything would be good between us again." The bitterness in his voice made me angry and it was an effort to keep my voice even.

"It's not about you," I snapped. "He's not angry with you; he's not angry with anyone. He's upset that his mum won't be at his wedding and that she's not here and she can't see who he grew up to be."

I was annoyed that it hadn't even occurred to Paul that it was a difficult time for Brian and that he was hurting. I was furious at myself for exactly the same reason. "He just misses his mum," I said sadly.

"Well at least we have that in common," he whispered. I cursed both Connor men as tears sprang to my eyes. Hopping onto the wall beside him, I rested my head on his shoulder. He took my hand

and squeezed it. "She'd have loved you."

"Come in and talk to Brian," I said.

"I don't think he wants to talk to me."

"Just come inside." I adopted my authoritative tone and it seemed to work for once. Brian was coming downstairs as we moved back inside. I felt like I was at a western showdown as we stood at opposite ends of the hallway.

Paul spoke first. "Marie said you'd like the rings …"

"They're perfect. Thanks," Brian replied.

"Do you still want to get dinner?" Paul looked at me and I wanted to shake him. I wanted to shake them both.

"I actually have a load of stuff to do," I said. "Why don't you two go?" They both gave me looks that said they knew exactly what I was up to, but neither commented. "Since Brian's not getting a stag night, I think he can at least have a night out with his dad."

"Sometimes it's easier just to do what she says," Brian said with a small smile.

By the time they left I was exhausted and collapsed in a heap on the couch. Hopefully they would finally manage to talk things through.

Chapter 41

When Julie rang to fill me in on the plans she'd made, her voice was full of worry.

"I found caterers but as it was so last-minute they can't do anything fancy, just a finger food buffet."

"That's fine," I said brightly.

"Paul sweet-talked a bakery into doing the cake. They wouldn't give us any choice at such short notice though, just a classic wedding cake style."

"That's good."

"We have the band that I spoke to you about … And I've ordered a marquee and tables and chairs to put in the garden. That will all arrive early on Saturday morning. I spoke to just about every florist in a ten mile radius and couldn't find anyone who could manage it …"

"It doesn't matter about flowers," I said quickly.

"It's sorted now. Paul went to the big florist in town and threw a load of money at them. They were suddenly available."

"So it's a family trait? Throwing money at problems?" I couldn't help but laugh.

"It worked! Anyway, have I missed anything?"

"Food, drinks, music, cake, flowers … what else could we need? You've done such an amazing job."

"I'm just worried. It all seems so thrown together. I don't know how it's going to turn out."

"It sounds just like my life! It will be great, I'm sure."

"Oh and this flipping rain. What if it rains on Saturday?" She sounded genuinely stressed and I felt guilty for putting her to so much trouble.

"Better it rains now; it'll be all out of the way by Saturday."

"It's forecast to rain all week."

"Stop worrying," I said. "Everything will be perfect, I know it."

"We've booked out all the rooms at the pub. I think your friends will all fit in there. If I've miscalculated then we've got room with us. And I thought maybe you'd want Sophie and your mum to stay at our place with you on Friday night. However you want to do it is fine. And what about your friend, Grace? There was a question mark after her name on the guest list."

"She can't make it," I said sadly. I'd tried to call her again but got no answer. Part of me was furious at her and another part of me was devastated by the thought of her not being at the wedding.

"Do you think she might change her mind?"

"I'd hoped so, but Brian tried to talk to her and they ended up having a big argument so it seems unlikely now. I need to stop dwelling on it, she isn't answering my calls so I can't do much about it."

"That's a shame. Why don't you write her an email? Even if it doesn't change anything, it's sometimes good to get everything off your chest."

"That's a good idea," I said. "I don't mean to sound down, I know how much effort you're going to and I can't wait." I really had been overwhelmed by everything she was doing. "Thank you so much."

"Don't thank me yet. It might be a total disaster."

I arranged to talk to her in a few days, or sooner if anything came up.

As the week went by, everything seemed to fall neatly into place. Jake and Michael arranged a minibus to drive our little gang up to Scotland together on Friday afternoon. They even had space for Mum and Aunt Kath, which meant that I would get a quiet drive up with Brian on Friday.

Chapter 42

I should have guessed that Sophie wouldn't have dropped the idea of a hen night so easily. On Thursday evening I arrived home to find Sophie and Brian all dressed up and chatting away in the kitchen.

"Surprise hen night?" I asked Sophie.

"Yes! Did you guess?"

"Not until just now," I said as I wrapped my arms around Brian's waist.

"You really thought I'd let you miss out on a hen night? What kind of a friend do you think I am?"

I rested my head on Brian's chest. "I'm not sure I've got the energy for a night out." I was still upset about the situation with Grace and part of the reason I'd decided against a hen night was because I thought it would be weird without her there. As Julie suggested, I'd sent Grace a long email telling her how I felt, but I still hadn't heard anything from her.

"Don't worry," Sophie said. "It's not going to be a wild one. Your mum and Aunt Kath are coming. Oh, and Anne," she added.

"You've not planned anything inappropriate have you?"

"It's a hen night." She rolled her eyes at me. "What would be inappropriate?"

"My mum would be mortified if a stripper turned

up," I said. "And Linda too."

"That's funny because your mum had a specific request for a fireman." Sophie grinned at me and I couldn't decide if she was joking or not. I shouldn't really put anything past my mum. "Anyway Brian insisted on helping me plan the night so I'm afraid it's going to be very boring."

I looked up at Brian. "You were in on it?"

"Yes," he said with a cheeky grin.

"And what will *you* be doing this evening?"

"I may have some sort of stag evening," he said, raising an eyebrow. "Let's see what Jake and Michael have in store for me."

***

Sophie insisted on choosing an outfit for me. I was wearing a cute little green dress and black heels when I left the house with Linda and Sophie. Taxi Dave was waiting outside with a big grin on his face.

"Your chariot awaits!" he said.

I turned and beamed at Brian in the doorway. He shrugged and gave me a boyish smile. "Have fun!"

"We will!" Sophie laughed as she opened the car door.

"Where are we going?" I asked as I squeezed into the back of the taxi with Sophie and Linda.

"A restaurant," Sophie said. "All very tame, I'm afraid. It's Brian's fault. We can ditch the old ladies later and go and dance the night away."

"Helen asked me to give you these." Dave turned in his seat and handed me a shopping bag.

I reached into the bag to see what my old friend

the taxi dispatcher had sent me. There were a pair of pink fairy wings, a tiara and a black whip. "I'm not sure I want to ask about this …" I said, holding up the whip.

"She said to apologise; she didn't have time to go shopping. These are just a few bits she had lying around." He smiled sheepishly. "It's usually best not to ask too many questions with Helen."

I wriggled into my fairy wings and secured the tiara on my head. "I think I'm going to get drunk and accidentally lose the whip!"

"I'll have it," Sophie said, taking it from me.

In town we pulled into a side street that I'd never even noticed before. "I'll be back later to take you to your next destination," Dave told us cheerfully.

"We're going in here?" I craned my neck to look at the neon sign hanging over the dingy black door. "Cuban Revolution," I said, reading the sign. "It looks dodgy."

"You can blame Brian," Sophie said cheerfully as she hopped out of the taxi.

"What do we owe you, Dave?" I asked.

"Brian took care of it. I'll see you later!" He pulled away and left us standing on the quiet street.

"Come on then." Linda opened the door. There was a little entrance hall shrouded by a black curtain, which I pulled aside.

The mellow tones of a saxophone immediately drew my attention to the band as my eyes adjusted to the low lighting. Smoke machines stood at either side of the musicians, sending out a hazy fog that glowed under the orange lights scattered around the room.

A cheerful waitress approached us. "Are you here for the hen night?"

"How did you guess?" Sophie asked, swinging the whip over her shoulder. She turned to apologise as she almost took Linda's eye out.

"Which one of you is Marie?" the petite waitress asked with a huge grin.

"That'll be me," I said.

"The rest of your party are already here."

We followed her across the room, weaving between tables made from old wooden barrels. I was surprised at how busy it was and my mouth watered as I glanced at plates of quesadillas and nachos being delivered to a table.

We passed the bar and I saw my mum, Anne and Aunt Kath perched on high stools around our table.

I waved and said a collective *hello* before turning to the waitress.

"I'm not sure what your policy is," I whispered, "but I don't want any strippers turning up. I've got my mum here."

"There are no strippers planned that I know of," she said, smiling. "But there'll be dancing and that can get pretty steamy."

I glanced at the couple dancing provocatively on the small dance floor in front of the musicians.

"I heard you're a fan of tequila," the waitress said.

"I'm not sure *fan* is the right word," I replied. "It's kind of a love-hate relationship. Love it at the time. Hate it the next day."

"So you're saying you'd love some?" she asked, happily.

"I think that's what I was getting at." I shifted my

gaze back to the dancers and was mesmerised by a dark-haired woman in a striking orange dress who was perfectly in time with the music. I would definitely need tequila.

Anne beamed at me as I pulled up a stool. "We love it here!"

"I really want to dance," Mum said. "I've got my tap shoes on."

"Why tap-dancing shoes?" I asked as she stuck out a leg to show me.

"Brian said there'd be dancing and I found these at a second hand shop."

"Lovely. Maybe we'll have a drink first."

Sophie cheered as the waitress appeared with a tray of shots and slid it onto the table.

"I don't think everyone wants tequila ..." I started to tell the waitress. "Never mind," I said as hands shot out to grab at them.

"I'll bring you some tapas," the waitress said. "Just let me know what you want more of and I'll keep it coming."

I reached for a shot of tequila to knock back with everyone else.

"Sophie, get me another of those, will you?" Anne said.

"Me too," Mum called as Sophie stood up.

"No," I shouted. "Mum can't have another. Ignore her!"

"I'll have another too!" Linda chimed in.

"No, no, no!" I wasn't sure the night was going to be as tedious as Sophie anticipated.

"Don't worry," Sophie said later, as we sat at the table, sipping mojitos and watching the rest of our party dancing up a storm in front of the band. "We'll ditch the old ladies in a bit and go find some proper fun. And strippers!"

"This is fun enough for me." I felt the warm fuzzy feelings flow through me. I couldn't decide if it was the tequila or just sitting with Sophie and watching everyone having so much fun, but I felt great. "I love this place!"

"I heard you might be in need of a dance partner?" A tall, toned guy appeared next to me in snug jeans and tight T-shirt.

"Don't even try and protest," Sophie warned me.

I gave him my hand and followed him to the dance floor where I spent a hilarious ten minutes trying to follow his instructions.

"Switch off your brain," he said as he stopped and looked me in the eyes. "Don't think. Just feel the music."

"Sorry." I snorted with laughter at his words. "I'm trying!" He lowered his hands to my hips in an attempt to guide me. "I think I've got it," I said. "My mum might need some help though ..." I pulled her over to him before slipping away. I went to find the toilets and pulled out my phone once I was away from the noise.

Grace's voicemail beeped for me to leave a message and I felt awkward. "I'm out on my hen night," I said into the phone. "I keep thinking about you and I wish you were here. I hope you're okay …"

I pressed the phone to my ear, wondering what else to say before finally ending the call. I missed Grace but I was determined not to dwell on her absence and let it ruin my night. Taking a deep breath, I moved back into the bustle of the large room and slapped on a smile as I joined Sophie and Linda who were dancing freely to the music.

"I can't believe I never knew this place existed," I said as the energy from the dance floor lifted my spirits.

"I'm still wondering how Brian knows about it!" Sophie said. She had a point.

Anne and Aunt Kath joined us and we did our best at Salsa dancing. I got the feeling that the place attracted a regular clientele; there were some amazing dancers and many people seemed to know each other. There was a nice mix of couples dancing, as well as individuals. A young guy came over and said hello to us before grabbing Anne for a dance and making her blush like a schoolgirl as she attempted to move her hips to the music. He danced with us all before moving back to his friends.

"I think I'll have to go," Aunt Kath finally said. "I've had a lovely time but it's getting late. I'm going to take your mum with me." We looked at Mum who was dancing with a curly-haired man about half her age.

"Time to go, Mum!" I called. She followed us back to our table.

"I think it's time we all went home now," Sophie said through a fake yawn. "We've got a big day tomorrow, so we shouldn't be out too late. It's a long drive up to Scotland. I'm going to make sure Marie gets home safely. Kath, Is it okay if Anne shares a taxi with you?"

"Of course."

The cool night air was refreshing when we stepped out into the street. Dave was sitting in his taxi waiting for us.

"See you all tomorrow!" I shouted as I fell into the car.

Dave passed me a black eye mask with a lacy edge.

"What's this for?" I asked, holding it up.

"Just put it on." Sophie laughed as she climbed into the taxi beside me.

"Go on," Linda said. She took it and pulled it over my eyes.

"What's going on?" I asked.

"All will be revealed," Sophie said.

"You better not be taking me somewhere dodgy," I said into the darkness. "Did Brian plan this bit, or was it you?"

When Sophie spoke, there was mischief in her voice. "Brian and I came to a compromise for the next part of the night."

We weren't driving for long before we stopped. Sophie guided me out of the car. It was disconcertingly quiet and I moved hesitantly through the darkness of my blindfold.

A door opened and we stepped into somewhere warm and musty-smelling. "Where on earth are we?"

"Wait and see." Sophie took my outstretched hands and led me slowly forwards. Linda had a reassuring hand on my back. When Sophie stifled a laugh, I instinctively drew back.

"Come on," she said. "We're almost there." She went quiet then and her hands dropped away from mine.

Oh, god. Where am I? Flailing in the darkness, my hands landed on warm flesh. I flinched and pulled back.

"Sophie! I said no strippers! It gives me the creeps. I don't want to touch some random beefed up guy."

"The random beefed up guy isn't deaf," Sophie said, laughing.

"Sorry. No offense," I said.

Sophie nudged me forward and forced my hand to caress the torso of the random beefed up guy.

"Actually not that beefed up," I remarked as my hand ran over a smattering of chest hair. Muffled laughter rippled around the room and I tried to retrieve my hand. Sophie's iron grip forced my hand down his torso, getting steadily lower.

A cheer rose from elsewhere in the room and I was confused by the fact that it sounded distinctly male.

"Sophie!" I pulled back and heard another snicker from over my right shoulder just as Sophie and Linda started laughing hysterically.

My hands were free and I was about to make a grab for my blindfold. I paused. Then I reached my hand out again. I could feel the gentle rise and fall of his chest and traced a line down his torso before stopping and moving lightly to tickle his ribs.

He laughed and snatched at my hand. "Alright! Enough!" His voice warm and familiar.

I grinned up at Brian as I lifted the blindfold.

He laughed. "Not that beefed up?"

I shook my head in amusement as I registered

301

where we were.

"Hi, Gerry!" I waved at the barman of the dingy little pub. It was on the road where I used to live with Grace. I'd had one or two interesting evenings there with Brian back when we were still getting to know each other.

"What kind of hen night is this?" I asked, looking round at Jake, Michael and Jeff. There were also a group of random old men who gave me a wave before they went back to playing cards in the corner.

"I told you a night without you didn't sound like much fun." Brian fastened the buttons on his shirt.

"You'd make a terrible stripper," I said.

"I know. I'm far too shy. And apparently not beefy enough!" He winked at me.

"Who needs a drink?" Gerry shouted, prompting everyone to move towards the bar.

"Can I just have some water?" I asked pathetically.

"No!" came the collective reply. I squeezed my arms tighter around Brian's waist as he kissed the top of my head.

"One more drink," I said. "Then I need my bed."

"I think you told me that once before in this place," Brian said. I grinned as I remembered our first night out together. We'd had leaving drinks with Grace and James before they left for New York. The night had ended up fairly wild.

"Come on." Michael took my hand and pulled me away from Brian. "I need someone to dance with me."

He led me over to an open section of the room and we began boogying along to the music. Everyone followed and I laughed as Jeff took my hand and twirled me round.

"I might need to take him home soon," Sophie said, rolling her eyes.

"I'm fine," Jeff said, slurring his words. "I'm just having fun!" He wrapped his arms around Sophie who snaked her arms around his neck and swayed to the music with him. I couldn't stop smiling as I danced with everyone. We danced and drank and laughed; singing loudly to the classic pop tunes on the jukebox. It was exactly the sort of hen night I never knew I wanted.

A hazy drunk feeling enveloped me as we stood outside the pub saying our goodbyes. Brian was on the phone to taxi Dave when I noticed Jeff sitting at a picnic table with a cigarette in his hand.

"They'll kill you," I said as I plonked myself down next to him

"It's more likely Sophie will kill me if she catches me," he said.

"Hurry up then, she's only gone to find her whip. She'll be out any second." He took a long drag before he stubbed the cigarette out.

"It's only when I'm drunk," he said sheepishly.

"Thanks for being annoying and childish," I blurted out.

He grinned at me, and his head rolled slightly. "When am I ever annoying and childish?"

"When you sent me into fat club instead of speed dating."

"Oh, yeah! You were very angry!"

"I was a little bit annoyed," I said with a smile.

"I'm very sorry," he said. "Look what I did to

your life …"

"I know. I could have had really cool friends by now if it weren't for you."

"No, you couldn't." He reached over and ruffled my hair.

I pushed him away. "You are so drunk!"

"No, I'm not." He reached for the packet of cigarettes in his top pocket.

"Jeff!" Sophie's voice boomed around us and he threw the cigarettes at me.

"I said I don't want one, Marie!" He did his best to look serious. "I don't smoke anymore. Stop trying to tempt me."

"Come on, you fool," Sophie said affectionately. "We can walk to your place from here. If you can still walk!"

He wobbled when he got up, and put an arm around Sophie to steady himself.

We all shouted goodbye as Sophie and Jeff stumbled away. Linda climbed into a taxi with Michael and Jake.

"I told Dave we'd start walking." Brian slung an arm around my shoulders and led me up the road in the direction of Grace's house.

"I had such a brilliant night," I said.

"So my planning wasn't too bad?"

"You did a great job. It was perfect."

We stopped outside Grace's house and leaned against the front wall. She'd rented the place out and it was strange to think of someone else living there. Even though I loved my new home, I sometimes missed that cosy little house. It held a lot of fond memories for me.

"Remember the night we got drunk at Gerry's pub and ended up bringing the bird home?" Brian said. I laughed, thinking of how horrified I been to find the budgie in the kitchen the next morning with no recollection of how it got there.

"That was first night we woke up together," I said.

Brian nodded. "I promised myself that the next time I woke up with you, I'd make sure you looked happier about it!"

"I was slightly hungover. And I didn't like you all that much back then."

"Thank goodness that changed." He smiled as I turned to kiss him. Then I moved my attention to the road to look out for Dave. "Thanks for making me talk to my dad," Brian said, suddenly serious.

"So you did talk to him?" I'd not managed to get much out of him after his night out with Paul, although he'd said they had a good time and he seemed much happier. I'd assumed it all went well.

"Yeah. We talked about a lot of things. It was good."

"I'm glad. And you're welcome." We moved towards the road as Dave's car came into view and slowed in front of us.

Climbing in, I told Dave I'd had the best night of my life. Then I promptly fell asleep on Brian's shoulder.

Chapter 43

"So we passed up on a wedding in Mauritius because you were worried about the weather?" Brian squinted at the road ahead as the rain bounced off the windscreen. It was Friday afternoon and we were on our way to Scotland. The rain didn't bother me. I felt like there was nothing in the world that could dampen my spirits.

I'd even decided to stop worrying about the situation with Grace. In my email to her, I'd been totally honest with her and I felt better for it.

The ball was in her court and I couldn't let myself dwell on it anymore. The weekend was about Brian and me. Anyone who couldn't be happy for us wasn't worth worrying about. Or at least that's what I kept telling myself.

"The rain will stop," I told Brian confidently. "It will be blue skies and sunshine tomorrow. I can feel it in my bones."

"We needn't bother checking the weather forecast then!"

I smiled and reached to squeeze Brian's hand. "I can't believe we're getting married tomorrow."

It was still raining when we pulled up in front of Paul and Julie's house. It was grey and bleak and the house looked suddenly creepy through the haze of wind and rain.

I laughed as I ran from the car to the house, wrapping my arms around Abby who was waiting for us. "Lovely weather for a wedding," I said.

She nodded to Brian in greeting. "Mum's really stressed."

"What's wrong?" I asked.

"The rain." Her eyebrows furrowed as she looked at me with a puzzled expression.

"Oh, that! It'll be fine … It'll have to stop soon."

Julie moved into the hallway. Her shoulder sagged as she sighed.

"It's fine," I said as I embraced her. "I don't believe any nonsense about rain on your wedding day being bad luck. If it rains, it rains. Who cares?"

"Come in and have a cuppa." She hugged Brian and moved back down the hall, avoiding eye contact. I think she had tears in her eyes. "Celia's here; our vicar. She wanted to meet you before tomorrow."

Paul gave me a big hug. He looked much more relaxed than the women of the house.

Celia was a large, jolly-looking woman. "You picked a good weekend!" she said, smiling at me.

"How bad is it?" Brian asked after shaking hands with his dad.

"It's quite bad." Julie sniffed as she busied herself making a pot of tea.

"What's going on?" I realised I was missing something.

Julie's eyes darted to Brian before she spoke.

"The church is a mess. More slates have blown off.

the roof. It's leaking so badly that they had to clear everything out. They've taken the pews and everything."

"Oh, well we knew it wasn't going to be all polished and perfect," I said cheerfully. "It'll be fine."

Julie stopped what she was doing to look at me. "The builders arrived this morning to secure the roof and ended up having to remove the rest of the tiles. There's no roof."

"Oh," I whispered.

Brian slumped into a chair at the kitchen table.

I pulled out a chair and looked at Celia. "Do we need a roof? Really?"

I felt all eyes on me, probably trying to decide if I had lost the plot entirely. "I'm serious," I said. "It will be like getting married in some old church ruins. It sounds romantic, doesn't it?"

"I guess…" Julie glanced at Brian and Paul who shrugged. "If the sun came out it might be okay … What do you think Celia?"

"I think you're determined to get married this weekend." She beamed at me. "The church doesn't need a roof for that to happen!"

I liked Celia immediately. She seemed to understand me even though we'd only just met.

"Honestly, I don't care if things aren't perfect." I turned to Julie, who looked like she had the weight of the world on her shoulders. "We don't need seats up there; people can stand. And if it's raining, we can stand with umbrellas! Everything will be great. But you all need to stop worrying so much. The sun will come out tomorrow, I just know it. For once in my life everything is going to fall into place."

I'm not sure why I was suddenly so positive but I had the feeling that everything would be fine. Perhaps I just really needed everything to work out because I couldn't face the thought of Grace being right.

***

In the evening we went to the pub and found our friends and family had arrived. They were having a merry old time with Kenny the barman, who I'd been introduced to on our last visit.

I introduced Paul and Julie to Mum and Aunt Kath. They were happily making small talk when Abby bounded over to be introduced.

"Oh, I brought presents for you!" Mum moved towards the bar to retrieve a carrier bag.

"You didn't need to get us presents," Julie said, surprised.

"I wanted to," Mum said. "I made them myself." She pulled a cushion out of the bag and turned it to check the front before handing it to Paul. It had a knitted square with a 'P' on the front and was very ugly in my opinion. I had a stash of them at home. Mum made them for just about every person she met. She pulled out matching ones for Julie and Abby and the three of them managed to be very enthusiastic.

"I love it," Abby said. "Did you really make it yourself?" I was slightly confused by the idea that Abby would find that hard to believe. They didn't exactly look professional.

"Yes," Mum said proudly. "I love making them. They're my speciality."

"That's really clever." Abby turned it over in her hands to inspect it. "Thanks! Mum tried to teach me to knit once but I only managed a thin scarf."

"I could teach you," Mum offered.

"Really?" Abby's eyes went wide and I smiled at how adorably geeky she was.

We ate dinner in the pub and I was stuck in a boring conversation about work with Linda's husband, George, when the door burst open.

My jaw dropped when Jason waltzed in.

"I made it!" He shook his hair, sending raindrops flying all around. He grinned and bounced up and down enthusiastically. "I'm so excited!"

I laughed loudly and rushed over for a hug. "I'm so glad you're here."

He raised an eyebrow. "You look surprised to see me."

"I'm a bit surprised," I admitted. "I thought you had to do the doggy fitness class tomorrow."

He stared at me. "So that's your excuse for not inviting me, is it?"

"I didn't think you'd be able to make it," I said, cringing. I realised how happy I was to have him here. Not inviting him had been a stupid oversight on my part.

"Well I spoke to your mum and she said I could come as her date. So here I am!"

"I'm sorry. I'm an idiot!" I felt tears prick my eyes and hoped I wasn't about to fall apart again. "I'm really glad you made it. Thank you so much for coming."

"Well, I'm not going to let you forget this! And it's not difficult for me to torture you for a bit of payback."

I laughed. "I'll do as many sit ups as you want!"

"I think I can find it in my heart to forgive you. Anyway, I brought you a present. Just a little something I found at the airport ..." He broke into a huge smile. "Go and look outside!"

"I'm intrigued." I reached for the door.

For a moment I just stood and stared. Then I burst into tears and flung myself at Grace. She was standing under an umbrella, crying her eyes out.

"I'm so sorry," she sobbed.

"Me too," I said through tears. "It doesn't matter. I can't believe you're here."

"I can't believe I nearly didn't come," she cried as I pulled her in out of the rain.

A cheer went up from my friends and I turned and grinned at them. None of them had ever been overly fond of Grace but they knew how much it meant to me to have her there.

"I'm really sorry." She cried even more as Brian approached her.

"It's okay." He embraced her tightly. "I'm glad you're here."

"It's not really okay." She sniffed as she pulled away. "I shouldn't have shouted at you."

"I'll get over it," Brian said.

"It doesn't matter." I took her hand and guided her towards the bar. "We need wine over here, please!"

Kenny grinned at me and poured two glasses of wine, leaving the bottle on the bar for us.

"So what happened?" I asked.

"My life is a mess." She wiped at her eyes. "Everything just seems to be going wrong. I hate my job and things aren't great with James and then all the trouble with the wedding date. I think I took it out on you and Brian."

"It's fine," I said. "We're thick-skinned."

"Yesterday I couldn't stop going over our argument in my head. I was sitting at work and realised that you were right: I have always been puzzled by your attitude to everything. I always thought that at some point you'd grow up and be more sensible."

"Thanks a lot!"

"I know. I realised how terrible that was. You shouldn't change. I decided that I should try things your way. So, I thought 'what would Marie do?'" She stopped to take a sip of wine. "Then I just got up and walked out of work. I went home and packed and went to the airport. And here I am!"

"I can't believe it." I laughed and gave her another hug. "I felt so bad for having a go at you and I hated the thought of you not being here."

"I wasn't sure I was going to make it! I couldn't find a taxi to bring me here from the airport. They were all refusing because there's so much flooding; the roads are terrible. Then I bumped into Jason, having the same problem, so we teamed up and offered double the fare. It wasn't too difficult after that."

"I'm so excited now everyone is here. Come on, let's be sociable." I picked up the wine bottle and we moved to sit with everyone else.

It was one of the best evenings of my life. The

atmosphere was so relaxed. Jokes were thrown around and everyone seemed to be having a great time. It was amazing to have all my friends and family together in one place. I was a bit emotional when we decided it was time to call it a night and get some beauty sleep. Grace and Sophie decided they would come and stay at Julie and Paul's place with me and I asked Linda to come up in the morning to help me get ready.

Jeff made a big show of being upset about being left alone for the night. Then he turned and high-fived Brian as he gestured to the bar.

"Just behave yourself," Sophie growled at him.

"You too!" I told Brian.

"Maybe just one more drink," he said innocently.

"See you at our wedding!" I smiled up at him and he gave me a long kiss goodbye, only pulling away when the wolf-whistles and catcalls got really loud around us.

"Alright! I'm going." I put my coat on and headed out of the pub and into the pouring rain. We hurried up the road back to the house but were soaked to the bone by the time we got up there.

Julie made hot chocolate for us all before we went to bed. I was totally content with the world as I drifted off into a peaceful slumber.

Chapter 44

There was a huge smile on my face when I woke on what I thought would be my wedding day. I'd honestly believed the weather would turn and we'd be bathed in glorious sunshine for the entire day. The possibility of more rain hadn't really registered with me.

I wandered to the window and pulled the curtains open. It didn't even look like rain anymore. It was more like a waterfall cascading from the sky.

There was a light knock at my door before Julie wandered in, followed by Abby, Sophie and Grace. They joined me at the window and we stood in silence for a while.

"It's bound to stop soon." I turned and smiled at their miserable faces. Abby put a hand to her mouth to try and stop herself, but the laughter escaped in a high-pitched squeal and I joined her.

"We might need to think about postponing …" Julie's voice came out in a whisper.

I continued smiling. "It's just rain! Let's get some coffee." I skipped off down to the kitchen and they followed close behind me.

"I think we have a problem," Paul said firmly when I waltzed into the kitchen.

"Not you as well. This house is full of pessimists!"

He picked up a remote and unmuted the TV in the corner. I hadn't even noticed it was on. The screen was filled with pictures of flooding. There were whole villages under water and dramatic scenes of people up to their waists in water.

"We're high," Paul said. "So we're not at risk of flooding but–" The phone rang and Julie reached to answer it. I stared at the TV screen and only vaguely heard Julie murmuring into the phone.

"The caterers can't get here," she said after hanging up the phone. It rang again almost immediately. "Nor can the band."

It went on like that over the next hour until everyone who was supposed to arrive had called and given their apologies. I showered and got dressed. The rain didn't ease up one bit.

"Let's go down to the pub," I said. "I still don't want to call it off. Let me at least talk to Brian first."

"It's bad luck to see him before the wedding," Abby told me innocently. I grinned at her and laughed. She looked out of the window and then smiled awkwardly.

Paul and Julie agreed that we would go down to the pub. I think they were happy at the idea; they could pass me over to Brian and let him be the one to convince me it wasn't going to happen.

The atmosphere in the pub was pretty glum when we walked in. My friends were scattered around the place, clearly awaiting instructions. I headed for Brian who was cradling a whiskey at the bar.

"Bit early isn't it?" I said.

He smiled but looked totally washed out. "I think I messed up," he said quietly.